P9-CFP-058

FOREIGN ÉCLAIRS

JULIE HYZY

BERKLEY PRIME CRIME, NEW YORK

BERKLEY PRIME CRIME

An imprint of Penguin Random House LLC
375 Hudson Street, New York, New York 10014

FOREIGN ÉCLAIRS

A Berkley Prime Crime Book / published by arrangement with Tekno Books LLC

ISBN: 978-0-425-26240-5

PUBLISHING HISTORY
Berkley Prime Crime mass-market edition / January 2016

PRINTED IN THE UNITED STATES OF AMERICA

10 9 8 7 6 5 4 3 2 1

Interior text design by Laura K. Corless.

Penguin
Random
House

In memory of Marty Greenberg

ACKNOWLEDGMENTS

Ollie and I have been close friends for almost ten years. I'm lucky she came into my life and I hope she believes the same of me. Writing her stories has been a joy and a delight. I like to think we both learned a lot along the way.

Marty Greenberg was the genius behind the concept and I wish he were still here today to see where Ollie is now. I will be forever grateful to him for offering me the opportunity to write the White House Chef Mysteries.

I am equally grateful to my wonderful editor, Natalee Rosenstein at Berkley Prime Crime, for taking a chance on me. She's just the best and I'm incredibly fortunate to have been able to work with her for so long. Many thanks to Natalee, Michelle Vega, and the team at Berkley Prime Crime—Robin Barletta, Stacy Edwards, and Erica Horisk—awesome supporters of this series, some from the very beginning.

Many thanks as well to Larry Segriff at Tekno Books, who keeps everything running smoothly and is never too busy to answer e-mails.

Hugs and kisses to my family: Curt, Robyn, Sara, and Biz. Love you all.

CHAPTER 1

BUCKY SCOURED THE STAINLESS STEEL SURFACE of the kitchen's center countertop while I filled a panko-crusted skillet with hot water and set it aside to soak. Dinner had been delivered to the First Family about twenty minutes earlier. Once we finished cleaning up, our official White House duties were done for the day.

My unofficial duties, however, were about to begin.

"How late do you plan to stay tonight?" Bucky asked.

"Depends," I said, as I filled another used pan with sudsy water. Shutting off the spigot, I washed my hands before pulling down a stack of ingredient bowls from an overhead cabinet. Autumn's snappy weather had inspired me to conjure up a new vegetable soup recipe. "Josh probably won't make it down here until seven." I set the bowls atop the counter Bucky had just cleaned. "We used to spend entire afternoons working together, but these days I'm lucky if he has an hour to spare."

The president's eleven-and-a-half-year-old son and I had forged an alliance during a tense confrontation three years ago, shortly after his father had been elected. Since that time, Josh and I had become good friends. From day one, the youngster expressed interest in the culinary arts and I delighted in nurturing his talents. Lately, however, with the pressures of middle school and his father's reelection efforts, Josh's time in the kitchen with me had been limited.

"Doesn't it bother Gav that you devote so much of your free time to the First Family?" Bucky asked. "Granted, you're not technically newlyweds anymore, but between his job and yours, it's a wonder you get any time together."

"We talk about it, believe me." I laughed. "But this time at least, I'm not the one taking time away. He's out of town again."

"Where's he off to this time? Another trip to the winery?"

Being careful not to answer the question directly, I kept my back to my assistant and shrugged. "It's a good idea for him to spend time there. He left early this morning." My misdirection wasn't exactly a lie, but it wasn't the truth, either. I bit my lip, and hoped Bucky didn't press the issue.

Over the past year, Gav had spent a lot of time with Bill and Erma at Spencer's Vineyards, learning the business they intended to leave to him when they retired. But he wasn't out at the couple's Loudoun County winery today. Gav was on a clandestine assignment with his friend and mentor, Joe Yablonski. As always, I'd been sworn to secrecy.

"Ah, you're both still here."

I looked up as Peter Everett Sargeant strode into the kitchen, tablet in hand.

"Good," he continued before either of us had a chance to reply. "I have a few updates to share with you regarding candidates for the vacant chef position."

My second assistant and good friend, Cyan, had left us

shortly after the sequester ended, opting to pursue a more traditional culinary career. The departure of our talented and color contact lens–favoring friend had left a hole in our hearts and a void in our kitchen. Bucky and I had gotten by these past few months by putting in loads of extra time and relying on Service-By-Agreement chefs to plug our gaps. Although we'd interviewed a handful of promising candidates, we hadn't yet found the perfect fit.

Belatedly, it dawned on me that Sargeant was alone. "Is Margaret off work again today?" I asked. "Is everything okay?"

He twisted his mouth sideways, effectively wrinkling his nose. "Apparently Friday's family crisis is not yet resolved."

"Apparently?" I asked, picking up on the word and his undisguised disapproval. "She hasn't updated you? That's not like her."

Sargeant sniffed. "When she called in Friday, she fore-warned that she may be out for more than a day or two. I find it highly inconvenient, however. We have a great deal on our schedule tomorrow and I'm unable to count on her being here."

"Do you know what's up?" I asked. "Not that it's any of my business."

"It isn't. But no, I do not know the nature of the emergency. Margaret's distress overwhelmed the conversation and I thought it best to keep things brief." Tapping the tablet, he continued. "I'm here to let you know that Audrey Lund will be able to meet with us Wednesday. I'll provide more detail later. Is that satisfactory?"

"Yes, very."

Sargeant went on. "I've also arranged for us to interview another candidate tomorrow at two. I trust you'll make yourself available?" He waved a hand toward Bucky, who had wandered over to the computer station. "Mr. Reed should be able to handle the kitchen on his own at that time, correct?"

Bucky threw Sargeant a baleful glance before turning his attention to the monitor.

"Thanks, Peter," I said. "The sooner we find the right person for the job, the happier we'll be. Right, Bucky?"

He didn't answer.

"Bucky?"

Gripping his bald head, my assistant stared at the computer screen with an expression of scowling disbelief. A second later he leaped into action, hammering at the volume control key until the sound came up loud enough for us all to hear.

Sargeant and I flanked him. "What happened?" I asked.

"Looks bad. I don't know where . . ."

His thought trailed to silence as we watched the situation unfold on CNN. This kind of scene had become much too familiar of late and I struggled to figure out what was happening. Police officers attempted to establish control amid chaos, ambulances, and emergency vehicles. Bit by bit, as the camera panned and I caught sight of charred ruins, I realized this was no shooting incident.

Blackened, twisted metal fragments smoldered in the foreground. Farther back, firefighters aimed their powerful streams at a small building engulfed in flames. A giant concrete wall sitting immediately behind the garage-size structure held the flames in check.

In that gut-clenching way that memory teases us, I recognized that I'd seen this place before. Not in person, but like this—on television. On the news, perhaps. I moved closer to the screen to chase the recollection but that didn't help; it slipped away and danced beyond my grasp.

When the shot widened and I caught sight of barbed wire spooled across the top of the giant concrete wall, I sucked in a breath.

The news reporter spoke solemnly into the unsteady camera. "To update viewers just tuning in, we are live on the scene in Encotere, Wisconsin, where a bomb reportedly went off a little while ago, killing at least three people and injuring several others."

My stomach rolled over on itself.

"That's it," Bucky said. "That's why it looks so familiar."

That teasing memory that had quietly lured me in mere moments ago now roared up with a triumphant crash, bombarding me with powerful, terrifying recollections.

"It's Cenga Prison again, isn't it?" Bucky asked.

"Oh, dear," Sargeant said. "Are you sure?"

I couldn't find my voice. Instead, I stared at the screen, silently urging the news reporter to quit repeating himself and to share specifics. I nearly shouted *Who is responsible?* Why weren't they telling us more?

Three years ago, Armustan failed in an attempt to force President Hyden to release a terrorist imprisoned at Cenga Prison. Armustan may have set out to test our then-new president's resolve, but it'd also tested mine. Although I'd been partially responsible for the United States's eventual triumph, I'd never been able to forget the terror the president's son, Josh, and I had experienced that night.

I watched and waited, telling myself that the regime responsible for the attack had long been overthrown. But their countryman, the terrorist Farbod Ansari, remained incarcerated in Cenga Prison to this day. It *had* to be Armustan behind the bombing. And I had no doubt that this time its extremists were desperate to prevail.

We listened and listened again, but no more details came.

"Three people dead this time," I said when the newsman threw the story back to the studio. "What were they hoping to accomplish? They can't possibly believe that killing American citizens is going to help achieve their goals."

"You don't know that Armustan is behind this," Sargeant said.

"No?" I held out my hands. "Then why are they the first culprit that came to *your* mind?"

Flustered, Sargeant tried to backpedal. "Simply speculation at this point."

Bucky turned down the volume and picked up a dishcloth. "An educated guess is more like it," he said with a glance back at the fiery scene. He picked up one of the bowls and began drying it.

"Those are clean," I said. "I pulled them out for Josh."

"Oh, right." He dropped the bowl with a clang.

Sargeant excused himself. "Regardless of who is responsible, I imagine the president will require assistance. Which means I need to be in my office. Good night."

After he left, Bucky and I continued to watch the story develop. We learned almost nothing more. No specific details. No information on who had been killed, or why. The commentators merely offered rephrased regurgitations of the little they'd provided thus far.

"I'm tired of violence," Bucky said. "No matter where it is or who's responsible."

"The timing is suspicious," I said as thoughts began to form. "Think about it. When the terrorists from Armustan struck last time—"

"You say that so calmly. 'When the terrorists struck' makes it sound like an unfortunate happening at a distant location. Ollie, they *kidnapped* you. They kidnapped the president's son. Don't tell me that experience doesn't still give you nightmares."

He was right, but that was beside the point. "What I'm

getting at is that last time—yes, when they kidnapped me and Josh—it was shortly after President Hyden's inauguration."

Bucky nodded agreement.

"Elections are less than two months away," I said. "What better time to strike again? That's why I have no doubt that Armustan is behind this. They've had three years to regroup from their massive humiliation. Now they're back and they want to see the president fail."

"You really believe that?" Bucky asked. "Granted, their guy is still incarcerated there. I mean, I don't doubt that Armustan could be behind this bomb today, but you make it sound personal."

"I'm no expert on that region, but Gav has shared what he can. The Armustanian people are very proud. Dishonor to the family is considered justification for killing."

"Kind of like Klingons?"

The question surprised a laugh out of me. "Not exactly. But to extend the metaphor, if I were President Hyden I'd go to red alert." I glanced toward the doorway and lowered my voice. "When Josh shows up, I'll make sure to remind him how important it is to follow instructions from the Secret Service. Even though Josh is accompanied by trained professionals whenever he leaves the White House, he needs to remain aware, and wary, as well."

"Scare the kid, why don't you?"

"The Armustanians didn't hesitate when it came to threatening the Hyden kids last time."

As I said that, a Secret Service agent rounded the corner and stepped into the kitchen. "Chef Paras, I'm here to tell you that Josh will not be able to meet with you this evening."

I tightened my mouth. "Did something come up?" I asked.

"He changed his mind." The agent spread his hands. "Sorry."

When the man was gone, I grabbed the bowls I'd pulled out and returned them to their cabinet glad, at least, that I hadn't yet filled them with the ingredients I'd planned to use tonight.

"I know you're disappointed, Ollie," Bucky said. "But, remember, Josh is eleven and it's Sunday night. How much you want to bet he procrastinated all weekend and is finally catching up on homework right now?"

"Maybe you're right," I said, but my heart wasn't in it.

CHAPTER 2

A FLURRY OF SECRET SERVICE SLIPUPS OVER THE past several months—none of which, thankfully, had anything to do with me—had resulted in a major shakeup in the Presidential Protective Division, also known as the PPD.

Tom MacKenzie, who'd helmed the department for several years, and with whom I'd once been romantically involved, had been transferred to a new position in Florida. I hadn't heard from him since and didn't expect to.

Because one of the more egregious Secret Service lapses involved an armed intruder jumping the fence and making his way inside the White House before being apprehended, the complex's periphery had been fortified. Sturdy fence segments now ringed the property. These temporary barricades provided an extra layer of protection until permanent solutions could be implemented. Additionally, a slew of uniformed Division agents now patrolled this new perimeter around the clock.

Although the Secret Service had a long way to go to reclaim the stellar reputation it once possessed, the area immediately surrounding the White House was as protected as I'd ever seen. As I exited the front gate on Pennsylvania Avenue, I wished the nearby agents a good night and headed north on Madison Place, embarking on my regular trek to the McPherson Square Metro station.

I'd barely gotten as far as the statue of General Lafayette when I noticed a dozen or so young people gathered in a rough circle about fifty feet ahead of me. Two men at the group's center were arguing, their voices rising with each hurled insult. Supporters hooted. Opponents jeered.

My first thought was that the two combatants—who looked to be in their late twenties—were a little old for a street fight, but that didn't slow them down. I glanced around, hoping a Metro Police officer would intervene and stop the altercation before it escalated, but there was no one in authority to take control.

It seemed to me, of late, that as the level of protection around the White House increased, the level of police presence in Lafayette Square dropped. Maybe it was my imagination, but I'd noticed fewer and fewer cops patrolling the park these past months.

Could be a coincidence. Could be that officers were called away on emergencies in other areas—every single night I traipsed through here. But I believed that this represented a new trend. My suspicion was that, with increased security and so much firepower a short block away at the White House, the powers-that-be in charge of Metro Police chose to redirect personnel to areas of the city with higher crime rates. Who could blame them? Tight budgets often necessitated hard choices.

I debated moving to the other side of Madison Place to get

around the rowdy group, but the circle had fractured, spilling across the street as spectators joined the squabble. This was looking more and more like a gang confrontation.

Although the altercation itself seemed unlikely to threaten innocent bystanders, I preferred not to get close enough to test that theory. I had a choice. I could either attempt to barrel through their midst and hope for the best or make a wide circle around them to the left.

When one of them crashed a bottle against a tree and held the jagged glass aloft, my decision was made. As soon as I got safely past them, I'd call 911.

Vexed, and hoping the detour didn't cause me to miss my train, I picked up my pace and veered into the park, keeping alert for the vagrants who took up residence there. By and large, Lafayette Square was safe, but over the years I'd learned to be cautious.

From the intensifying grunts and shouts, it sounded as though the ruckus had escalated into a full-blown brawl. I swiftly made my way past the shrieking crowd, confident they hadn't noticed me at all.

I'd made it as far as the Kościuszko Statue when a cop car raced around the far corner, lights flashing, high beams spotlighting the gathered group. There was a brief mob-in-the-headlights moment before the miscreants scattered like pigeons from a barking dog. Another police car arrived on the scene and within seconds four officers began rounding up the troublemakers. Relieved, I started to make my way back to the Madison Place sidewalk.

I'd taken two steps toward the street when a man stepped in front of me. At the exact same moment, I was jerked from behind. The world blurred as I fell. My backside hit the ground, the impact reverberating up my spine. Instinctively, I cried out. Whoever grabbed me had the presence of mind to clap a hairy hand over my mouth. He dragged me into the shadows. His partner scanned the area for witnesses, then followed at a trot.

Ignoring the pain from my abductor's harsh grip, I fought, doing my best to scramble for leverage. Crouched behind me, my assailant's knee jammed hard between my shoulder blades as he jerked my left arm behind my back, effectively twisting me into submission. He whispered, "Be quiet," so close I could smell the sour heat of his breath against my cheek. "I don't have to hurt you, but I will."

Though I struggled and squirmed, he held tight. I couldn't see his face.

I *could* see his partner. For all the good it did me.

The man in front held tight to my ankles, using his body weight to pin my kicking legs to the ground. Some detached part of my psyche registered that he had words tattooed on his fingers. Like the Robert Mitchum character in *The Night of the Hunter.*

This man had a scarf covering his mouth and nose. His dark knitted cap covered what might have been sandy-colored hair, but in the dim light I couldn't be sure. His gaze was steady. The malevolent intensity in his light eyes made me try to cry out again, this time from fear rather than pain.

I squirmed, gurgling against the sweaty hand on my face, trying my best to generate commotion loud enough for someone to hear. The guy behind me twisted my arm tighter. "Hurry up," he said.

Fifteen seconds in the cold grass and already the damp began seeping through the fabric of my pants and into my skin. I shuddered as the Hunter character shifted position. He moved far too smoothly for this to have been the first time he'd orchestrated such an attack.

Before I had a chance to understand his intentions, he'd

trapped my legs with his own, freeing his hands. One second later, he withdrew a blade from his waistband. At least six inches long and two wide, its sharp, serrated business edge could inflict tremendous damage.

Summoning all the power I could, I writhed against my captor's crushing grasp, twisting my face away from the gleaming blade. I clenched my eyes, imagining the worst. My strangled cries for help went nowhere. They were lost in the cacophonic chaos taking place less than a half block away as police officers bellowed orders at the would-be fighters and their gangs.

Yanked forward by the band of my cross-body purse, I snapped my eyes open in time to see Hunter's blade slice through the handbag's narrow strap. The sudden release of tension sent me flying back against the hairy-knuckled guy's knees. He took the opportunity to tighten his grip even more. "Hurry up," he said again.

Hunter-guy yanked one end of the split strap, whipping the fabric out from under me. Shifting his weight off my legs, he stood.

The hairy knuckled guy shoved a thick wad of fabric into my mouth. A second later, he released my twisted arm and jumped to his feet. I fell backward onto the wet grass.

Laughing, Hairy Knuckles moved into my field of vision. Shorter and more muscular than his partner, he had a mop of dark hair and he, too, wore a scarf across his face. He grabbed my purse from the Hunter guy and danced it in the air between them. "Whatcha got in here, lady? Must be something good. Otherwise next time it won't go so easy." He pulled out a switchblade of his own and twisted it for effect. "Know what I mean?"

Hunter snatched the purse back, shoved it under his coat, and ran off. Hairy Knuckles shouted and ran after him.

The moment I was free, I tore at the gag. The dry fabric stuck to the inside of my mouth, making me cough and choke, stuttering my shouts for help. It was too late, anyway. They were gone. Swallowed up into the night.

I winced at the pain in my left arm when I boosted myself to my feet. The two thieves had been swift and efficient; the entire altercation had taken less than a minute.

Trembling, I steadied my breathing and shook my legs to get the blood moving in them again. My heart pounded hard and fast. I glanced around quickly as though expecting another ambush.

About a hundred feet west, two people strolled with their arms around each other, their backs to me. A bus rumbled east on H Street. The rest of Lafayette Square remained quiet and dark. Even the original disturbance that had set me off my path—the clash between the two gangs—was winding down.

I drew in a deep breath and fought off the delayed panic that always hit me post-skirmish. The fact that I recognized the reaction as normal infuriated me almost as much as the encounter had. Over the past few years, I'd fought off assassins, terrorists, angry dissidents, and a variety of conspirators, all of whom had devised far more sophisticated assaults than the blunt attack I'd just endured. I'd managed to outwit offenders who had greater resources and the benefit of surprise. And yet today, I'd failed to protect myself.

I didn't blame myself for their audacious violation. Of course not. But that didn't mean I wasn't angry about having gone through it. I consoled myself remembering one good thing I'd learned from my many and varied experiences: the importance of keeping my cell phone separate from my handbag.

As I hurried back to the White House, I pulled the device from my jacket pocket and dialed Gav.

CHAPTER 3

THE UNIFORMED AGENTS AT THE GATE COULDN'T have been more solicitous. One of them, Isaac, notified the PPD immediately and invited me to sit inside the guard house while we waited for an agent to arrive.

"You sure you're okay, Chef?" the young man asked for the second time. "You want anything? Coffee? Water?"

"I'm fine," I assured him. "I'm envisioning all the work ahead of me to cancel credit cards and replace my driver's license, though. It isn't a happy thought."

"You're lucky that's all they got," he said.

I knew he was doing his best to console me, so I smiled. "Very true."

"Is there anyone else you'd like me to call?"

I hesitated. There was no doubt that the Secret Service would turn this mugging investigation over to the Metro Police. The streets of D.C. were their jurisdiction, after all, and I had no quarrel with that. I could have easily called them myself and kept the White House out of it. But the freshly appointed head of the PPD had enacted strict new guidelines. He insisted that staffers report all suspicious behavior, no matter how inconsequential an incident might seem. Though this was hardly inconsequential, it wasn't a White House matter. Still, I took no chances. I wanted to get off on the right foot with this guy.

"No, thank you," I answered Isaac. "Believe it or not, I managed to hang onto this." I held my cell phone aloft. "While we wait, I'll alert my credit card companies, if you don't mind."

"Go right ahead," he said. "I've got reports to fill out here to keep me busy anyway."

As I took care of notifying my credit companies, I thought about Gav. When I'd phoned him on the trek back to the White House, my call had gone straight to voice mail. I'd been disappointed, though not surprised. After a quick mental debate, I sent a text asking him to call me, opting against leaving a message. He'd contact me when he could, and by then I'd be composed enough to relay the circumstances without worrying him overmuch.

If Gav and I were a typical couple with more traditional jobs, I might have left a message warning him about our credit card cancellations. I knew, however, that he'd left all of his personal effects with Yablonski's staff before he'd left town.

Gav hadn't been able to tell me much about the mission he was on, but I knew he was undercover this time. Anything that he owned directly, whether it be phone, jewelry, or clothing, was left behind whenever he slipped into a new identity.

Isaac glanced up when I put my phone away. "Did they get your White House ID?" he asked.

I reached into my jacket to pull out the lanyard that hung around my neck. "Nope. I keep that on me, too."

"Good thinking."

An agent I'd never met before arrived and introduced himself. Young and pale, wearing a black nylon jacket and a disinterested air, he informed me that Metro Police would take my statement back at the White House and that he was to escort me there.

"Are the Metro Police meeting us in the kitchen?" I asked.

"West Wing." Maintaining the lifeless expression, he held out his hand. "After you."

THE NEW HEAD OF THE PPD, NEVILLE WALKER, met me outside the Secret Service office in the West Wing. "Are you all right, Ms. Paras?" he asked as he led me in. "Is there anything you need?"

"I'd like my purse back," I said, "but I assume it and its contents are long gone."

Agent Walker was as tall as Gav, and similarly lean and muscular. His deep brown cheeks sported long, vertical creases instead of dimples, and his hair was super short with threads of gray at the temples. He showed square, even teeth when he smiled and looked exactly like his voice sounded: dark and powerful. "Are you sure you don't require medical assistance?"

"Thank you, but I'm more angry than anything." He seemed unconvinced, so I added, "They knocked me to the ground and twisted my arm a little, but otherwise didn't harm me."

He waited until I took a seat at his desk before lowering himself into the chair opposite. "You and I haven't had a chance to interact since I assumed this position." No longer smiling, he folded his hands atop his bare desktop with a precision I didn't know the gesture could effect.

"Not since you were introduced to the staff, no."

"Frankly, I'm surprised." Not only was his voice full-bodied, his words were measured. Every syllable rumbled with weight. "I've read the reports." Expressionless, he blinked. "All of them."

I didn't believe that required a reply, so I kept quiet.

"I expected the two of us to have collided long before today. To what do you attribute this extended period of quiet?"

Taken aback, I hesitated. "I don't know how to answer that."

"You suffered a personal attack. That's not in dispute."

Nor should it be. I pulled in my lips to keep silent.

He blinked again. "What threat do you believe the White House is facing this time?"

His eyes were like black holes, his dimple-streaks rendered invisible by his suddenly flat, blank face.

Having returned to the White House, where I felt safe, knowing that the police were on their way, I'd allowed myself to relax a little bit. Now I sat straighter, inching forward on my seat. "Agent Walker," I began in an equally quiet voice, as I folded my hands atop his desk, "are you attempting to intimidate me?"

He considered the question. "Are you intimidated?"

I couldn't read this man. At all. I flexed my jaw and told the truth. "A little. But not enough to back down from speaking my mind."

His eyebrows lifted as the corners of his mouth turned down. "Go on."

"I won't deny anything you've read about me in the reports you mentioned. Nor will I apologize for any actions I've taken in the past." I lifted my chin. "Or those I may take in the future." My gaze slid across the top of the desk's pristine surface looking for something to focus on besides the brick of his folded hands. What kind of person kept nothing at all on his workspace? "That said," I continued, "the attack tonight seemed to be one of opportunity. I didn't get the impression I'd been intentionally targeted."

We were interrupted by the arrival of two officers from the Metro Police. One male, one female, they wore plain clothes and introduced themselves as detectives Beem and Kager. Agent Walker invited them to sit.

As they did, Beem pulled out a notebook and pen. The detective settled a pair of reading glasses on the end of his bumpy nose and raised a tired gaze. "Sorry this happened to you, Ms. Paras," he intoned, then encouraged me to tell them everything from the moment I'd exited the White House gates. After I finished recounting the incident, I did my best to describe my attackers.

Half Beem's age, Kager had a narrow face and wore her fawn-colored hair pulled back into a lean ponytail. Like an exaggerated reflection from a funhouse mirror, she cut a slimmer, taller figure than seemed possible. She tapped a finger against her chin when I mentioned the tattoos. "You say you noticed letters," she repeated. "Were you able to make them out? Did his tattoos spell a word?"

"They pulled me into an area that wasn't brightly lit, and held me down in a shadowed spot." I could hear myself making excuses. I shook that off and answered directly. "No, I couldn't make out words, but I'm absolutely certain he had an E and an L on one hand, and a T on the other." I closed my eyes, remembering. "The E and L were on his right and the T on his left," I said when I opened my eyes again. "And I think the T was on his ring finger."

Beem continued to scribble notes, but I couldn't miss his pointed look to Kager, or the arch of one steel-wool brow. She acknowledged him with a nod. "The man with the tattoos," she asked, "was there anything else unusual about him? Mannerisms? Build?"

I tried to conjure any details I may have missed. Came up empty.

"What about his voice?" she asked.

"He didn't speak," I said. "Not a word. The guy behind me did all the talking."

The detectives shared another look that couldn't be missed.

"You know who attacked me, don't you?" I asked.

Kager held an index finger to her chin. "Hypothetically speaking, if we were able to arrange for a lineup tomorrow, would you be willing to come down to the station to make identification? I know they both wore scarves, but it's worth a try."

"I have a commitment at two," I said, remembering the interview Sargeant had set up. "It should last about an hour. Otherwise, yes, I will make myself available whenever you need."

The detectives stood, making ready to leave. "Thank you," Kager began. "We will be in touch."

"One moment." Walker's resonant baritone stopped the officers mid-step. He remained seated. "Before you arrived, Chef Paras indicated to me that she believes this attack was one of opportunity, rather than a premeditated personal assault."

Walker spoke so slowly, I couldn't tell whether he'd finished his thought, or intended to continue. The two detectives seemed to be stymied by the uncertainty as well. They waited.

Walker made deliberate eye contact with both of them. "I realize the question is premature, as you don't have any suspects in custody yet, but I would appreciate knowing your opinion on this matter."

Kager worked her narrow jaw. "It is too early to offer conjecture. What I can tell you is that there is a known gang member who matches the description Ms. Paras provided. And we can speculate about his companion. If it turns out that they are responsible for this attack, then we may be able to assume that tonight's altercation was motivated by opportunity."

"Thank you, Detective."

"Mind you," she added, "a low-level crime like this is beneath their . . . talents . . . if you will." Kager's round, wide-spaced eyes were the only non-skinny thing about her. She fixed her gaze on Walker. "The gang members in question are high-ranking soldiers in their organization. Simple muggings are generally delegated to kids hoping to prove themselves to gang leaders."

Walker listened quietly. "You will keep my office updated?"

"Of course," Kager said. After reminding me to double-check that I'd made all the necessary notifications to prevent identity theft, she wished me a good night. "We will call you tomorrow when we're ready for you to come in."

When they left, I prepared to leave. There was no way I would attempt another trip to the Metro. Tonight I would call a cab. "Thank you for your help, Agent Walker," I said, hoping that the "extended period of quiet" he'd alluded to earlier hadn't suffered a permanent interruption. The less time I spent in this man's office, the happier I'd be.

"Two more issues before you leave," he said. "First, I do not intend to make the same mistakes my predecessor did."

"I don't understand."

"As of this moment, all evidence suggests that you were simply in the wrong place at the wrong time this evening. That is the most likely scenario. I don't, however, care to leave questions unanswered, nor opportunities for investigation unexplored. Before you arrived, I called for an agent to escort you home. Romero is waiting for you in the lobby."

"Understood," I said, relieved. Even though I wasn't injured, it hadn't been easy to maintain a calm and unruffled air. Those two men tonight had me cold. They'd hijacked control. In the past, whenever I'd been confronted, I'd used my wits to either overpower my captor or figure a way out. This time there had been no opportunity. The intellect and instincts I'd come to depend on had been useless against two opponents who took me by surprise and immobilized me with strength and an intent to harm.

I'd gotten away with no more than a few bruises and a stack of credit card paperwork. Logic told me I was lucky, but I didn't feel that way right now.

When Walker didn't continue, I asked, "What's the second thing?"

"I believe people work better together when they feel comfortable around one another. I'd prefer it if we were on a first-name basis. That is, if you don't mind, Olivia?"

"I'd like that," I said. "But please, call me Ollie."

"Good. Is there anything else you need, Ollie?"

I managed a smile and a quick head shake. "Thank you for arranging for the ride home."

CHAPTER 4

I'D EXPECTED AGENT ROMERO TO DROP ME OFF in front of my apartment building, but she surprised me by insisting on accompanying me all the way in. "Agent Walker's orders," she said. "We aren't taking any chances."

"He seems very thorough," I said. She scanned the parking area, studied the apartment windows above, and kept a hand on her weapon as we made our way from the car to the front door. Neville Walker, apparently, wasn't the only conscientious new agent. "Have you worked with him before?"

She maintained light contact, the fingers of her free hand against the back of my jacket. "Most of us have." I knew she was referring to all the new Secret Service personnel currently staffing the PPD. "When he took the job, he brought a bunch of us in. He said he wanted people he could trust."

"And you're one of them."

Still not looking at me, she rested a hand on my arm to

slow me down. "One of many, but yes. Fortunate to have this opportunity. Hold up a minute."

I waited while she gave the parking area a final once-over, then studied the lobby of the apartment building, where James sat behind the round desk.

It was late enough in the evening for our drowsy doorman to have nodded off, so I was surprised to find him wide awake and clearly curious as to why I'd arrived with a Secret Service agent in tow.

"I had a little excitement this evening, James," I said after we'd exchanged greetings. "My purse was stolen, and I can't get into my apartment."

"Oh no, Ollie, what happened? Are you okay?"

"I'm perfectly fine," I said, not wanting to get into a detailed explanation. "Agent Romero was kind enough to give me a ride, but I'll need help getting in."

"Gav's not home, either, I take it?" James asked as he reached into a nearby drawer and pulled out a ring of keys. "He out on assignment or something?"

I smiled. "Or something."

After fiddling with the clinking bits of metal, he identified a golden key with my apartment number on it. "Here you go," he said, handing the entire collection across the desk. "I'd take you up myself, but I can't leave the floor for a while yet."

I took the keys from him. "What's up?"

"Had a couple of late deliveries this evening." He gestured with his chin at two lamp-size boxes sitting on the floor next to the desk. "They have the same return address but showed up separately. They are boxes number two and three of three."

I didn't understand, but didn't really need to. I had my ticket in. The sooner I was up in my apartment and alone, the happier I'd be.

"They made me sign for them, but I don't know who they belong to. I argued with the delivery guy until I turned blue, but he didn't have any more information than what's on the address label. You didn't order anything recently, did you?"

"Not three big boxes' worth." I started for the elevators. "There's nothing to indicate which tenant they're meant for?"

"Nope," James said. "They got the right address but no apartment number, no name. The delivery guy said all that information will probably be on the last one—box number *one* of three. He says he's seen that before. Until he comes back, I'm going to wait here. Don't want anyone stealing the two boxes. I signed for them. I'd be liable, you know."

"Whoever they belong to will probably come and claim them soon, anyway," I said.

"Sure hope so. Can't imagine how companies stay in business without putting the proper address on their packages."

Agent Romero and I remained quiet in the elevator as it made its slow ascent. "He shouldn't have given you the keys," she said as we cleared floor six, then seven, then eight. "He should never let them out of his sight. It's a security risk."

I couldn't argue; handing keys off *was* a risk. But most of us in the building had known one another for years and the vast majority of occupants were senior citizens. Fortunately for me, they'd been happy to welcome a young new neighbor when I'd first moved in. Especially once they learned I worked in the White House. Romero couldn't know any of that, nor could she know that I would trust any one of them with the ring of keys. Rather than defend James's actions, however, I changed the subject.

"You know that I'm married to Leonard Gavin, right?"

Romero had bobbed brown hair worn pinned back at the sides. Her pointed chin thrust too far forward—I could never remember if that signaled an underbite or overbite—giving her a constant air of smug disapproval. Her eyes never stopped moving. I couldn't imagine what threat could possibly exist in this elevator, but if one made itself known, I had no doubt Romero would spring into action before it got the chance to fully materialize.

"Everyone on the PPD is familiar with your personal dossier," she said, adding, "and with Special Agent Gavin's as well."

It didn't surprise me when she referred to Gav by his title. Although he'd been tapped to work with Yablonski again in recent weeks, his tenure there was more a long-term loan from the Secret Service than a permanent position. Gav was often brought in as an expert consultant in White House matters and thus hadn't been affected by the Secret Service shake-up that had tumbled the preceding team.

"Okay, good," I said, though the truth was it unnerved me to have so many strangers know so much about us. I couldn't help but wonder how deep that knowledge went. Did she have any idea that my husband's mission with Joe Yablonski was highly classified? And if she did, would she know where they had been sent? I assumed both men were in Wisconsin this evening at the scene of the Cenga bombing. Before that incident happened, though? No idea where they'd been. I never knew, and I certainly couldn't ask.

I was relieved to discover Mrs. Wentworth's door completely closed when Romero and I alighted at my floor. A moment later, I remembered that my elderly neighbor and her husband, Stan, were out of town for a family wedding. Good. Even though my nosy neighbor wouldn't blink at the sight of yet another Secret Service agent escorting me home, I preferred not having to explain my need for the master key tonight.

Agent Romero surprised me again by following me into my apartment. I sputtered, "Are you staying here overnight?

Agent Walker didn't mention anything about twenty-four-hour coverage."

I caught what might have been a fleeting smile. "Walk me through," she said. "Let's make sure the apartment is secure. Then I'll leave."

Walker hadn't been kidding about not taking chances. Following his orders, Agent Romero conducted a thorough inspection. She checked that my windows were locked—this despite the fact that I lived on the thirteenth floor—and ensured that no one was hiding under the bed or in a closet.

While she completed her survey, I dug out an old purse and began filling it with replacement items, including a beat-up wallet I'd tucked away months ago.

"To the best of your knowledge, nothing has been stolen?" she asked as we completed the tour and started back toward my front door. "Everything is exactly as you left it?"

"More or less." She blinked at my ambiguous answer, so I hurried to add, "My husband was still here when I took off for work this morning."

"Understood. Nothing inexplicably out of place then?"

"Nothing at all."

"You ought to have your locks changed immediately."

"It's on my to-do list." I couldn't wait to get her out of my apartment so that I could relax. "Speaking of keys, would you mind returning these to James on your way out?"

"No problem." She took them, then handed me a business card. Her first name was Tori. "If you need me, please don't hesitate to call."

"Thanks," I said, surprised by the gesture. "I hope I have no reason to."

She nodded. "Same here."

As soon as she was gone, I called the apartment building's superintendent, unsurprised when I was connected with the answering service. The woman on the other end assured me their locksmith would be more than willing to come out tonight. It wasn't the premium fee that made me hesitate, it was the fact that I was done in for the day. I didn't relish the thought of staying awake to await his arrival and through the subsequent lock replacement process.

Although I knew it was probably not the smartest decision I'd ever made, I decided to play the odds and set up an appointment for the morning.

The moment I hung up, I dialed James at the front desk and asked if he, or another of our doormen, would be willing to meet with the locksmith tomorrow in my stead. James said he'd be happy to.

"Thanks," I said. "I take it the agent returned your master key ring?"

"She did. And don't you worry about anyone getting in here tonight, Ollie. I'm on duty for another hour and then our overnight guard comes in. Nobody's getting past who doesn't belong."

"I appreciate that, James," I said. But before I went to bed, I wedged a heavy chair beneath the knob of my front door.

CHAPTER 5

"WHY IS IT ALWAYS YOU, OLLIE?" BUCKY ASKED
the next morning as we stacked pots and pans next to the sink.
"It's as though you have a great big neon arrow over your
head, pointing down, blinking 'Aim here.'"

"Don't even joke about that," I said. "It was bad enough
explaining the mugging to the new head of the PPD last night.
The last thing I need is for the staff to get wind of it. The
Secret Service will take any excuse to target me, I'm sure."

"Not a chance," Bucky said with a dismissive hand gesture. "You know you're safe here. At least as long as this
administration is in office. The Hydens love you."

"That's true, and I appreciate it," I said, "but we both
know that life around here can change in the space of a
heartbeat. Or with an election. I don't want to make enemies
of the Secret Service again. Not after I've worked so hard
to establish credibility."

"Once they catch the guys who robbed you last night, you'll feel better."

"I hope so."

We settled into a companionable silence as we puttered about the kitchen. Years of working together had allowed the three of us—Bucky, Cyan, and me—to establish patterns. Between the time we usually sent breakfast upstairs for the First Family and when we needed to begin preparing lunch, we enjoyed a short break in activity.

Ever since our team had dropped in number from three to two, however, Bucky and I found ourselves buzzing around the kitchen all day, even during our supposed down time.

Today promised a shot at our elusive lull. The president's kids, Abigail and Josh, were at school with the lunches we'd packed for them this morning. The First Lady's commitment at a hospital benefit kept her out of the residence all day and President Hyden, we'd just been advised, had departed the White House fifteen minutes ago via Marine One. He wasn't expected back until nightfall.

We had no idea where he'd gone, but it wasn't our business to know. All that mattered to us at this point was preparing dinner and ensuring that the kids' afterschool snacks made it upstairs before they did. That was hours away. For the first time in a long time, an extended period of calm stretched ahead of us.

Bucky folded his arms and made a face at the clock. "Would you mind if I ran out on an errand this morning? Brandy's birthday is coming up."

"I have that interview with Sargeant this afternoon at two o'clock," I reminded him, "and there's a chance I may have to view a lineup at some point today."

"Got it, Chief. I'll stay put."

"No, go ahead. I was just letting you know the parameters. With everyone gone today, we're safe. At least until this afternoon," I said. "What do you have planned for her?"

"Nothing yet. That's the problem. When you've been together for as long as we have, you start running out of ingenious ideas."

Gav and I hadn't had the chance to celebrate much together. Not yet, at least. I hoped someday to share Bucky's lament. "You'll think of something."

"You're sure it's okay?" Bucky asked as he untied his apron and began to unsnap his smock. "I'll be back well before two."

"Take your time and good luck."

Five minutes after Bucky left, Neville Walker's assistant called, summoning me to the Secret Service's West Wing office. I was surprised to find Kager and Beem waiting for me when I arrived.

"The detectives are back," Neville said unnecessarily. "They'd like you to look at some photos." He gestured me into the same chair I'd sat in last night as the two detectives resumed their positions.

"Feels like déjà vu," I said. "I thought you said I'd be called to come down to the station today."

The studiously silent Beem tugged at his lower lip. Kager shot me a chilly "yes, you're right, but that's not important right now" smile and said, "We're eager to close this case; and the sooner you make positive identification, the better. With that in mind, we brought photos of individuals and would appreciate it if you could take a look at them."

She opened a file folder and began laying mug shots across the top of Neville's desk in a slow, precise row. The Secret Service agent remained silent, but I caught a look in his eyes that I read as disconcerted surprise.

When she laid the fifth photo down, I said, "That's him. That's the man with the tattooed fingers. The one I thought of as Hunter because of the movie *The Night of the Hunter.*"

Kager and Beem exchanged a glance. "You're certain?" she asked. "You told us he wore a scarf."

"I can't explain it," I said. "But his eyes. The shape of his forehead, maybe. I can't tell you why, but I recognized him immediately."

"He's the one you claimed didn't speak, is that correct?"

"Right. He didn't say a word."

She gathered the photos back up and began laying down another set. "Do you think you'll be able to recognize the other man?"

The guy with the hairy knuckles had remained behind me for most of the assault. I hadn't gotten up close and personal with him—or his face—the way I had with Hunter. "I'll do my best."

She placed a series of photos down, and although I studied them closely, not one hit me the way the first photo had. "I'm sorry," I said.

Dismissing my apology, she scooped up the pictures and began laying out another row. "Oh," I said, "I thought we were done. Hey—" I pointed to the third photo. "Him. I can't swear to it like I did with the other guy, but he feels familiar."

The two detectives exchanged yet another one of their confounding looks. Beem stood. Kager gathered up the pictures then stood, too. "As soon as we arrange for the lineup, we will be in touch," she said.

"Hold on a minute." Neville didn't get up. "Chef Paras and I were under the impression that the lineup would take place today. Has something changed?" He held a hand out toward the folder Kager had tucked under her arm. "Are the individuals Ms. Paras identified the same ones you originally suspected and intended to bring in?"

Kager shook her head. "I'm not at liberty to say."

"Then"—Neville folded his hands again as precisely as before—"tell me this much: Are you here today because you've been *unsuccessful* in picking up these persons of interest?"

Kager scratched at one eyebrow with the tip of a fingernail. "We will be in touch once we've assembled a suitable lineup," she said.

"That didn't answer my question."

"The less I share about our investigation, the less we color Ms. Paras's recollections. I'm sure you understand."

Neville stared. "As long as *you* understand how important it is to the White House to have these two criminals apprehended and charged as soon as possible."

Beem tilted his head toward the door. Kager turned to me. "I'm sure we'll be in touch soon."

When they left, I stood up. "I don't like it," Neville said before I could turn for the door. He fingered an ear lobe and stared at the wall. "They know these guys, they know where they live. There's no reason why they couldn't have rousted them and hauled them in today."

"What's the holdup then?" I asked. "Excuse the pun."

Neville glared, but allowed a quick grin. "That's what I want to know. Even if these two detectives don't deal directly with this gang, they have the resources to find them. Shouldn't take more than a couple of hours."

"Unless the criminals left town?" I asked. "Or someone is hiding them?"

"Possible, but unlikely." He continued to tug at his ear lobe. "I don't like it," he said again. "When is Agent Gavin expected to return?"

I didn't know, and said so.

"Has he been apprised of the situation?"

"I haven't had a chance to talk with him," I said. "He's completely out of touch."

Neville offered a wry smile. "Part of the job," he said. "Tough to have a family when the country always has to come first."

I didn't know how to respond to that, so I didn't.

A HALF HOUR BEFORE I NEEDED TO BE UPSTAIRS with Sargeant, Bucky returned to the kitchen empty-handed. "Browsing the stores didn't do me any good," he said. "I have less than a week to figure out what to get Brandy."

"I'll bet you come up with the perfect idea," I said. "Think about what she always talks about. What's important to her?"

"Hmm," he said. "Easier said than done."

I turned at a brisk knock at our doorway. "Chef Paras?"

Elaine stood there. One of our administrative assistants, she'd worked in the White House longer than I'd been alive. Taller and heavier than me, with silvery hair pulled back in a low pony, she wore rhinestone-studded cat's-eye glasses and an apologetic air.

"I'm sorry to bother you," she said with a smile and a swift glance at her watch, "but the candidate for the assistant chef position is here. Mr. Sargeant would like to know if you're free to start the interview early."

"That's fine." I stripped off my apron and conferred with Bucky before heading upstairs with Elaine.

"Mr. Sargeant will be very pleased," she said as we made our way up the quiet stairway. "He has a particularly busy schedule this afternoon."

"I take it Margaret isn't back yet?"

She shook her head. "Mr. Sargeant has been trying to reach her to find out when she expects to return."

"Margaret is always so on top of things," I said. "I'm surprised she hasn't kept him better informed."

Elaine pursed her lips and gave a one-shoulder shrug. "Family emergencies turn a person's life upside down. It's hard to predict how people will react in a crisis."

"I'm sorry for whatever she's going through."

"You may go right in," Elaine said when we reached the chief usher's office. "They're waiting for you."

AFTER WELCOMING CANDIDATES AND MAKING appropriate introductions, Sargeant liked to open interviews by summarizing general expectations of all White House employees. It was a good icebreaker and usually served as an effective segue for questions.

When Sargeant finished his intro, he turned the meeting over to me.

If old-school pizza ads could come alive, then one of them sat before us now. Nicholas Dulkin looked like a blend of every smiling, chubby, mustachioed chef caricature out there. Most candidates sat up straight and a little bit forward during the interview process, conveying eagerness or perhaps their discomfort. Dulkin sat back, hands folded across his prodigious middle, twiddling his thumbs.

Maybe it was a nervous habit, maybe he wasn't attempting to personify boredom. I reminded myself to give him the benefit of the doubt.

Dulkin answered my questions well enough; there was no doubt that this chef had the chops. I couldn't help wondering, however, why a professional of his caliber would seek a junior position. So I asked.

He shifted his weight. "The White House kitchen is, of course, the most prestigious in the nation, possibly the world."

Sargeant and I waited for him to continue.

He smoothed his mustache with the back of his thumb, one side at a time. "The chance to prepare meals for our president is every chef's dream, isn't it?"

I didn't sense outright prevarication from him, but I couldn't allow that sort of non-answer to slide. "Are you telling us that working here has always been your dream?"

"If that's the case, please clarify." Sargeant donned his reading glasses to sift through the Secret Service's reports on the man. "You don't seem to have ever sought a position at the White House before this."

Dulkin smoothed his mustache again, darting a glance at Sargeant, who watched with his characteristic squirrel-like alertness. "I have spent all of my adult life in kitchens and I have—with utter modesty—created spectacular meals for hundreds of important guests. I could easily continue to do so and retire comfortably whenever I wanted."

We waited for the "but."

Instead, he rolled his shoulders. "I'm not married and have few family ties. There is nothing for me at home. Each day I travel to my workplace and if I'm successful—which I usually am—I enhance our guests' lives a little bit. The time has come for me to take stock and to ask myself how to enhance my own life."

"How do you expect working at the White House to do that for you?" I asked.

"It's not just the White House." He met my gaze. "It's also working with you."

"Oh?" Sargeant's chin tilted up. "Do you care to expand on that?"

"I hesitate to admit this . . ."

"Please," Sargeant said, with feigned solicitude, "we're eager to know what makes you tick."

A flush crawled into Dulkin's high cheeks, even as he maintained eye contact. "I have had a good life. A successful life. But most kitchens do not afford the opportunity for intrigue and excitement that your kitchen does." He pointed inward, with both hands. "I'm middle-aged and out of shape. Your Secret Service would never hire me. And yet . . . you." Unfolding his hands, he stretched them toward me. "Like me, you are a chef and yet unlike me, you've been involved in world events. Your legacy will live on. I am forgotten by the time a diner sits down to his next meal."

Taken aback, it took me a moment to find my voice. "Am I to understand that you see this White House position as some sort of gateway to intrigue?"

"It sounds ridiculous when you put it that way." His face, glowing with perspiration now, continued to redden. "But, in a way, yes. I want a legacy. I want to have done something important and big. I want to be known for more than I am now. You have accomplished so much for someone so young. I can learn from you."

To my great surprise, Sargeant appeared amused rather than perturbed by Dulkin's impassioned speech. His brows came together briefly, and he jotted a note on the papers before him. "I see. Thank you for your candor, Mr. Dulkin."

"I'm probably the top candidate you'll interview." He talked faster now. Using the back of his hand to wipe at his glistening hairline, Dulkin's gaze jumped back and forth between us. "I wouldn't go looking for trouble. I hope you understand that. Have I ruined my chances by admitting that I long for a more meaningful life?"

Before Sargeant or I could respond, Elaine stepped into the office. "Excuse me, sir. You have a phone call."

Sargeant's head snapped up. "I told you we were not to be disturbed."

The assistant didn't cower or apologize. She held a pen tightly clasped in one fist and gripped the doorknob with her other hand. The look in the woman's eyes underscored her point even before she spoke again. She widened the door, this time addressing me and Dulkin. "Would you both please join me out here to allow Mr. Sargeant privacy for his phone call?"

CHAPTER 6

WHEN SARGEANT OPENED HIS OFFICE DOOR A
few minutes later, Dulkin jumped to his feet, displaying undisguised impatience to resume the interview. I remained rooted
in my chair, rattled by the expression on our chief usher's face.
I'd witnessed Sargeant suffer devastating news in the past, and
I recognized that look on him now. Something terrible had
happened.

Dulkin barely had time to open his mouth before Sargeant
held his hand up, palm out. "Elaine will escort you out," he
said to the man. "We will be in touch."

Dulkin glanced to me. "That's it then?"

If this man harbored any delusions of becoming the next
James Bond, he needed to work on his observational skills.
"Yes." I touched his arm. "Let's go." To Elaine, I said, "I'll be
happy to see Mr. Dulkin out."

"No, Ollie." Sargeant's snappish tone and uncharacteristic

use of my nickname stopped me cold. Pinching the bridge of his nose, he turned away. "In my office, please."

He shut the door behind us. "Please sit," he said as he lowered himself into his chair. "I know I need to."

I reclaimed my spot across from him, feeling my heart rate accelerate in fear of the unknown. He peeled his reading glasses off and threw them to the desk, never making eye contact with me. Using both hands he rubbed his face slowly. Very slowly.

I remained silent as long as I could. "What happened, Peter?"

"A moment, please." Through the space between his wrists, I watched his Adam's apple bob. He kept his face down, shifting his fingers to massage his eye sockets before moving them to his temples. His ministrations went on for an unbearably long time before he finally raised his gaze to meet mine.

He struggled to speak. "I have just been notified that Margaret is dead."

My hand flew to my mouth.

Times like these, my gut processes information faster than my mind can form words. How could her family emergency have produced such a result? Had she actually been ill herself and reluctant to admit it? How could a person who seemed perfectly healthy have succumbed so quickly?

As though he'd heard the cyclone of questions roaring through my brain, Sargeant waved the air between us with one hand while covering his eyes with the other. "No," he said. "It's not like that." He drew in a deep breath and looked up at me again. "Margaret was murdered."

"What?" The worthless exclamation plopped out, helping no one and serving no purpose whatsoever. Condemning my instinctive response, I struggled for control of my wits and emotions as I searched for better words. "Tell me what you know."

"Very little." The downturned edges of his mouth quivered as he fought to maintain control. "Neville Walker made the notification after the Metro Police contacted him. We have few details at this point, but the police seem to believe that she was killed over the weekend." He pulled in a deep breath through his nose and blinked several times. "That would certainly explain why she hadn't been in contact."

"I'm so sorry to hear this," I said when I found my voice again. "Where did it happen? That is, did her death have something to do with the emergency that called her away?"

He shook his head. "There was no family emergency. When the police contacted Margaret's next of kin, they said that they hadn't heard from her in more than a week."

"Then why . . ."

Before I could ask the question, Sargeant answered it. "We don't know. Because Margaret was employed here, the Secret Service will be working with Metro Police on this matter. There are any number of possible scenarios to explain her fabrication. None of them good."

WHEN I RETURNED TO THE KITCHEN, BUCKY grinned. "Hey, I've got good news for you." One second later, his cheery expression faded. Immediately solicitous, he pulled out the chair we kept near the computer and encouraged me to sit. "What happened?"

When I told him, he gripped the nearby counter for support. "Murdered? Are they sure?"

I didn't know anything beyond what Sargeant had told me. "I doubt they'd make such a grave statement without cause."

The two of us sat silently for a long moment.

"She and I didn't really get along, you know," I said quietly.

"I mean, she was dependable and good at her job, but as a person . . . I didn't particularly care for her."

"She irked a lot of people. That's not to say that anyone here would have wished her ill. Never that."

"I know. But now I wish I would have tried harder to break through to her. People like Margaret who go out of their way to put other people down, usually do so because they're unhappy with themselves, or their lives."

"What happened to her isn't your fault, Ollie."

"I know that."

"Then don't blame yourself."

I rubbed my forehead. "I should have tried harder."

"I know it isn't right to speak ill of the dead, but I'm not one to confer sainthood on a person just because they're no longer around," he said. "You were kinder to her than she deserved."

"I thought I'd lead by example," I said with a rueful chuckle. "Does that sound conceited or what? I truly believed that over time she would come to understand that there was no need to . . ."

"Not everyone can be turned around, Chief, no matter how much you want to believe otherwise."

I shook myself. We still had dinner to prepare. I would mourn Margaret in my own way, but later. "You said something about good news?" I asked.

"It was," Bucky said. "Not sure how you'll feel about it now. Secret Service came down to let you know that Josh offered to bring a treat to school tomorrow and wants to make it himself. He asked if you might have time for him today. I knew how much you missed working with him, so I said that would be fine. If, in light of what's happened, you'd rather not, I'm sure he would understand."

I ran a hand up and through my hair. Of all days for Josh to come work in the kitchen. "No, it's good." I straightened. "Working with him will help me focus on the positive."

JOSH SHOWED UP A COUPLE OF HOURS LATER. He hadn't grown much taller in the nearly three years we'd known him, but though the dark hair and eyes stayed the same, the gangly little boy was gone. Over the past year, he'd picked up weight and a habit of shrugging when he answered a question. Although I wouldn't call him chubby, he could no longer be characterized as lean.

Whenever the president's son joined us, his Secret Service detachment escorted him to the kitchen. Once there, however, they usually stepped outside of the working area in order to allow Josh privacy and all of us room to move. Two agents accompanied him today. I'd never met either of the men, but they had evidently been instructed on the how-to of the situation. They quickly withdrew from the room.

After greeting me and Bucky, Josh asked, "You got my message, right?"

"I did," I said. "Good to see you. How's school going?"

With his back to me as he pulled an apron from our stash, he lifted one shoulder. "It's okay."

"What would you like to make today?" I asked. "This is for the kids at school, right?"

Bucky and I had come up with a few options for today's project—new recipes we were convinced Josh would enjoy preparing—but before I could suggest any, Josh finished tying the apron and said, "I was thinking we'd do a quick batch of those brownie bites—you know which ones I mean?"

"The ones we usually garnish with pecans?" I asked.

"That's it. Those are pretty easy."

I could make brownie bites in my sleep. Josh could, too. In terms of adventure, this project rated a big fat zero. "Does anyone in your classroom have a nut allergy?" I asked. "If you want, we could come up with a new treat. Chocolate but without the added nuts. Wouldn't that be fun?"

"Can't we just keep the nuts off?" he asked, with the ever-present shrug. "I don't need anything weird or fancy. Just normal brownies."

"No problem," I said, fighting disappointment. Behind Josh, Bucky raised his eyebrows; I knew he read my mind. "How many do you need?"

"We could double the recipe and leave some home, I guess. That would work."

"What sort of garnish would you like?" I asked. "You remember those mini-leaves Marcel used to decorate your grandmother's birthday cake last week? They look really cool, and are perfect for fall. We may have enough left over."

"The gold ones?" he asked with alarm. "No, that's way too much. Plain brownies are fine. I don't want anything special."

Nothing special. Got it. "Okay," I said. "Let's get started."

We went through the motions of gathering, measuring, and combining ingredients in near silence. Josh was a polite enough kid to reply to my questions, but offered nothing in terms of flavor. His answers were quick and covered minimal ground.

I did learn that not all the students from his grammar school had automatically moved up to the same middle school. There were, in fact, only two boys from the old school who shared classes with him now. I also learned that Josh hadn't yet found any extracurricular activities to participate in. He tolerated math and music. Hated gym.

By the time the brownies came out of the oven, we'd already prepared the frosting and apparently exhausted our conversation. "Do you mind if I take these upstairs and finish there?" Josh asked. "I have homework."

"Sure," I said. "Let me pack things up so you don't burn your fingers."

He looked as though he wanted to protest, but allowed me to place the still-hot muffin pans onto one of the rolling carts we used to send food up to the First Family. I covered the frosting bowl and tucked that onto the shelf below.

As if by magic, Josh's Secret Service escorts arrived along with a butler to help manage the transport. "I could do this myself you know," Josh said under his breath. "I'm not completely helpless."

"People like to feel needed," I said.

He shrugged.

"See you next time, Josh," I said as they departed.

He turned and shot me a smile over his shoulder. "Thanks."

As soon as the elevator door closed behind them, Bucky said, "Well, wasn't that fun?"

"I feel awful," I said. "And I can't tell if it's because this was the most lackluster visit with Josh I've ever had, or if it's because I'm relieved it's over." I pulled the stool out from beneath the computer, sat down, and massaged my forehead with both hands. "Maybe it was me. I mean, after the news about Margaret today, my heart wasn't in this."

"It wasn't you, Ollie," Bucky said. "He's a good kid, but tonight he wanted to be anywhere but here. That was painfully obvious."

"It was, wasn't it?" I frowned at the ceiling. "I've never been an almost-twelve-year-old boy—"

"I have," Bucky said. "Even now, all these years later, I remember how much I hated middle school. And compared to

Josh, I had it easy. My father wasn't the president of the United States."

"I wish I could do something for him."

"You can't. Not this time."

"I worry about him."

"He's a good kid," Bucky said again. "Trust me. He'll come around."

CHAPTER 7

A STAFF MEMO WENT OUT INFORMING ALL PERsonnel that White House access codes and passwords were to be changed. That happened often enough around here, but after Margaret's untimely and violent death, it was a crucial precaution.

Agent Neville Walker called me, personally, to inform me of another necessary safety measure. "I'm assigning an agent to escort you to and from the White House."

I didn't argue. "After today's news about Margaret, I admit to being skittish walking alone in the dark," I said. "But I do hope to regain my self-sufficiency soon."

"Until we know more about your attack and whether it was in any way tied to what happened to Ms. Brown, we will take every precaution."

"You don't really believe they could be related, do you? The police are pretty sure they know who the gangbangers are."

Neville cleared his throat. "Until we have more information, you will be escorted to and from home."

"Understood," I said. "Thank you."

He hung up.

When it was time to leave I was pleased to discover I'd been assigned Agent Romero, the same agent I'd gotten to know yesterday. "How are you?" I asked when she showed up in the kitchen. "Looks like you're stuck with me again."

"I'm happy to see to your safety," she said. "Have you gotten your locks changed?"

"I'm to pick up my new keys from James at the front desk tonight. The locksmith replaced both the handle and the deadbolt locks."

"Good decision," she said.

Agent Romero allowed me to sit in the passenger seat rather than insist I ride in the back. I'd had enough experience with both spots and much preferred sitting up front, where I felt less like a prisoner and more like an equal.

Agent Romero and I chatted amiably for a few minutes when my cell phone came alive with its default ringtone. I didn't recognize the number on display.

I had high hopes, but answered cautiously. "Hello?"

"It's me," Gav said.

Flushed with relief and happiness, I broke into a smile I knew he couldn't see. "It's good to hear from you."

"Listen, I only have a minute but I wanted to let you know I won't be home tonight."

"Not again," I said before I could stop the plaintive tone. "Sorry, sorry," I amended. "I understand." And I did.

"Two things," he said. "I heard about Margaret Brown."

"I wondered if you knew."

"And I've been updated about what happened to you."

"Who told you?" I asked.

"Neville Walker," he said. "You and I need to talk more when I finally get home. I may not be able to call again before then. In the meantime, please be careful."

"I am."

"You're being escorted to and from home, right?"

"As we speak."

"Good. Neville said he'd take care of that." I could almost hear him nod. "I'm sorry I can't say more right now. It's touch-and-go at my location."

I wanted to ask if he was in Wisconsin at the Cenga Prison bombing site. Of course, I couldn't. "I'm thinking about you," was the best I could manage.

"I'm thinking about you, too. Always," he said. "I'll be home as soon as I can, but please, be extra careful."

"Don't worry. I'm sure all this extra precaution is unnecessary."

"Ollie. It's you we're talking about." Before I could reply to that, he said, "Gotta go. Love you."

"Love you, too."

When I hung up, I looked longingly at my phone before tucking it back into my pocket.

Smiling, Romero kept her eyes on the road. "Gavin's a good man."

"The best," I said.

THE FOLLOWING MORNING, AFTER BREAKFAST had been served and the kitchen cleaned, Bucky and I began poring over plans for the week's menus.

"Mrs. Hyden has two working lunches we need to talk about."

"We didn't plan for those last week?"

"Newly scheduled for this week. It's a good thing we're so

flexible," I said with a smile. "Tuesday at noon and Thursday at one-thirty. With the weather turning cooler, and the fact that the Tuesday meeting will likely run long, how about a hearty dish? I'd like to offer her something substantial, like chicken chili."

"Got it." Bucky scribbled notes on our working copy. "For Thursday, though, we probably ought to go lighter. The First Lady often mentions how much she enjoys finger sandwiches. Maybe we can work them in?"

"Exactly what I was thinking. How about an assortment of sandwiches served along with our mushroom-tomato bisque?"

The kitchen phone rang. I reached for it as Bucky answered me. "We haven't made that soup in a while," he said, continuing to jot notes. "Good idea."

"Chef Paras?" Elaine said when I answered. "I hope I'm not interrupting you."

"What can I do for you?" I asked.

"Mr. Sargeant and Agent Walker would like to meet with you in Mr. Sargeant's office."

I made a "Yikes" face at Bucky as I asked, "Right now?"

"Yes, if that's not too much of an imposition." Elaine knew as well as I did that I had no choice in the matter. Although I appreciated the older woman's gentle approach, it was in such stark contrast to what we'd become accustomed to from Margaret that I couldn't help draw comparisons. Which made me think about Margaret's brutal murder.

I cradled the phone between my shoulder and ear as I untied my apron. "I'll be right up."

SARGEANT'S OFFICE WASN'T VERY BIG. THOUGH the space accommodated three adults with relative ease, it grew more cramped with each additional arrival. That's why, when Elaine ushered me in, I stopped at the doorway, surprised to find myself the fifth to join the meeting.

"Come in, Olivia." Sargeant sat behind his desk. He had his reading glasses in his right hand and gestured me in with his left. "I understand you've met Detectives Beem and Kager."

"Yes," I said, shaking hands with the two officers. Extra chairs had been brought in and I nodded a greeting to Neville Walker as I slipped into the only empty seat, next to him. Kager sat nearest the door to my right, Beem sat behind us, farthest from the desk.

Sargeant waited for Elaine to shut the office door. "Ms. Paras," he began, adopting a more formal tone. "There has been a development that the detectives, Agent Walker, and I believe you should be made aware of."

"Does this have to do with Margaret?" I asked.

Neville answered me. "Detectives Kager and Beem are not involved in investigating Ms. Brown's homicide."

"Then this"—I made a circular motion with my index finger—"has to do with my purse being stolen?" As unlikely as that seemed, it was the only conclusion that made sense.

"Yes, the detectives have a few more questions for you."

With Neville to my left, Kager to my right, Sargeant across from me, and Beem in the back, I couldn't make eye contact with all of them without turning and twisting in my seat while I talked. "I still haven't been called to identify my attackers, so I assume that means you haven't picked them up yet." Settling my attention on Kager, I asked, "What's going on?"

She pulled up a canvas bag that had been leaning against her chair and drew something out. "Does this belong to you?"

In her palm she held a set of car keys on an Eiffel Tower keychain.

"Yes, that's mine," I said. Although I didn't use my little car often, I always kept the keys in my purse. About to pluck them from her, I stopped myself. "But shouldn't that be in an evidence bag?"

"No." After handing the keys to me, she leaned forward, resting her elbows on the tops of her knees. I got the impression she wanted to secure my undivided attention. "The two men you identified as responsible for your attack Sunday night are dead."

"Both of them? Oh no." The entire room fell silent while I digested the information. Reading between the lines, I hazarded a guess, "Not by natural causes, I take it?"

She made eye contact with Neville as she answered me. "The two men were killed, execution style, in a manner not inconsistent with gang warfare."

"Not inconsistent with gang warfare," I repeated. "Wow. That's some careful wording. I have to ask why you're qualifying it that way. Is there something about their deaths that casts doubt on a gang hit?"

From over my shoulder, Neville said, "I told you she was sharp."

Kager's expression didn't change. "When we were here the first time, we withheld the men's names so as to avoid compromising the identification process." Pulling the mug shots from her folder, she placed them on Sargeant's desk and pointed to the one I'd referred to as Hunter. "This is Viceboy," she said. "He had an unusual voice, and we believe that's the reason he never said a word during the purse-snatch."

She tapped the other photo. "And this is Dagger." I recognized him as the one with the hairy knuckles. "Their bodies were found out of their territory. Very far beyond their borders. More telling than that, however, is the fact that there's no chatter on the street about this hit. No one seems to know anything."

Beem piped up from the back of the room. "When it's

an act of revenge, you hear talk. They *want* to get the word out. This time, nothing."

"What does that mean?" I asked.

"For us, it means *your* case is closed."

"And yet, here we are," I said slowly. "I assume there's more to the story."

Kager made a so-so motion. "Every once in a while we come up against a situation like this one, where an act of gang violence doesn't fit the pattern. Chances are the two victims were taken down by a rival gang. It happens all the time."

I waited.

Neville leaned on Sargeant's desk. I sat back to give him room. "The Secret Service would appreciate it greatly if you and Detective Beem kept us advised of your progress in this investigation."

"As I said, our involvement is over and our case is closed. The homicides took place outside our jurisdiction," Kager said. "We won't be handling that."

Neville blinked a few times and gave a thoughtful nod. "Let's try this again. The Secret Service would appreciate it *greatly* if you and Detective Beem kept us informed as the homicide investigation progresses."

She expelled one of those half-breaths that precedes a refusal. "Agent Walker," she began.

Agent Walker rapped his fingers on Sargeant's desk, commanding the floor. "We aren't interested in gang warfare, if indeed that's what's going on here. We're concerned as to whether or not Ms. Paras's attack is connected to another staff member's homicide."

"I assure you—" Kager said.

"You cannot assure me of anything yet, can you, Detective?" he said smoothly. "I understand that both Ms. Brown's homicide and the two gang members' executions occurred out of your jurisdiction. We are in touch with authorities from both areas. I'm not asking you to overstep your boundaries. What I am asking you is to not let this matter drop."

Kager lifted both hands in a helpless gesture. "There's little else we can do."

Sargeant cleared his throat. "The White House would appreciate your cooperation in this matter. We would consider it a personal favor."

Kager glanced toward the back of the room and her partner. "Beem?" she asked. "What do you say?"

The older detective shook his head. "As my partner stated, the investigation into the attack on Ms. Paras is now closed," he said.

Sargeant got to his feet. "Then this meeting is at an end." He used his reading glasses to point the way out. "Thank you for your time, Detectives."

Clearly surprised by the swift dismissal, the two officers stood. Beem turned back when he got to the door. "A personal favor to the White House, you say?"

Sargeant nodded.

"My partner and I will do what we can. There may be resources we can tap into to follow up," Beem said. "That's the best we can offer."

"Then we look forward to receiving updates," Sargeant replied. "Thank you."

When they were gone, Sargeant returned to his seat. I faced the two men. "What don't I know?"

Neville ran his thumb and index finger down the corners of his mouth. "Margaret Brown's murder has us very concerned. Not only because of the loss of one of our own," he said, "but because of the circumstances of her death."

"What kind of circumstances?"

"Tell her." Sargeant leaned both elbows on his desk, his

forehead propped in his palms, rubbing his eyes. "It's better she knows what's going on."

"I agree," Neville said. "Margaret was killed in her home on Friday."

"She called in Friday, didn't she?" I directed my comment to Sargeant but he didn't look up. "The family emergency?"

"That's right," Neville said. "Whoever killed Ms. Brown must have ordered her to notify the White House that she'd be absent so that no one would come looking for her. That tells us that those responsible either targeted Margaret because of her position here, or panicked when she told them where she worked."

When Sargeant looked up again, I was startled by the pouchy bags beneath his eyes. "She may have tried to bargain her way out."

"She may have," Neville allowed. "Evidence from the murder site leads us to believe that whoever killed her took his time. Additionally, there are indications that at least two individuals were involved. Margaret did not die quickly."

I raised a fist to my lips. I had no words.

"Margaret Brown's position here gave her access to a great deal of privileged information. While we mourn her loss, our primary concern right now must be security. We know whoever killed her took her White House–issued cell phone."

"Before you ask," Sargeant added, "no, we are unable to locate it. They've either turned it off or managed to disable the GPS. Until the device comes back online, we're in the dark."

"We have the means to track any attempts to infiltrate our systems," Neville said. "But if it turns out that Ms. Brown was incentivized to share classified information . . ."

"Incentivized?" I asked. "Is that what you mean by 'bargained'? That they told her they'd let her go if she shared information?"

Neville shot a glance toward Sargeant before answering. "She did not die quickly," he said again. "We don't know what transpired in her home, or what additional information she divulged to her killers, if any. The knowledge Margaret possessed goes far beyond access codes and passwords. Everything she knew about day-to-day life here at the White House could now be in criminal hands. And that puts us all at risk."

I started to ask a question, but he silenced me with a look.

"The potential for a breach here is enormous. Understand that we have already taken steps to adjust the First Family's schedule. Every activity they had scheduled outside the White House has now been changed. But that's merely the tip of the iceberg. Margaret held a wealth of personal knowledge of staff members: who arrives at what time, which establishments people frequent after work"—he lowered his chin to deliver a meaningful look—"which Metro line the executive chef takes home every night."

"You don't think—"

"We must consider the possibility," he said, cutting me off. "Until proven otherwise, we must operate under the assumption that you were targeted for a reason. Think about it, Ollie. High-ranking gang members don't usually bother with purse-snatchings. And then those two men are found murdered, far away from their home turf, and no other gang claims responsibility?"

"You think those two were hired to attack me?"

"It's a theory," Neville said. "One I'm not ready to dismiss, no matter what the Metro Police will have us believe."

"But what could they have possibly wanted from me?" I asked. "There was nothing sensitive in my purse." I pressed a hand against my chest, where my White House ID sat beneath my smock. "My phone was in my pocket, and my lanyard was around my neck."

"And where are the two gangbangers now? Dead. Because they failed?" Neville let that sink in. "I'd say that's entirely possible."

"If you're right, then who's behind all this?" I asked.

Neville and Sargeant exchanged another look. "We're working on that," Neville said. "But until we know more, we will do our utmost to keep you safe."

CHAPTER 8

NEVILLE AND SARGEANT ASKED ME TO KEEP THE specifics about Margaret's death to myself. They assured me that an additional staff memo would be issued later in the day informing everyone about Margaret's untimely death, and urging all White House employees to exercise caution. Additionally, there would be the ever-present reminder to report any suspicious activity no matter how small.

By the time Bucky and I finished sending up today's chicken chili for the First Lady's lunch meeting, the memo arrived in our inboxes.

"Wow," Bucky said when he read it. "Reading this makes it sound like they suspect Margaret was killed *because* she worked at the White House." He lifted an eyebrow in an unspoken question.

"Take it seriously, okay? Be careful. You and Brandy both have ties to the White House. If you think anything seems a little wonky, don't hesitate to call for help."

"What aren't you telling me?" he asked.

I placed a finger to my lips. "You know the drill."

He frowned.

"Just promise you'll be extra vigilant, okay?" I asked.

"You got it, Chief."

WHEN I RETURNED TO THE KITCHEN AFTER MY second trip to Sargeant's office that day, Bucky perked up. "How did it go?"

I shook my head, sorry to disappoint him. "I didn't think hiring a chef would prove this difficult," I said. "Wait, let me rephrase that: I knew it would be impossible to replace Cyan, but I never thought we'd have such a hard time finding a qualified person to do the job."

"I thought our human resources team vetted all these candidates before setting up interviews."

"They did," I said. "It's not that these individuals aren't accomplished, or that they aren't capable of handling the job, it's the personality quirks that won't work here."

"Oh, come on. You've run this kitchen with amazing efficiency no matter who worked here. Even when dealing with the likes of Virgil."

"My point exactly," I said as I donned a fresh apron. "We were all miserable with him around. There's no way I will allow that kind of negativity in my kitchen again. I had such high hopes for this Audrey Lund, too." About to scour the grill, I stopped and looked around. "Wow. Already done. You've been busy."

"Getting there," he said as he sanitized the center worktop.

"Looks like all that's left is the sink," I said, turning the faucet on. "I'll take care of this."

"I understood your hesitations about that James Bond wannabe, but what was up with the woman you interviewed today?"

"Where do I begin?" I asked with a laugh.

"How about by telling your husband how much you've missed him?"

I spun. Gav stood in the doorway. I took a second to shut off the flowing water, then wiped my hands on my apron. Before I could start toward him, he'd crossed the kitchen to wrap me in a hug.

"I've missed you," I said. "More than you know."

He pressed his face into the top of my head and made an indecipherable noise. "I needed to get back. To see for myself that you were safe."

"For the record, I'm safe, too, Agent Gavin," Bucky called from across the room.

Gav lifted his head, chuckling. "Sorry, Bucky. Good to see you."

As we parted, Bucky grinned. Waving the dish towel he was holding, he said, "Oh, please. Don't let me interrupt the happy homecoming."

"When did you get back?" I asked.

"Not long ago," Gav said. "I stopped in to talk with Neville. He's agreed to allow me to take over escort duties while I'm here."

"Makes it sound as though you expect to be called away any minute. Do you?"

"Hard to say." Gav shot a fleeting glance toward Bucky.

My assistant waved the dish towel again. "Go," he said. "You two have a lot of catching up to do, and you clearly can't talk in front of me."

"Are you sure?" I asked.

"I'll finish up here, no worries."

"Thanks, Bucky. You're the best."

"Yes, I am." This time he shook the dish towel. "And don't you forget it."

I WAS SURPRISED TO SEE GAV'S CAR PARKED just beyond the Southwest Appointment Gate. "Not a government-issue vehicle today?" I asked.

He smiled at me as he settled behind the steering wheel. "Nope."

"Can I surmise that you stopped back at the office and picked up all your personal belongings before you came to meet me?"

"Surmise at will," he said.

He pulled out into traffic, and I didn't even attempt to tamp down my good cheer. "Can I further surmise that this means you plan to be home for a while?"

"That I do."

If he hadn't been in the middle of a left turn at that moment, I would have thrown my arms around him. Instead, I sighed with deep contentment. "How is it that I lived blissfully on my own for nearly two decades and now that we're married I can barely endure a single day we're apart?"

His smile was as wide as mine. "I don't understand it, either. But I'm not about to complain."

I settled deeper into the passenger seat. "Agent Romero is pleasant enough, but you're far better company."

"Speaking of your added protection," he said, "did you get the locks changed?"

"I did." I told him that a new set of keys awaited him at home. "You know that the Metro Police are convinced I was simply in the wrong place at the wrong time."

Gav took his eyes off the road long enough to give me a sharp glance. "What do you think?"

"I don't know. I'd be willing to chalk it up as bad luck if it weren't for the Margaret situation."

Gav worked his jaw. "If the two incidents are related, we have to ask why they let you go." He turned to me again, briefly. "It tears me apart to have to say it, but they could have killed you. They didn't. Why not?"

"Maybe because I wasn't targeted. Maybe because this *was* a mere purse-snatching."

Gav stared ahead, accelerating as traffic cleared. "You have no idea how much I hope that's true. But we can't relax our guard until we know for certain."

"Neville and Sargeant are pushing the two detectives to find out more. They aren't thrilled, but seem willing."

"I know. Neville briefed me."

"Merely professional courtesy? Or is there more going on behind the scenes?" I studied him. "Seems unusual for the head of PPD to consult with you personally on this one. Unless there's more to it."

"You, my dear wife, are too sharp for your own good." When he turned to me this time I caught the glint in his eyes that told me he was pleased by the question. "We can't tie Margaret's murder or your attack to any of the global issues we're dealing with, yet. But that doesn't mean they aren't related."

"Do you really believe such a thing is likely?"

"More than likely," he said. "But suspecting a connection doesn't mean one exists."

I watched him navigate the busy roads for a minute. "You may not be able to answer this, but were you in Wisconsin? At the Cenga Prison bombing site?"

"I can answer that. Yes, I was."

"And was Armustan behind the attack?"

"Joe Yablonski is still in Wisconsin, finishing up paperwork," he said, not answering my question. Adopting a far-too-casual tone, he added, "He's arranged to have our apartment building watched around the clock."

"Whoa," I said. "What's going on?"

Grimacing, Gav made a right turn. "Let's hope it's nothing."

BACK AT THE APARTMENT, WE COVERED LESS-dire topics, including my frustrated attempts to hire Cyan's replacement.

"You've been shorthanded for quite a while now," Gav said as the two of us worked together to cobble dinner out of refrigerator leftovers. "She left almost immediately after the sequester ended, didn't she?"

"The scare at Blair House was too much for her." I peeled back the cover of a bowl. Green beans. How long ago had we made these? I sniffed. Not bad. Removing the cover completely, I set the bowl next in line for the microwave. "Cyan often lamented that the job takes everything from us: our time, our hearts, our lives. I think the terror she went through in fear for her life—literally—was too much to bear."

As we warmed what was left of a roast, the last few helpings of mashed potatoes, and the green beans, I told Gav about Nick Dulkin's interview and how the man had admitted to seeing himself as a kitchen-based warrior against terror.

"That's what you are," Gav said around a mouthful of potatoes. "Admit it."

"There's a big difference. I don't set out to get into trouble. It finds me."

"Which is another reason why I'm glad Joe ordered surveillance." Gav circled his fork in the air to encompass our building. "This time, we hope to take down that trouble before it sets its sights on you."

Back to the subject of the kitchen, I told Gav about the

second candidate we'd interviewed. "Another miss," I said. "She's worked at some of the most prestigious restaurants in the world, but hasn't stayed in any one position for longer than six months."

"Did you ask her about that?"

"Of course," I said. "She admitted that she has a small problem."

Gav cocked an eyebrow.

"When the pressure gets to be too much, she starts singing."

Gav nearly coughed out his food.

"She claims she can't help it, and oftentimes doesn't even know she's doing it. But when things get tense—like the last hour before a big dinner, for instance—she bursts into song."

"Like a human teakettle?"

I laughed. "Precisely. Seems she has a predilection for Gilbert and Sullivan and Elton John."

Having put down his utensils, Gav sat back and laughed. "And considering the kind of pressure you face in that kitchen on a daily basis—"

"We'd be serenaded nonstop, yes," I said. "I liked her, though. Her personality seemed like a good fit for us. But, I don't know. That singing thing could get old fast."

"At least she has good taste in music."

I pushed a few green beans to the middle of my plate and frowned at them. "Which is more than can be said for my taste in dinner tonight. I wish I would have planned something better for your first night home."

"Right about now, nothing could possibly be better," he said. "I'm back after being away and we're together. This, to me, is a perfectly wonderful meal. But"—he leaned forward—"what would you say to going out tomorrow night?"

"You know I never refuse dinner out."

"Good. You've had a crazy week. So have I. Let's let someone else take care of feeding us."

"Love it," I said. "Do you have anywhere in mind?"

"We haven't been to Suzette's in a long time."

"You're right," I said. "Do you think Jason's completely forgotten us by now? How long has it been? At least two months. More than that, I'll bet." I picked up the kitchen phone. "Let's make reservations. You know how busy it can get, even on a weeknight."

Gav watched me, grinning. "I'm sure Jason hasn't forgotten us. At least not completely."

Suzette's warm and witty owner answered the phone himself. "Ollie," Jason gushed when he came on the line. "Wonderful to hear from you. How's married life treating you?"

"Fabulous, as always," I said, picturing the gregarious restaurateur. Jason had a deep voice and rumbling laugh. If I'd never met him I would have pictured a Santa-size fifty-year-old. Jason, however, was just shy of forty with a slim build and shaved head. He resembled a skinny cue ball with glasses. "But it's been too long since we've seen you," I said. "Would you have room for us tomorrow night?"

Shortly after Gav and I had begun seeing one another, we'd stumbled upon Jason's establishment not far from the apartment. Suzette's quickly became our go-to restaurant. We'd gotten to know Jason from his stopping by our table on our weekly, sometimes twice-weekly, visits. The food was delicious and comforting, the former apartment space cozy and warm, with its chic blue linens and creaking wood floors. Thick-painted radiators dotted the perimeter. They served as steamy reminders of another time, another life, when the refurbished two-story had originally been built.

"Of course," Jason said. Then, as though he'd read my mind, added, "I assume you'd prefer the table in the window?"

We had a favorite table. It sat by itself up a step from the main level, tucked into the front window. Not only did it provide a wonderful street panorama, allowing us to people watch as we dined, its solitary setting made it the perfect spot for private conversation.

"We would love that, Jason," I said. "If that's at all possible . . ."

"I will make sure your favorite table is ready when you are. What time will you be joining us?"

In my haste to call, I'd neglected to nail down the details. I turned to Gav. "I have another interview scheduled late in the day tomorrow. But I could be out by six-thirty."

"Let's make it for seven then," he said.

Into the phone, I said, "Would seven o'clock work, Jason?"

"You're in the book as of right now. I can't wait to see you both."

"Same here. We've missed Suzette's."

"Music to my ears," Jason said. "See you tomorrow."

I hung up and turned to Gav. "How about tomorrow night we pretend we're a normal couple on a normal date? No worries about murderers or purse-snatchers. What do you say?"

Gav stood and wrapped an arm around my waist. He smiled, but his eyes weren't in it. "I wish we could."

CHAPTER 9

"YOU'RE IN A CHEERY MOOD," BUCKY SAID LATE
Wednesday afternoon as we prepared the First Family's dinner
entrée: pork chops with apple, walnut, and Gorgonzola salsa.
With as much assembled ahead of time as possible, we were
waiting until just before serving time to cook the chops.

"I am," I said. "Everything went right today. Perfectly right.
Do you know how seldom that happens? No timing issues. No
missing ingredients. I've got a date with my handsome husband
a few hours from now, and I plan to enjoy every minute."

"That man is good for you," Bucky said. "I've never seen
you as happy as you've been since the two of you got together."

"I never expected this sort of completeness in my life.
Sounds pretty sappy, doesn't it?"

"Not at all. You deserve this. You both do."

"You know . . ." I tapped a finger against my lips. "I'm
feeling so lighthearted I could practically burst into song."

"What are you? Alto? Soprano? Are you considering

hiring that chef to harmonize?" Bucky asked as laughter grabbed hold of him. "Dinner and a show in the White House kitchen every night. I love it!"

"I'm feeling a little guilty about rejecting that woman," I said. "Well, I haven't actually turned her down yet, but I intend to." Glancing around the quiet space, I asked, "How bad could it be?"

"She hasn't been able to hold onto a position for longer than six months, remember," he said, still grinning. "Wanna bet she doesn't limit herself to low-level humming?"

"You're probably right; poor thing. If she wants a career in a high-pressure environment she'd have to learn to control that habit."

Bucky looked up at the clock. "Speaking of interviews, you have another one coming up in about a half hour. Let's hope the third time is the charm."

"That's exactly—"

The kitchen phone rang. As I reached for the receiver, I groaned. "It's Sargeant. Let's hope candidate number three hasn't canceled."

"Olivia," Sargeant said when I answered, "would it be possible for you to come to my office a little early?"

"Has the candidate arrived already?"

"No. I have another matter to discuss with you before the interview begins." He didn't provide any further information but the tone of his voice led me to believe this "other matter" had nothing to do with hiring a new chef.

"I'll be up there shortly."

"Very good," he said.

"What's up now?" Bucky asked when I replaced the receiver.

"No idea." I rubbed my forehead. "I suppose I'll find out soon enough, though. Will you be okay handling the rest of dinner on your own?"

"Piece of cake."

"Thanks." Pulling off my apron and checking my smock, as I had so many times this week before heading to meet with Peter Sargeant, I mused aloud, "This is what I get for expounding on how perfectly the day was going."

"It might be nothing," Bucky said.

"Ewww." I noticed a starburst-shaped splatter near my collar, which sent me scrambling for a new smock. "Maybe." I tore off the old one and pulled on the new. "How do I look?"

"Like a chef I'd want to work for," Bucky said. "Good luck with the interview."

"Third time's the charm," I reminded him. "Keep the good thought."

I ARRIVED AT SARGEANT'S OFFICE LESS THAN five minutes later. Elaine greeted me warmly and told me to go right in and shut the door.

"Uh-oh," I said as I took a seat across from him. "Closed doors usually portend bad news."

Like last time, he held his reading glasses in one hand while he rubbed his eyes with the other. "Paul Vasquez made this job look so easy," he said before looking up at me. Sargeant had been in the position of chief usher for more than a year but, to me, it seemed as though he'd aged at least five in the interim.

"What happened?" I asked.

He donned his glasses to read from his notes. "Detective Beem called me about a half hour ago. He and Detective Kager were able to uncover more information about the two men who attacked you."

"Viceboy and Dagger."

"It appears that the duo was actually a trio."

Sitting up straighter, I conjured an image from Sunday

night. "There weren't three," I said. "I watched the two men run away. There was no one else with them."

"The third member of the group is either another general or a gang lieutenant, but may not have been with Viceboy and Dagger when they robbed you. The detectives have reason to believe this individual may be able to shed light on the situation. They plan to pick him up for questioning."

"He wasn't with them, but he's able to help with the investigation? I don't understand."

"The detectives have apparently taken our request to heart and are pursuing the matter with more enthusiasm than they exhibited last time they were here. Detective Beem wanted me to know that he and Kager would be following up personally with this third gang associate."

"Does this guy have a name?"

Sargeant frowned at his notes. "Cutthroat."

"Lovely."

"They're hoping Cutthroat will be able to tell us what Viceboy and Dagger were doing so far off their turf when they were executed, and why two gang generals would risk stealing a purse when they had minions willing to do that kind of dirty work for them."

"I appreciate the update," I said. "I think your comment about it being a favor to the White House is what piqued their interest. Thank you for that, by the way."

He nodded. "I'm pleased they haven't dropped the matter. Agent Walker and I haven't had much luck connecting with the team investigating Viceboy and Dagger's case, but we are in contact with the team handling Margaret's murder."

"Any news there?" I asked.

Sargeant bunched his mouth and took a deep breath before answering. "I've seen photos of the crime scene. Before you ask, trust me, Olivia: You don't want any part of them.

There's nothing to be gained, and the images will haunt you for years. I know they'll haunt me." He pulled his glasses off his face and rubbed his eyes again. "Her home was ransacked—vandalized. She died at the hands of monsters. I hope whoever tormented her suffers the same fate."

There was nothing I could say except, "I'm sorry."

Elaine tapped on the door, opened it, and peeked in. "Ms. Catalano is here for her interview."

Sargeant took another deep breath. "Thank you, Elaine. Please send her in." When his assistant left, he made eye contact with me. "We're overdue for good news. Let's hope this candidate is a winner."

SARGEANT AND I ASKED LOTTIE CATALANO most of our standard questions and she delivered thoughtful, intelligent answers to all of them. Older than Cyan by a few years—closer to my age, probably—Lottie had a small mouth, pink, puffy cheeks, and a tendency to bite her bottom lip. Her face was damp with perspiration, but her eyes were alert.

We were about three-quarters of the way through the interview when Sargeant asked about her availability. The sooner she could start the better, but everyone understood the need to provide a current employer with appropriate notice.

For the first time during the interview, Lottie winced. "I hope you both understand how very much I desire to work here," she said.

Sargeant and I exchanged a glance. There was a "but" screaming behind her words.

"Go ahead," he said.

"I first learned about the job opening three weeks ago," she said. "I applied immediately, of course. I never dreamed I'd be called in for an interview, but here I am."

We both waited.

"*Four* weeks ago," she said, stressing the word, "my husband and I put a bid on a house." She bit her lip. "In California. His parents are out there, and our daughter is almost three. We believed it would be a good environment for our little family. Our bid was accepted, and we began making plans to move."

"Why did you apply for this position if you knew you were relocating?"

She lifted both hands. "I couldn't *not* apply," she said. "This would be a dream job for me. I put my name in fully knowing that even if I were lucky enough to wrangle an interview, I would most likely be unable to actually accept the job. When the White House called me last week to schedule today's interview, I couldn't find it in my heart to refuse. I just couldn't."

I watched my high hopes for hiring this woman shred into tatters around me.

"The thing is," she went on, "two days before that, our Realtor called. The house inspector uncovered a problem. A big one. I won't bore you with all the details, but right now it looks as though our plans are in flux."

"Oh?" My mood brightened. "You mean there's a chance you may be staying in D.C.?"

She kept her hands in her lap, but her fingers never stopped moving. "If the house purchase doesn't go through and if I'm hired here, then there's no question: We'll stay."

"That's a lot of ifs." Sargeant's back was rigid and his words were sharp.

"I wanted to be as up-front about my situation as possible. Contractually, we're required to allow the home sellers a chance to resolve the problem before we can walk away from the deal. If we cancel before then, we stand to lose a lot of money we can't afford. Until we know which way it will go, I'm in limbo." Her gaze flicked from me to Sargeant, back to me. "I completely understand if this situation disqualifies me from consideration, and I apologize for wasting your time."

Years of working with Sargeant provided me with insight to his moods. His darkening brow, the exactitude with which he folded his hands atop his desk, and the set of his jaw presaged a storm about to blow.

Jumping in before he could quash Lottie Catalano's hope with a scathing dismissal, I said, "We truly appreciate your honesty." Getting to my feet, I said, "I hope we have the opportunity to discuss this further. Will you keep us updated on your situation?"

Lottie's visible panic transformed into a glow of excitement as she stood to shake my hand. "Yes, of course I will. I'd be happy to. The minute I know anything I will be in touch. Thank you."

Looking like someone who'd taken a large bite of an unripe persimmon, Sargeant got up and shook Lottie's hand. "My office will contact you soon." He pressed a button to summon Elaine.

"Thank you again," she said as Sargeant's assistant opened the door. "I was so excited to move to California, but now I really hope we get to stay here."

From the doorway, Elaine offered a bland smile as she ushered Lottie out. "This way," she said.

When Lottie and Elaine were gone, I glanced at my watch. The interview hadn't run as long as expected, which meant I might even have time to run a comb through my hair before dinner tonight with Gav. "She was great," I said. "I'm selfishly hoping her house deal falls through."

Hands held aloft, Sargeant dropped into his seat with a *thud*. "Doesn't that foolish woman realize how much we deal with every single day of our lives? How dare she waste our time when she has no idea if she'll be able to take the job if offered?" Hands still held high, he shook them. "This isn't a game we're playing here. If she couldn't commit, she should never have agreed to this meeting. How dare she?"

I sat quietly, watching my former nemesis manage his meltdown. Feisty, short-tempered, and quick to find fault, Sargeant had aggressively nipped at my heels since his first day at the White House. We'd barely tolerated one another for the first couple of years, but after several tense moments that required us to work together in order to survive, we'd achieved a truce. Better than a truce, in my opinion. Though I could have never predicted such a thing, I now considered Sargeant a friend. And though he'd be loath to admit it, I suspected he felt the same.

"Who hired you?" I asked.

"What, me?" he asked. He blinked a couple of times as though to reorient himself. "Paul, of course."

"What was it like? When you got the call to come interview here? Were you excited? Were you nervous?"

He leaned forward, wagging a finger at me. "I know what you're attempting, Ms. Paras," he said. "It won't work. We need our employees to be cognizant of how their choices impact others, impact our efficiency, impact the White House itself. This behavior Ms. Catalano displayed—this selfishness—is unacceptable. There's too much at stake."

"It's a once-in-a-lifetime opportunity, Peter. I don't blame her for keeping her options open. You know what they say about fortune favoring the bold."

"There's no doubt you ascribe to that sentiment," he said, but there was no bite to his tone. He waved a hand in front of his face. "She was the best we've talked with so far. I suppose we can forgive this indiscretion of hers, but if she's hired, I will hold you responsible for ensuring she knows not to play fast and loose with us again."

"Fast and loose? Really, Peter."

Not looking at me, he shrugged, sat back, and vigorously

rubbed his chin. "Margaret's death has hit me harder than I care to admit," he said quietly. "I fooled myself into believing that we were safe because we work here."

I didn't interrupt, but he waved the air again as though I had.

"Yes, yes, I'm not dismissing your proclivity to get into trouble. Who could forget any of that?" he asked rhetorically. "And, although it's easy to cast blame, it wasn't until you and I found ourselves fighting for our lives together that I began to understand that these things are rarely your fault." Eyebrow arched, he shot me a pointed look. "Note, I said 'rarely,' not 'never.'"

"Thanks for understanding," I said with only a hint of sarcasm.

"But this," he said, shaking his head. "What happened to Margaret strikes at the very heart of this house."

"Are you sure she was targeted because she worked here?"

"It's looking more and more likely though we don't know for certain. Not yet at least. All we have is speculation." He heaved a deep sigh. "Maybe Cyan was smart to get out when she did."

"You don't believe that, do you?" I asked.

He sat up, rubbed the bridge of his nose, and shook his shoulders. "My apologies, Olivia. It's been a rough few days."

"It has."

"Does it get any easier?" he asked.

I thought about the many times I'd fought for my life. About the people I'd known who'd been hurt or killed along the way. "Not easier. Never easier."

His eyes were creased, dark, and pouchy with wrinkles. "I didn't think so."

CHAPTER 10

BUCKY MET ME AT THE BOTTOM OF THE STAIR-way. "Got a call from upstairs," he said. "Josh wants to know if he can come cook with you this evening."

"Tonight?" After the lackluster experience last time, I'd been convinced Josh wouldn't visit the kitchen again for months. I glanced at my watch.

"I started to mention the fact that you and Gav had dinner plans, but he sounded weird, so I held off."

"He called down to the kitchen himself?" I asked.

"I thought that was unusual, too, which is why I figured it would be better if you talked with him. I told him you were with Sargeant, but that you'd call as soon as you got back."

"That's odd," I said. "An assistant usually calls down here on his behalf."

"And lately, he cancels last minute."

I followed Bucky into the kitchen, where I drummed the countertop and stared down at its shine for a few seconds.

"There's got to be a reason he called out of the blue." Wrinkling my nose at the clock, I did some mental math. "I can't turn him down," I said to Bucky. "Even if it messes up my dinner plans."

"You're a soft touch."

"Yeah?" I pulled my phone from my pocket and dialed Gav. "Don't let it get out." When Gav answered I told him the situation and asked if he would mind if we delayed dinner.

"Wait that long for sustenance?" he asked. "I'm liable to wilt away."

"Ha-ha. Do you think Jason will still be able to fit us in?"

"Leave it to me," he said. "And good luck with Josh."

While I called upstairs to tell Josh I had a free hour, Bucky finished cleaning the kitchen. "Don't know why I bother if you're about to mess it all up again," he said good-naturedly when I hung up.

"He'll be down in a couple minutes," I said. "How did the rest of dinner prep go, by the way?"

"Smooth as silk," he said. "And the interview?"

I turned to our bookshelf, seeking inspiration. "Good," I said. "I'll tell you more later. Right now I need to come up with a plan for Josh. Any suggestions?"

"What about that soup you thought he'd enjoy making? The idea you had the other night?"

"That'll take too long." I tapped fingers against my lips. "I told Gav I'd keep it under an hour. I need something quick yet fun."

By the time Josh showed up, I'd pulled out three of my favorite cookbooks. "Hey, Ollie," he said from the doorway. He raised a hand in greeting and attempted a smile that fell flat.

"Josh, come on in," I said. Pointing to the open books strewn across the center workspace, I asked, "Glad we could make tonight work. I have about an hour. What are you in the mood to make?"

As the Secret Service contingent did their cursory inspection of the kitchen, Bucky lifted his chin in greeting. "Hi, Josh. How's school?"

Was it me, or did Josh seem surprised and disappointed to see Bucky there?

"Good, I guess," Josh said. He waited for the Secret Service agents to disappear around the corner before making his way over to glance at the books. I was no mind reader, but I could tell his heart wasn't in the task.

Bucky and I exchanged a look and I could tell that my assistant had picked up the same vibe I had. He untied his apron and unsnapped his smock. "I hate to leave before the fun begins, but I still haven't figured out the perfect gift for Brandy. More shopping ahead of me tonight." He rolled his eyes. "My favorite thing."

Josh visibly relaxed. "Good luck," he said.

"Thanks," Bucky replied with a wave. "See you tomorrow, Ollie."

The kitchen grew unnaturally quiet as Josh breezed through the cookbooks. He sent furtive glances toward the doorway while flipping pages too quickly to register content.

I knew his Secret Service bodyguards were probably out of earshot, but I made a spur-of-the-moment decision and crossed the room to our computer. "Anything catch your eye?" I asked.

"Um . . . not yet." When he got to the final page he didn't push it away and turn to the second book. Instead, he flipped back to the beginning and resumed his mindless paging. "I'm sure there's something in here . . ."

Loading a music website, I turned to him. "What do you like? Classic rock? Country? Hip hop? Smooth jazz?"

His eyes brightened and a corner of his mouth turned up. Still, he shrugged.

"Okay then," I said. "You're stuck with what I pick." I entered my choice into the search bar: soundtracks from animated features. First up was an Academy Award winner with catchy lyrics and an earworm-worthy tune. Grabbing a giant spoon, I held it like a rock star clutching a microphone. "If you don't pick something to work on soon, I'm liable to start singing."

Finally, a shadow of a smile. Josh sent another quick glance toward the doorway. "Can we turn it a little louder?" he said.

"You got it." I turned up the volume, returned the spoon to its place, and took up a position across the workspace from the First Son. Tapping the open book in front of him, I asked, "There's nothing in there for you today, is there?"

He pushed the books to the side and leaned forward heavily, resting both elbows on the shiny stainless counter, his gawky maneuvers bringing to mind a collapsed marionette.

"You don't have any more of those brownies, do you?" he asked. "To eat, I mean. Not to make."

"No brownies, but Marcel has been experimenting with different cupcake combinations this week before holiday entertaining begins in earnest. He left a few samples here for us to taste test." Opening the small refrigeration unit to my right, I read Marcel's tiny hand-printed descriptions of each flavor aloud. Josh perked up at the mention of German chocolate.

"I like coconut," he said.

I plated his choice and placed it in front of him. "You need a fork?"

"Nah," he said. "I mean: No thank you."

"It's okay, Josh. We're casual down here."

He peeled back the cupcake's paper holder and took a

big bite. "You're not having any?" he asked around a mouthful of chocolate. He used the back of his hand to wipe frosting off his nose before I could hand him a napkin.

I chuckled. We *were* casual down here, all right. "Bucky and I have gotten a little cupcaked-out this week," I said, opting not to mention my dinner plans.

As he plowed through the treat, demolishing it with preteen gusto, I gathered the cookbooks and returned them to the shelf.

"By the way, how did the brownies go over at school? Were your classmates suitably impressed that you made them?"

"I guess." The shrug was back. As was his leaden expression. "They ate them. It was fine."

Something clearly not fine was going on in his life. The theme song from a jungle-based film warbled in the background. "Tell me what's going on."

Not looking at me, he played with the chocolate bits left on his plate, rolling them together to make one giant crumb. "I overheard Dad talking about you the other night. Did something happen in the park on Sunday?"

Weighing my options, I answered slowly. "What did you hear?"

"That you were attacked again." The crumb had snowballed to about the size of a macadamia nut. He played with it, rolling it back and forth on the plate. "He said you were okay, though. You are, right?"

"I'm fine. They got my purse is all."

Using the pad of his index finger, he picked up tiny shreds of chocolate that still clung to the plate, popped them into his mouth, then scoured for more. He rolled the giant crumb of chocolate around one more time before devouring that as well. "How come you didn't say anything about it when I was here on Monday?"

"I don't want to burden you with that kind of news."

Elbows back on the countertop, he propped his chin in one hand and played with the empty plate with the other. "Plus, I wasn't exactly talkative Monday night, was I?" When he looked up at me, there was an apology in his dark eyes.

"It's okay, Josh. Seems like you had a lot on your mind."

He shot a glance at the doorway, then lowered his voice. "You pretend things don't bother you when they really do."

It wasn't exactly a question, but I said, "Sometimes." Leaning both elbows on the counter, I mirrored his posture.

"Isn't that really hard to do? I mean, when people say and do mean things, how do you keep from letting them know it gets to you?"

I wanted to ask what had prompted the question, but I sensed it best to tread lightly. "It depends," I said. "Usually, if the person is someone I care about, I *do* let them know. Small problems can grow into big ones if they aren't addressed, and the truth is that the people who love us want us to be happy."

He nodded and shrugged.

"When that happens," I said, "I try to be fair, and try to keep myself from sounding as though I'm placing blame." My turn to shrug. "I'm sure I'm not always successful, but I find it's best to explain how circumstances affect me, rather than try to tell people what I think they're doing wrong."

"What about people you don't care about? I mean . . . you care what they *think* and what they say, but you don't really care about them personally? Not family. More like somebody you work with, or go to school with?"

Continuing to play with the plate, he pressed his index finger hard enough along the edge to tip the opposite edge upward. He made small circles with his finger, causing the dish to spin like a small satellite seeking signal.

"If someone I don't care about hurts me," I continued,

"and if I believe it's deliberate, I do my best to ignore them. People who intentionally hurt others usually do so because they're unhappy themselves."

"Doesn't mean it hurts less to hear it."

"Good point," I said. "The thing is, people like that thrive on negativity. They can never get enough. If you feed them by letting them know they got to you, they'll keep coming back for more. When I can, I try to simply cut those people out of my life."

He frowned. "What about a person you have to like?"

"You don't *have* to like anyone," I said. "But I think I know what you mean. It gets messy when we don't like a person at work, or school, or wherever. And if that person is purposely mean, it can be really tough."

"Yeah."

"Are kids at school giving you trouble, Josh?"

He stopped spinning the plate, allowing the elevated end to drop, clunking against steel. "Everybody wanted to be my friend the first day," he said. "I mean, I know why. Duh. Probably all their parents told them to make friends with the president's son. Gives them the chance to brag."

I smiled. The kid was perceptive.

"That was okay," he said with yet another shrug. "They all wanted to ask me about living in the White House and what it was like having Secret Service guys hanging around all the time. But then one of them—his name is Seth— started asking different questions."

"Like what?"

Josh sent another look toward the door. "They can't hear me, right?"

"Not with the radio on."

"I mean, I know they're supposed to keep me safe, and let me be as normal as possible, but I'm eleven. My father is the president of the United States. I know they're not supposed to, but you think they *won't* tell him if there's a problem?"

The weight of this conversation settled on me. Josh couldn't have made it more clear that he expected me to keep his confidence.

"Go ahead," I said. "Tell me more about this Seth kid."

Despite my assurances that the radio—now bouncing to the beat of singing fish—would cover our conversation, Josh dropped his voice to a whisper. "He started out friendly like the rest of the kids, but then he started picking on my dad. Saying he's useless and he should never have run for office and that anyone who voted for him was stupid."

"Sounds to me like Seth is a jerk."

Josh almost smiled. "I like that you say what you think. Too many grown-ups try to be too polite all the time." He mimed gagging himself.

I laughed, then sobered. "What else is Seth saying?"

Josh began playing with the plate again. "He says my dad's a loser and that he's screwing up our country. He says my dad won't win this next election and that I'll be kicked out of school because I'm a loser, too."

The despair in his voice cut my heart.

"You know the truth, Josh. Your dad is a good man and a strong leader. But no matter how hard he tries, or how much he accomplishes, there will be people who disagree with him. That's okay. That's normal. That's the way our system works. If he's defeated in this next election, that doesn't mean he's a loser. It means that the country decided to work with someone else."

"I know that," Josh said with more than a little strain. "But the other kids are listening to Seth and telling me what a bad president my dad is and how he should be kicked out of office."

When he looked up at me with shiny eyes, I wanted to

wrap him in a hug and promise I'd find a way to protect him from Seth.

"How do you react when he says these things?" I asked.

Shrug. "I never know what to say. Nothing makes him stop. I wish Dad wasn't running for reelection. I wish we could leave here and just be normal again."

"Have you told your parents any of this?"

He shook his head. "They would feel like they had to *do* something. If they did, it would only make things worse."

I came around to his side of the countertop and put my hand on his shoulder. "Give them a chance. They were kids once, too. They'll understand. And believe me, they need to know what you're going through."

He nodded as though he'd expected me to say that.

"You'll get through this," I said. "I promise you will. It won't be easy, but as long as you stay true to yourself and don't give in to the Seths of the world, you'll be okay."

CHAPTER 11

GAV SHOWED UP IN THE KITCHEN LESS THAN a minute after Josh left. "Your timing is amazing," I said.

"One of the perks of the job," he said as he came over to give me a kiss. "I get to loiter in the White House without anyone chasing me off. I've been here for about fifteen minutes, but didn't want to rush you."

"I appreciate that," I said as I peeled off my apron and smock then tossed them into the laundry. "Josh and I had a nice chat."

"What did you wind up making?" He looked around the still-pristine kitchen. "Whatever it was, you sure cleaned up fast."

"No cooking today." When he cocked an eyebrow in question, I shook my head. "It's classified," I said.

"Sounds serious."

"What do you remember about middle school?" I asked.

"Three of the most miserable years of my life."

"Exactly. 'Nuff said."

I pulled a vivid blue V-neck sweater over my lightweight shirt. Eyeing Gav's charcoal suit and shiny shoes, I glanced down at my dark slacks. "I originally planned to change clothes at home, but with the time crunch, this is as dressed up as I'm going to get. Is that okay?"

"You look wonderful. And besides, we're going to Suzette's, not a reception at the Kennedy Center."

"So Jason was able to accommodate the delay?"

"Yep." He looked at his watch. "You ready?"

WHILE WE DROVE TO CRYSTAL CITY, WE DIS-cussed our days, and I shared my hopes about hiring Lottie Catalano to fill Cyan's spot. Gav agreed that it didn't seem right to wish for someone's home purchase to fall through, but said he hoped for the best.

A fire engine clanged, rushing up the street as we parked Gav's car in our apartment building's lot. With mild temps and the air soft with the scent of autumn, it would be a lovely evening for the quick walk to Suzette's. For the briefest moment, I considered running upstairs long enough to switch out of my work clothes into something nicer, but decided not to delay.

"You sure you don't mind being seen with me?" I teased.

He squeezed my hand. "I'm the luckiest guy in the world."

We walked no more than thirty steps when I turned to look behind me. "Is that *another* siren?" A fire engine roared past us in a blaze of lights, its horn warning automobiles and pedestrians to get out of its way. "That's the third one to pass us in the last minute."

Two blocks ahead, a police car racing toward us took a hairpin left turn. Seconds later, another followed. "What-ever's going on, it's big," Gav said.

At the next intersection, through a clearing, he pointed south over the top of the nearby buildings where gray smoke twisted into the dark sky. "It looks like the beginnings of a fire." He gave a quizzical look. "Or the end of one. But why all the heavy equipment if it's under control?"

"That has to be near Suzette's," I said. "The same street, for sure."

He gripped my hand a little tighter. "Let's see what's going on."

As we picked up our pace, an ambulance rushed by, followed by two more police cars.

At the end of the block, we turned right and stopped in our tracks. "What is going on?" I asked.

Gav didn't answer. Before us, the entire street was in chaos. Emergency lights flashed from every direction, nearly blinding me. The next block—where we were headed—was completely obstructed. Cops shouted, trying to establish order, urging people back and away. But from what?

The lingering smoke, though dissipated, was acrid and biting. I coughed, clutching Gav's arm. "Look."

Suzette's restaurant was located three buildings in from the corner where we stood. Or, at least, it had been. The front of the establishment was missing. Reduced to rubble. Utterly destroyed. The former cheerful doorway and the bright front window was now a blackened and charred mess.

It hurt to breathe. "Gav? What happened?"

A cop shouted for us to get away. When we didn't immediately comply, he started toward us. "Move along, folks. You can't be here."

Gav pulled out his ID. "I want to talk with whoever's in charge."

The cop hesitated a split second. "Over there." He pointed ten feet west, where three men in suits huddled. Their arms were crossed, and they wore solemn expressions. "One of them."

Our favorite restaurant looked as though some Godzilla-like creature had reached over and clawed the entire front of the two-story building away. The front of the apartment above the restaurant had been sheared off, leaving the rooms open to the elements, looking sad and vulnerable, like a destroyed home in a war zone.

"What about Jason?" I asked. "Where is he? I hope he's all right."

Gav didn't speak as we picked through uneven chunks of concrete and piles of debris I couldn't begin to identify.

"Gavin," one of the men said when he spotted us. I didn't recognize him, but from his appraising glance I got the impression he recognized me. "What are you doing here?"

"We had dinner plans, Cummings," Gav responded. He acknowledged the two other men with a nod. "What happened?"

Cummings stepped away from his group and gestured for us to join him. "Wish I knew," he said quietly. "Call came in about twenty minutes ago about a gas explosion." He shook his head and lowered his voice. "This was no gas explosion."

Gav and I were still holding hands. His grip tightened and his jaw clenched. "What was it?"

Joe Yablonski stepped into our group. "That's the question we need to answer, isn't it?" The big man nodded a greeting to each of us. "Agent Cummings, Agent Gavin. Ms. Paras."

"Joe," Gav said. "What are you doing here?"

"Taking control of the situation. And I'll need your eyes and ears on this one," he said. Turning to Agent Cummings, he said, "Would you please see Ms. Paras safely home?"

"But—" I said.

Yablonski's eyes were just as steely as I remembered.

"No arguments, Ms. Paras." To Cummings, he said, "I want an agent outside her door around the clock. Call in whoever you need."

"Yes, sir," Cummings said.

Yablonski turned to Gav. "Let's go."

"It'll be okay, Ollie," Gav said as he broke away.

I wanted to hug him, but Yablonski's sharp rebuke to Cummings—"Get going"—forestalled that plan.

I called to Gav as Yablonski led him away. "Be safe."

Without breaking stride, he turned. "I will."

TWO HOURS LATER, AFTER WATCHING NEWS coverage of the explosion on every possible station and refreshing my browser again and again, hoping for updates that never came, I began to pace. Every media outlet parroted the same story: gas explosion at a neighborhood restaurant. Five people injured and taken to area hospitals. No one confirmed dead. Not yet, at least. Gas company officials investigating. Authorities keeping the public far away until the area was safe again.

Cummings's words taunted me: "This was no gas explosion."

Then what was it?

I checked the time on my cell phone for probably the forty-third time in the past half hour. I desperately wanted to call Gav, but knew that I couldn't. When he was busy with Yablonski, he had no time for interruptions. He'd call me when he could.

My stomach growled, reminding me that I hadn't eaten anything since lunch. When Agent Cummings had brought me back, food had been the last thing on my mind. He'd walked through my apartment exactly the way Agent Romero had the.first time she'd brought me home, and he assured me that he, or a colleague, would remain outside my door all night.

That was small consolation now when what I wanted most was to have my husband here.

Almost as though I'd willed it so, my cell phone came alive in my hand. Gav's ring. "Are you okay?" I asked the moment we connected.

"I'm fine," he said in a far more brusque tone than I would have expected. "Have you eaten?"

Startled by the question, I hesitated. "No, but—"

"Meet me at the car," he said. "We'll grab something."

"But—"

"Ollie." His tone was off. Way off.

"Okay," I said. "How soon?"

"Two minutes."

I hung up, grabbed my coat and keys, and flung open the front door, having momentarily forgotten about my body-guard. Agent Romero stood there. "Cummings had to go," she said. "Looks like you're stuck with me again."

"Gav's meeting me downstairs," I said by way of expla-nation.

She frowned. A second later, her phone rang. She held a finger up, indicating that I should wait while she answered. Less than thirty seconds later, she ended the call. "I'm to escort you to him."

Romero and I took the elevator down and, true to her word, she stayed by my side until Gav wrapped his arms around me, thereby relieving her of duty. "Thank you very much," he said. "Are you here all night?"

"Yes, sir," she said. "Have a nice dinner. I'll see you both when you return."

The moment we broke apart, I asked, "What in the world is going on?"

Gav didn't answer. Instead, he held out his hand. "Let me see your phone."

I gave it to him.

He examined it closely. "This hasn't been out of your possession recently, has it?"

"Not at all. I keep it with me wherever I go. This was in my pocket when my purse was stolen."

"What about at the White House? Do you ever leave it unattended?"

"No, never."

He handed it back. "When you made our dinner reservations for Suzette's, did you use this or the apartment's landline?"

I thought back. "The landline."

"Let's walk," he said.

He led me through the sea of parked cars to the main street. The same street we'd taken earlier this evening. Instead of heading south, however, we walked north. Gav and I were notoriously quick-paced, but tonight we strolled.

The air had cooled tremendously. I shivered. "Tell me what's going on."

He waited until we got to a bench. "Have a seat," he said. When I did, he made a slow circuit around it before sitting down next to me.

"Jason is okay. He was pretty badly injured, but he'll make it. His restaurant, on the other hand . . ." Gav sat forward, elbows on knees, hands clasped. "I hope he has good insurance."

I waited for him to continue, knowing he would at his own pace.

"There was no gas leak," he said after a pause. "But I assume you already knew that."

"Got that impression, yes."

"Suzette's was destroyed by an IED."

I knew from the first time Gav and I had worked together, long before we even liked each other, that an IED was an improvised explosive device.

"Who would want to target Suzette's?"

"Here's where it gets interesting." Tension tightened his face, deepening his cheeks and accentuating his jawline. A vein throbbed at his throat. He raised his eyes, checking the area around us again. "Remember how we talked about signature bombs? And how we can sometimes trace a bomb to its creator through an analysis of its components and composition?"

I nodded.

"Our forensics team will be analyzing the debris to confirm, but Yablonski and I are convinced that the bomb that destroyed Suzette's today was created by the same person who set off the bomb at Cenga Prison on Sunday."

When I gasped, Gav turned to face me. "I wasn't able to share specifics when you asked, but after tonight, Yablonski is greenlighting including you in the investigation." He took both my hands. "The bomb that went off at Cenga Prison was almost certainly the work of Armustanian terrorists."

"Which means that the bomb at Suzette's was theirs, too?"

"Yes."

Realization crashed, humming in my ears and quickening my heart. I stiffened, but Gav held tight to my hands as I reasoned it out. "Yablonski is allowing you to tell me all this because *we* are targets?"

He nodded.

I turned away, picturing the destruction I'd seen tonight. "The front of Suzette's was blown off. Our table," I said. "If Josh hadn't asked to work with me in the kitchen—if we hadn't been delayed, we would have been there tonight when the bomb went off."

Gav nodded again.

"The Armustanians knew our plans, didn't they?" I asked. "And that's why you asked which phone I used to make the reservation. The landline. They're taping our phone calls?"

Still holding my hands, he spoke quietly. "We believe it may be worse than that. We believe that when your purse was stolen, they were after your keys. We believe they bugged the entire apartment."

"But I had the locks changed the next morning, remember? Agent Romero and I walked through the entire apartment that night to make sure no one was—" My hands flew out of Gav's into the air as the answer came to me. "Of course. They *were* in our apartment that night. They let themselves in while I was busy giving my statement to the Secret Service and the police."

"Most likely, yes."

Snippets from that evening came back to me in a rush. "James mentioned confusion in the lobby that evening. How much do you want to bet that it was a distraction to allow someone to sneak past him unnoticed?"

Gav looked sad. "As a doorman, James is ineffectual at best. Even on a good day he tends to fall asleep at his post."

The bombers had been in our apartment. And I'd never suspected it. My stomach somersaulted. "They've been listening to everything, haven't they?" I sucked in a breath as horror set my gut spinning again, this time shooting bile up the back of my throat. "Cameras? Do you think there are cameras in our apartment?"

He pulled me close. "We will find out. I promise you."

Now I glanced around, fearful that we were being watched. Certain that we were.

"What do we do?"

"For now, we head back to the apartment."

"And rip out every single listening and watching device they put there."

"Unfortunately not," he said. He pulled me closer. "Yablonski is calling in a few favors, and he's making arrangements as we speak. You and I need to go home and wait for him to contact us. Until we get further instructions, we have to pretend as though we have no idea we're being watched or listened to."

"You've got to be kidding."

"I'm sorry. You're going to have to trust me on this one."

"You know I do."

I hung my head and closed my eyes. Except for the traffic and the wind shushing through the trees, the evening was silent. My stomach growled.

Gav patted my knee. "Let's get something to eat while we're out. The less time we spend in the apartment, the better."

CHAPTER 12

WE STARTED BACK FOR OUR APARTMENT AFTER having devoured far more food than was good for us. Our favorite Mexican place specialized in takeout but provided two small Formica tables and four wobbly aluminum chairs for those rare patrons who chose to dine in. We'd occupied one of the tables for more than an hour, consuming tacos, burritos, chips, salsa, and guacamole, little of which I actually tasted.

Agent Romero met us outside the elevator when we alighted at our floor. "One of us will be out here all night if you need anything," she assured us. "You can both sleep soundly knowing we have agents stationed around the building. No one who shouldn't be here is getting in."

We thanked her and let ourselves into the apartment the same way we always did. And yet, the clank of our keys into the ceramic bowl on the table inside the door sounded different. The very air smelled different. Breathing felt different.

Talking, however, was the absolute worst. The pressure to behave normally—to pretend we had no inkling we were being observed while every nerve in my body twisted with tension—made forming casual conversation virtually impossible.

Gav had expressed his strong belief that whoever had established surveillance had placed only a handful of listening devices around the apartment and would not have had the time to set up cameras.

Still, to be safe, we agreed to keep our actions as benign as possible. That meant no pantomiming messages. No writing notes. If the bad guys *were* watching, they needed to be convinced that we didn't suspect a thing.

We hung up our coats in silence and moved toward the kitchen, bumping into each other when we both started through the doorway at once.

"You first," Gav said.

"No, after you."

He tried to smile, but it was as forced as my gesture signaling him to go ahead.

Gav walked through the kitchen into the living room, where he turned on the television. I opened the refrigerator and stared in, seeing nothing.

Updates screamed from the TV. Our eavesdroppers had to have realized by now that we'd escaped being blown to bits. I kept my fingers crossed they wouldn't try to redouble their efforts tonight.

"I hope Jason has good insurance," Gav said.

Okay, here we go.

Gav's comment about insurance at Suzette's signaled the start to our agreed-upon script—the one we'd worked out over dinner because we had no choice: We *had* to discuss the bombing. Avoiding the topic would have only raised suspicion.

I poured two glasses of water from the carafe in the fridge and handed one to Gav as I joined him in the living room. No wine for us tonight. We needed to stay alert.

Every television news station cheerfully reported that no diners had been seated at the front table at the time of the explosion and that no one had been killed in the "gas explosion." On-camera experts theorized that if anyone had been dining in that space when the blast occurred, casualties would have been a certainty.

I delivered my line: "I can't imagine how that happened. Aren't there safeguards in place to prevent gas explosions?"

Gav stood in front of the TV, arms folded. "These things happen."

"Can you imagine if we'd gotten to the restaurant on time tonight?" I gave a shudder that wasn't complete affectation. "The gas company should do a better job of protecting the public."

"Shush," he said, pointing to the TV. "I'm watching."

Gav would never tell me to shush, but our eavesdroppers didn't know that.

"We were right there, less than a half hour after it happened." I injected a trace of whine into my voice. "What more do you need to know?"

"There's nothing more I *need* to know," he said, answering my huffy tone in kind. "Can't you just be quiet for five minutes? I want to watch this."

"Fine. Cuddle up with your TV. See how much comfort it gives you tonight."

I slammed my water onto the coffee table and stormed into our bedroom.

It didn't matter that the squabble was bogus; exchanging sharp words with Gav unsettled me more than I cared to admit. This fabricated argument was our best cover. How better to prevent awkward, stilted conversation than by avoiding conversation entirely? If our eavesdroppers believed we were angry with each other, they'd accept our silent treatment as a reasonable consequence.

Sitting on my side of the bed, I stared up at the ceiling, doing my best to look like a beleaguered wife. At this time of night, I would normally get comfortable in my sleepwear, but the idea of undressing where I might be observed froze me in place. The thought of how many times I'd done so since Sunday night turned my stomach.

I blew out a breath of frustration and reminded myself of Gav's theory that the Armustanians hadn't had time to install cameras. I wanted to believe that.

Rather than get changed, I made my way to the other bedroom, where I turned on my computer and pulled up one of my favorite recipe sites.

You want a peephole into my life you lowlifes? Here it is.

I browsed recipes until my vision blurred. My bones were tired, my spirit drained. I cast a look at the doorway, wishing I could talk with Gav. Really talk. But I needed to sleep and I knew he needed to, too.

Steeling myself, I pulled out the long-sleeved T-shirt and cotton pants I usually slept in, and began making my way to the bathroom. Surely they wouldn't have set up a camera in there.

"Hey." Gav stood in the doorway, frowning. "I'm going out."

"What?" I covered my surprise with indignation. "At this time of night?"

Gav's proclamation could mean only one thing: Yablonski must have texted and wanted to meet with him. Although we'd anticipated that possibility, the likelihood had grown dimmer with each passing minute.

"I need air," he said.

"It's so late."

He met my eyes and held up two fingers. "For the second time: I need air."

Two fingers. I was to come, too.

"Oh, really?" I said with a snarl. "Seems a little fishy to be wandering outside by yourself."

He shrugged and walked away.

"What? The television isn't enough company for you anymore?" I called to his back.

"Cut me a little slack, would you?" he shouted in return. "One of my buddies is in town. He just texted that he wants to meet for a beer. Nothing wrong with that."

"Fine." I got up and followed. "I'm coming along. I could use a drink."

"You'll be bored out of your wits."

"So? You're not the only one who had a rough night, you know."

He shrugged. "Suit yourself."

Romero nearly jumped when the two of us exited the apartment. She glanced at her watch. "Is everything all right?" she asked.

"We're going out," Gav said. "You're to remain here."

"Sir?"

"You have your orders."

"Yes, sir," she said, but I could tell she didn't like it.

Gav strode past his car without giving it a glance. I kept up with him, knowing better than to ask what was up. When we were almost to the end of the parking row, he turned and opened the passenger door of a dark blue Ford. "Your chariot, ma'am," he said.

Once I was in, he came around and sat in the driver's seat. He dug beneath it until he came up with a set of keys.

"Yablonski?" I asked.

He nodded as he started the car. "Can't take the chance that they bugged either of our vehicles. Unlikely, but not worth the risk."

I rested my head back and sighed deeply. "I cannot believe how hard it is to stay in that apartment," I said as we pulled out of the lot. "Even my thoughts feel formal and stilted."

"I know," he said, checking his rearview mirror.

"Please don't tell me we're being followed."

He checked both side mirrors, then the rearview one again. "That's the nice thing about late-night meetings. Makes it way easier to spot a tail. The only vehicle behind us is the one that's supposed to be there. We're clear."

Gav hadn't gotten into specifics at the Mexican restaurant and every inch of me was crawling with curiosity. "What's going on? Can you tell me now?"

He gave a curt nod. "As I mentioned before, there's no doubt Armustan was behind Sunday's bombing at Cenga Prison. Yablonski and I are convinced that they're responsible for tonight's attack as well."

"And for some unknown reason, they're targeting us," I said.

"Not us." He shot me a sideways look. "You."

"Me?" I nearly shot out of my seatbelt. "But why?"

"Remember when we talked about how Armustanians value family honor above all else and how they swear to avenge their loved ones' deaths?"

"I never killed any Armustanians."

"No, you didn't." He took a last-minute left on a yellow light and checked his mirrors again. "You did, however, kill their plan to kidnap Josh."

"And for that they've declared war on me? They should blame their operatives or whoever devised the plan in the first place. The fact that it failed wasn't my fault." I thought about that. "Well, not entirely. It was a bad plan to begin with. You don't kidnap the president's children. You don't touch children."

Gav waited for me to finish my tirade. "They *did* blame the person who devised the plan. Remember when I told you about the Armustanian regime being overthrown?"

"Of course."

"Its leader was overthrown because of you."

I had no words. "Explain."

"You, Ollie, singlehandedly foiled the kidnapping attempt causing Armustan to lose its last chance to negotiate Farbod Ansari's release. When that happened, its leader fell into disgrace. He'd failed, badly. Angry Armustanians rose up, murdered him, then paraded his body through the streets. A very public humiliation."

"A blow to the family honor," I repeated quietly. "Who is the relative coming after me? And why now?"

We'd crossed the Potomac into D.C. and were now heading north.

"His name is Kern and he seeks to avenge his brother's death by overthrowing the new regime and reclaiming his family's power." Gav turned to me. "You didn't just save Josh's life that night. You took down an entire faction—what had been the most powerful faction in Armustan until that point. The new leadership is on shaky ground. Kern stands a good chance of gaining control." He made eye contact. "If he can succeed, that is."

Raindrops pattered the windshield as we sped through the night. I worked to process everything Gav had said. After a couple of miles, he turned right.

"Kern's success comes with my death, is that it?"

Gav's face was grim. "Armustan's ultimate goal has always been to free Farbod Ansari from prison, make no mistake about that." He kept his eyes on the road. "Kern's objective is to seize control of his country using any means at his disposal. We believe he intends to use you to achieve his goals, though how, we can only guess. What's important, as far as you're concerned, however, is that to Kern you represent the loss of family honor. That makes you a personal target."

"Which is why he won't give up until I'm dead." Ahead, the shiny pavement reflected the watery streetlights, smeared and bright. "None of this makes sense. If the Armustanians did arrange to have my purse stolen, then why am I still alive? They could have killed me right then and there."

"I'm hoping Yablonski has answers for us," he said.

Gav slowed as we encountered a residential area where two-story brick houses were set so close together there were no gangways between buildings. Identical in style, the homes formed a line of giant, sleepy faces. Their wooden, spindled porches were shadowed teeth; their front door noses sat between tall window eyes, all shaded closed this time of night. Above the windows, half roofs jutted forward, their heavy overhangs resembling angry brows. Like the buildings were frowning at us.

"I hope he does, too," I said. "By the way, where exactly are we going?"

Two blocks later, Gav parallel parked in front of one of the squat, silent homes. "We're here."

CHAPTER 13

GAV LED ME TO A HOUSE IN THE MIDDLE OF the block. As we ascended the concrete steps, a woman stepped out of the porch shadows.

"Good evening, Agent Gavin, Ms. Paras." She opened the front door for us as another agent stepped out of a far corner to take her place. "Follow me."

The small front hallway was not much bigger than an elevator car. Smelling of damp pets and old carpeting, it offered just enough light to keep us from tripping over one another. Our guide waited for Gav to close the front door behind us before she opened the one in front of her.

Though considerably more spacious than the hallway, the room we found ourselves in was also small and only slightly better lit. Three pieces of art—the kind one might find at an ART SALE TODAY stand by the side of the road—decorated bare, cracked walls. A sagging, patterned sofa sat along the far side. Heavy brocade draperies framed the front windows and, behind the fabric, the shades were down. There was a low table, a television on a stand, and a fog of stale cigarettes. The bare floor creaked under our feet.

Ahead and to our left, the galley kitchen featured almond appliances, fluorescent lighting, and the white trimmed-in-oak cabinetry that had been all the rage in the 1970s. Slightly shabby with its worn linoleum and dated fixtures, the narrow space was nonetheless clean. I sniffed the air. Bleach. An improvement over the musty welcome at the front door.

The agent turned and gestured to our right into what I presumed was the dining room. "In here."

Yablonski sat on a folding chair at the center of a long, collapsible table. He had a laptop open to his right and paperwork piles everywhere else. The plaster walls in this windowless, rectangular room had been painted a high-gloss white that reflected the bleak illumination from four bare, high-wattage bulbs overhead. I blinked in the brightness.

"Come on in," he said, waving us into the two folding chairs opposite him. "So it seems we're required to work together again, doesn't it, Ollie? I'm sure you're delighted by the prospect."

His words sang with sarcasm, but his gaze was warm.

"Always a pleasure to work with you, Joe. I only wish it were under better circumstances."

"Someday, perhaps," he said. He glanced over the top of my head and nodded to the agent who had brought us in. "That will be all."

She ducked out of the room. A few seconds later, I heard the front door open and close.

"Let me tell you what we've uncovered in the few short hours since you both neatly avoided assassination. Well done, by the way." He turned to me first, "Ollie, let's go back to the night of your mugging. You identified two assailants, am I correct?"

"Yes, Viceboy and Dagger," I said, "but both of them are dead. Executed gangland style, according to the Metro Police."

"Mr. Sargeant informed you of the existence of a third gang member, correct?"

"He did. He said the police would try to pick this person up and question him. I believe his name is Cutthroat."

"Mr. Cutthroat is in custody. He's refusing to say a word to the detectives, but I'm convinced he'll talk with us."

"Us?" I asked. "He's here?"

"Not yet." He turned his attention to his laptop and navigated using his touchpad. Swiveling the computer around, he asked, "Do you recognize these men?"

The question had been directed to me. There were three faces on the screen. I studied them but none looked familiar. "No." I turned to Gav. "You?"

He made a low noise that, in any other situation, could have been amusement.

Before he could answer, I slapped my forehead. "Of course you do."

He had an arm around the back of my chair and used his fingers to rub my shoulder. "I haven't met any of them in person, though."

Yablonski identified each of the men in turn as he pointed to their photos. When he got to the last one on the far right, he said, "And this is Kern. Their leader. It's not a clear image, but it's the best we've got. We have every reason to believe that he stayed back in Armustan and chose not to accompany his lieutenants on this mission, but we don't want to overlook the possibility that he may be in the United States."

Kern didn't face the camera directly. His attention seemed to be focused on something low and to his left; I couldn't get a good look at his eyes. Although the photo was blurred, there was no missing the wavy brown hair that hung past his shoulders, his full, bushy beard, and the heavy mustache that covered his lips. From this hazy image it was impossible to determine the man's age; he could have been twenty-four or forty-seven. So I asked. "How old is he?"

"Our best guess—thirty-two," Gav said.

A door opened at the back of the house. Angry protestations followed, along with the unmistakable sounds of bodies scuffling and struggling. Alert, I sat up straight, but when Yablonski didn't seem to be bothered, I relaxed.

A male voice: "Where is this place?" More scuffling. "Who are you? What do you want with me?"

"Right on time." Yablonski stood. He made his way to the rear of the home and spoke to the new arrivals. "Up here."

I turned to Gav. "What's going on?"

Before he could answer, Yablonski returned to the room, carrying another folding chair. He opened it, placed it at the head of the long table, and resumed his original seat.

A moment later, two agents half-dragged, half-carried a rangy young man into the room. He shouted profanities and struggled against his captors, his eyes wide with panic.

Shackled, with his hands cuffed behind, the guy wouldn't have gotten far even if he had managed to break away, but I can't say that I blamed him for trying. He smelled of hot fear and cold dread. His face shone with perspiration. Beneath his open leather jacket, his T-shirt was stained with sweat.

Yablonski pointed to the folding chair he'd set up. "Have a seat, Mr. Cutthroat."

I watched as the ferocious-eyed young man took in the stark room, its temporary furnishings, and Yablonski's apparent authority. As the two agents pushed him into the chair, he glanced at Gav, then at me. I could tell my presence puzzled him most of all. "What's going on? Who are you people?"

Yablonski brought his face close to Cutthroat's. "Right now we're your best friends."

A sheen of perspiration gathered along Cutthroat's upper lip. He had wide-set eyes and a sharp, straight nose. Scar tissue from an old wound zigzagged from near his right ear down to his chest. I wondered if that injury was how he'd gotten his name.

"You can't hold me. I know my rights."

Unruffled, Yablonski regarded him thoughtfully. "You want us to let you go?" He sat back, crossing his arms. "Fine."

Cutthroat glanced up at the two agents flanking him, as though he expected them to snap to it and release him from his bonds. They stared straight ahead as though they hadn't heard a word.

Yablonski cleared his throat. "But before we do, let me ask you this: Where will you hide?"

"Hide?" Cutthroat asked. He slid a quizzical glance at me and Gav again. "What do you mean?"

Yablonski wrinkled his face and scratched his forehead. "I mean, Detectives Beem and Kager were able to find you and pick you up less than a day after they learned of your existence. How long do you think it will take the men who killed Dagger and Viceboy to hunt you down?"

Cutthroat looked ready to jump out of his own skin. His gaze darted about the room as though looking for an exit. "I don't know what you're talking about," he said, convincing no one.

Yablonski leaned forward again, resting his thick arms on the table, never taking his eyes off the fidgety captive. "You know what they did to your friends," he said. "How long do you think you'll stay alive out there once they find out about you? Hmm?" He waited for that to sink in.

"I didn't have anything to do with Viceboy and Dagger getting offed."

"You and your friends went back a long way, didn't you?" Yablonski shuffled through papers. "Look what I have here." He held up a photograph of a grade-school class where three boys' faces had been circled in red. "Did you first meet Bobby and Roger in Ms. Winchell's second-grade class," he asked as he tapped the photo, "or do the three of you go back even further, Steven?"

At the mention of each of the gang members' real names, Cutthroat/Steven flinched. "I didn't have anything to do with them getting killed," he said again.

"We know you didn't," Yablonski said smoothly. "But if you can tell us who did, we might be able to offer you protection."

Cutthroat shook his head, more in an expression of disbelief than of refusal.

Yablonski turned to his laptop and navigated the touchscreen again. From my vantage point, I could see that he'd returned to the three photos he'd shown me earlier. Turning the laptop around to face Cutthroat, he asked, "Do you recognize any of these men?"

The young man leaned back, fear in his eyes. "The one on the left and the one in the middle," he said. "They killed Viceboy and Dagger."

"What about the man on the right?"

Cutthroat squinted. "I never saw him."

"You're sure?"

"That's not a real good picture. He could be anybody, but uh-uh. I don't think I ever saw that guy."

"How do you *know* the two other men killed your friends?" Yablonski asked.

Pain worked its way across Cutthroat's face. His eyes hardened and his mouth tightened in a way that made it seem he was trying not to break down in front of us. "I watched them do it." His Adam's apple bounced up and down, twice. "I was supposed to stay on the outside, to make sure Viceboy and Dagger stayed safe." He gestured toward the laptop with his chin. "But these guys . . . there was no forewarning."

"Why did the two men kill your friends?"

Cutthroat looked away. He shrugged.

"Steven," Yablonski said, his gray face darkening with impatience, "your friends made some bad decisions and it got them killed. Do yourself a favor and make the right decision now." He spoke slowly, allowing every syllable to settle before moving to the next. "I can help you. I can offer you protection."

"Nobody can protect me."

"I can," Yablonski said. "I've done it before with much bigger fish than you. All you have to do is tell us everything you know. From the start."

He waited while Cutthroat fidgeted and bit his lip.

"Take us back to the beginning, Steven," Yablonski said. "Tell us everything you know. What did Viceboy and Dagger get into?"

"Who are you, anyway?" Cutthroat asked. He turned and pointed his chin toward us. "Who are they?"

"I told you before: Right now, we're your best friends. Your buddies got in way over their heads. Once they stepped in, they had no chance of getting out alive. But you do. One chance. And this is it."

Cutthroat seemed to be waging an inner war with himself. Arguments played across his features so clearly I could almost hear them. "Listen," he finally said, "I told them—I told Viceboy and Dagger—that they were messing with the wrong people."

Yablonski nodded. "From the beginning," he said.

Cutthroat took a deep breath. He tossed a look over his shoulder. "Can I get these cuffs off? And a cigarette?"

"Cigarettes will kill you. Aren't we here to prevent that? You can have water," Yablonski said, but he allowed the cuffs to be removed. One of the agents stepped out and returned a moment later with four bottles of water.

"Now," Yablonski said when we were settled. "Talk."

Sometimes leaning on the table, sometimes gesturing with lanky arms, Cutthroat told us about how Viceboy and Dagger had been approached by the two men. "They promised money—lots of money—and guns. The kind that are hard to get."

"Where were you?" Yablonski asked. "During these negotiations, I mean?"

"I had to take my grandmother to the hospital that day," Cutthroat said with a frown. "But when I got back Dagger and V—we used to call him that for short—told me about these guys and the money we were looking at. They didn't try to cut me out. They wouldn't. The three of us always worked together. We came up in the ranks together and had each other's backs." He gave a shrug as though it didn't matter, but the look in his eyes made him look lonely and forlorn.

Yablonski tapped his computer screen. "When did you finally meet these two men?"

"Never did. They didn't know about me. V thought it would be better if I stayed on the outside to make sure the two guys made good on their promises. I was their backup, y'know. I stayed out of sight when they met up, but I was always around."

Even though I didn't know where any of this was going, I was too fascinated to interrupt.

"When was this?" Yablonski asked.

Cutthroat took a deep drink of his water. "A week ago

maybe?" He studied the ceiling for answers. "Yeah, a week ago last Tuesday. That's when my grandma fell and I had to take her in." He looked at me and at Gav. "She's okay, by the way. No broken hip or anything. Just a lot of bruising."

"Glad to hear it," I said.

"Back to the story," Yablonski said.

"Those two guys?" Cutthroat lifted his chin to indicate the two men in the photos. "They were bad news. Really bad. Viceboy and Dagger hooked up with them again a couple days later. That's when I saw them in person for the first time and when I heard what they wanted." Cutthroat shook his head. "Weird accents. No idea what country they were from, but nobody asked. These guys were scary. There was this look in their eyes." He affected a shudder. "Never seen anything like it."

"What did they want?"

Cutthroat worked his jaw. "How do I know you won't take everything I tell you and use it against me?"

"You don't," Yablonski said, folding his arms. "But what have you got to lose? Now tell me: What did they want?"

"They were crazy, these guys. Kept talking about a woman they wanted killed, but kept talking about how it had to be done a certain way."

"More detail, please," Yablonski said.

Cutthroat leaned forward. "They came in with this plan. They wanted Viceboy and Dagger to kill this woman—"

"Her name?"

He shook his head. "I don't remember. Somebody who worked in the White House and—"

I sucked in a breath. Although the disclosure came as no real surprise, it was still shocking to hear him admit it aloud.

Cutthroat's gaze settled on me.

Gav squeezed my hand.

"Back to the kill job," Yablonski said without looking at me. "Why did they need Viceboy and Dagger? Why couldn't these two men simply kill their target on their own?"

"They said it was because they didn't know the streets out here. I thought it was because they were setting my friends up, y'know, so the killing couldn't be traced to them. And that's exactly what happened." Before Yablonski could say anything, Cutthroat went on, "I told Dagger and V that they were messing with the wrong people. I told them that we can't go after people in the White House. I tried to talk them out of it, but they went ahead because the money was too good to walk away from."

"You're here, and they're dead," Yablonski said. "Looks like you made the better decision. Keep going."

I wanted Yablonski to ask why the two men had only stolen my purse rather than kill me when they'd had the chance. But Cutthroat started talking again.

"So V and Dagger broke into some *other* lady's house. Somebody who worked in the White House, too. I wasn't there, I swear I wasn't." He glanced around the room as though looking for us to say we believed him. "Once they had her tied up they called the foreign guys, who came to ask her questions."

"What kind of questions?" Yablonski asked.

"I wasn't there, remember?" Cutthroat said. "I can only tell you what my buddies told me later. They said she was real scared and that the foreign guys promised her that if she told them everything they'd let her live. So she did."

"Did what?"

"Tell them everything. Like who worked at the White House and how many guards are usually around and what she does at work. That kind of stuff. V said that the two guys were especially interested in some chef and they asked a load of questions about her. Dagger thought that was funny—like maybe they wanted to learn how to cook some secret recipe or something—but the lady told them about how the chef is married to some special undercover agent. That's when the big-money guys got really excited."

Cutthroat looked around at all of us again as he took another swig of his water. "They killed that lady, the one whose house they broke into," he said. "But you probably already knew that. The two guys told V and Dagger that they'd have another job for them soon, and they'd be in touch. The next day, they told them to steal a purse and get the chef lady's keys. No idea what they planned to do to her, but that's what they wanted. Next thing I know, my friends are dead."

"I thought you were supposed to be their backup," Yablonski said. "What happened?"

"They took Dagger and V out to this warehouse miles away from our turf. Said that's where the guns were hidden and it wasn't safe to bring them out in the open. I was supposed to follow behind without anybody seeing me, which was tough. I was too far back, I guess. By the time I found a place to hide my car and sneak in, Viceboy and Dagger were dead." His voice cracked. "I was too late."

"Tell me more about what Viceboy and Dagger told you before they died," Yablonski said. "About the woman they killed and about the chef. Anything you remember about that? Anything at all."

Cutthroat stared at his hands, which he fisted and stretched several times. "Viceboy told me that the main target was this lady chef, and that the two foreigners wanted to know everything about her first—like her schedule and stuff—so that they could make a big spectacle out of offing her in public." He looked up. "And they were only hitting this other lady— the first one, the one who they killed in her house—to get that information. Like I said, they were really excited to find out the chef was married to some Secret Service dude. It, like, changed the whole plan."

Yablonski scratched his forehead. "Take him upstairs," he said to the agents.

"Wait, what's going on? What's upstairs?" Cutthroat asked, panicked again. "You said you'd keep me safe if I told you everything."

"Upstairs is a bedroom. This is a safe house. I wager you couldn't do better tonight, given your circumstances."

The agents replaced the young man's handcuffs. "Do I have to have these on?"

Yablonski didn't answer. "You will remain here indefinitely in case we have further questions. After we're satisfied, we will make arrangements for safe housing elsewhere."

Cutthroat seemed almost disappointed that his moment in the spotlight was over.

I'd been sitting rigidly, trying so hard not to react to what Cutthroat was saying, that the moment he was gone, I nearly collapsed. The room roared around me, blocking out all but the rushing realization: Margaret had been targeted because she had information on me. It was my fault she was dead. I couldn't think. I couldn't breathe.

"They killed Margaret to get to me," I whispered.

Sick to my stomach, I felt Gav's hand on my back.

Yablonski heaved a noisy sigh. "I don't know whether this makes it worse, or better, but if they hadn't targeted Margaret first, if they hadn't learned of your relationship with Agent Gavin, you most likely would be dead by now."

I looked up. "What do you mean?"

"They had the means, they had the element of surprise, and—as proven by their attack on you in the park—they had the opportunity, but they held off. Why?" Yablonski spread his hands. "Based on what Cutthroat told us, the plan to bug your apartment came *after* Margaret spilled about Gav. She bought you some time. She bought us time, too."

"With her life."

Yablonski closed his eyes for slightly longer than a blink. When he opened them again they were dead, flat, unreadable. Exactly the way Gav's were when he struggled with emotion. "Then let us ensure her life wasn't lost in vain." He turned to Gav. "Your cover is blown, Agent Gavin. There's no doubt about it."

Gav flexed his jaw, but said nothing.

"These two," Yablonski said as he tapped his laptop screen, "are clearly aware of who you really are. You can no longer glide in and out of our investigations with fake identification and a plausible cover story. They're onto you, which makes your current role in the organization a liability rather than an asset."

Gav straightened to stare at Yablonski. "That's why they tried to kill us tonight, isn't it? That's why they'll continue to come after us until we're dead." His eyes blazed and his body vibrated with anger. "I want to get out there right now and kill both those men with my bare hands."

"Perfectly understandable," Yablonski said. "But until we come up with a plan for how to proceed, you will follow orders. And that means you're behind a desk until further notice." He tapped the third photo on his laptop screen. "Have you told Ollie about Kern and his plans to overthrow the current regime in Armustan?"

"I have."

He nodded. To me, he said, "Then you know this is a blood feud we're facing. Kern is honor-bound to kill you."

"So I gather," I said.

"Now the hard part."

"Hard part?" I repeated. "Haven't we gone through enough for one night?"

"I'm afraid the worst is yet to come." He blinked those flat, dead eyes. "Unless we can come up with a plan to eliminate the threat against you once and for all, you won't be able to resume your regular life. You can't. It would be impossible to protect you. Do you understand what I'm saying?"

I did, but I didn't want to. "But you have a plan, right?"

"Not yet. That will take time and considerable effort. And you need to know that, ultimately, we may not be able to do anything except hide you. Permanently. You know what I'm getting at?"

Though worded differently, it was the same question again.

"What do we do now?" I asked, deflecting.

"Until we come up with a suitable plan to capture these men, you will both need to return to your apartment and pretend nothing's wrong."

"You're joking," I said.

"I wish I were. Think about it. We have one shot at bringing them in," he said.

I could see the pieces coming together. I didn't like it, but I couldn't argue the logic as he laid it all out for me.

"As long as Kern's soldiers believe their surveillance hasn't been compromised," he said, "we retain a measure of control. We feed them what we want them to know. If we lose that tenuous connection—if they become skittish and decide to cut and run—we're in the dark again. There's only one thing for certain: They won't give up. They'll kill you or die trying. We have this one chance—our only chance—to reel these terrorists in."

"What is it, then?" I asked. "The plan, I mean?"

He glanced at his watch again. "We have details to work out, and you both need sleep. I should have more information for you tomorrow. Trust me," he said. "We will have you two covered every minute of every day until these men are stopped. You will be safe. But I need your full cooperation. Do I have it?"

Gav took my hand as we got to our feet. I faced Yablonski. "What other choice is there?"

CHAPTER 14

BACK AT THE APARTMENT, GAV AND I MADE light conversation—for the benefit of our listeners—about how happy we were to have made up after our argument and how our late evening out at the bar enjoying a few drinks had smoothed all the roughness between us.

As we prepared for bed, I reminded myself of Gav's assurances and tried hard not to think about anyone watching me change clothes. We talked about the devastation left by the gas leak and how walking into that scene had caused us both so much stress.

We kissed good night and shut off the lights. Tucking into Gav's warm body, I knew it would be a long time before my heart and mind settled enough to allow me sufficient peace to sleep.

"We're together, Ollie," he whispered into my hair. "That's all that matters."

* * *

EVEN THOUGH I WAS EXHAUSTED FROM THE wee-hour interrogation, and even though I could have called on Bucky to handle breakfast without me, I set out on time for my shift at the White House. I couldn't stand being in our apartment a moment longer than necessary.

Agent Lynch, a young man who had relieved Agent Romero during the night, escorted me in. He didn't speak much and had a habit of addressing me as "ma'am" whenever he did. A second Secret Service contingent—in a dark sedan—followed us the entire way.

Gav had taken off in the same car we'd used last night. He had a team following him as well. His first stop was the Secret Service office near the Gallery Place Metro station for a lengthy debriefing on all his contacts and interactions with Armustanian citizens over the past few years. Although he didn't complain, I knew how angry he was that all his efforts—all the connections he'd made—were now compromised. His frustration level—and mine—were almost more than I could bear.

An e-mail message from Sargeant was waiting for me when I arrived in the kitchen. Time-stamped very early this morning, it was a request to call him immediately. I did.

"What's up, Peter?" I asked.

"I'm putting hiring on hold for the entire White House," he said. "That includes the kitchen position."

"What's going on? I haven't heard anything in the news about a hiring freeze."

"Neville Walker and I discussed your predicament last night."

"My 'predicament'?"

"Ms. Paras," he said with heavy disappointment, "must you be so obtuse? With all that has transpired with the Armustanian factions responsible for Margaret's death and who have targeted you, we can't take any chances, can we?"

"He called you?"

"At four o'clock this morning, yes."

"I'm so sorry, Peter."

"Please," he said, stopping my apology. "We have bigger issues at stake here, and we hope to all sleep more soundly once this situation is resolved. In the meantime, however, security concerns rule the day. All interviewing has been halted."

"What about Lottie Catalano? She's not an unknown quantity. I don't want to lose the opportunity to hire her if her house contract falls through."

"Collateral damage," he said. "We can do no more than hope for the best and trust that we will be able to resume normal operations soon."

Disappointed but resigned, I hung up.

Bucky walked in a few minutes later. "What's up now?" he asked. "You look as though you've been up all night."

"I have," I said, too emotionally exhausted to pretend otherwise.

He donned an apron and a gentle tone. "Tell me," he said. "You know I won't breathe a word."

I thought back to the last time we in the White House kitchen had been threatened. That had been nearly a year ago but Cyan's lament about how this job took everything from us—our time, our lives, our hearts—resonated now louder than ever. I understood her need to walk away from the constant pressure and—what had turned out to be—ever-present danger. Bucky had never expressed a similar desire to break free of the White House's hold, but that didn't mean he didn't harbor similar thoughts.

"Let's get started on breakfast," I said.

"Ah, you can't tell me. Is that it?"

"I have plenty to tell you," I said. "But it's easier to talk when I'm doing something."

I pulled out a frying pan and placed it atop the stove. After all we'd been through, Bucky deserved to know the truth. Except for details dealing with Gav's undercover work, and Yablonski's name, I told him everything.

"OLLIE," BUCKY SAID WHEN THE BUTLERS SWEPT breakfast away, "this is too much. You've been in rough patches before, but nothing on this scale."

"The Secret Service has been relentlessly protective of us," I said. "Neville Walker has seen to that. Even when Gav's with me, I'm not considered safe. We have a security detail watching us around the clock."

"Don't you think the Armustanians have noticed your bodyguards? Don't you think that alerts them that we're onto their plans?"

"Absolutely," I said. "But that doesn't mean they'll give up. They're waiting for their moment. And when it comes, they'll strike."

"What can you do?"

"That's the worst of it," I said. "Nothing. We can't do anything until we get word from the higher-ups. They're working on a plan now."

"I wish they'd hurry."

"Good morning," Sargeant said. Bucky and I turned as our chief usher strode into the room. He held a tablet in his hand and wore his typical persnickety sneer. "From the hushed conversation you two were engaged in before I arrived, may I presume that Mr. Reed is fully informed on recent events?"

If Sargeant planned to ream me out for having shared so much with Bucky, so be it. I didn't have it in me to lie. "Of course I did," I said.

"Good," Sargeant said, surprising me. "Then I won't have to dance around these updates. With the bombing at Cenga Prison, what we know thus far about Margaret's murder, and the recent attempt on your life, Ollie, the White House is effectively on lockdown. The president has agreed to act on the advice of his counselors and will depart for Camp David with his family as soon as breakfast is over. Nonessential staff members will be sent home until further notice. They're being told that the residence needs to be fumigated but that the procedure is to be kept quiet."

"And people are buying that?" Bucky asked.

"Most of our personnel do as they're told," he said with a glaring frown. "A habit I do wish more of you embraced."

"I'm very glad that decision's been made." I said.

"This means, of course, that until further notice, both of you are freed from your kitchen duties. With the First Family off premises and no official dinners to organize, you have no meals to prepare." He wagged a finger at us. "How much time you both spend here at the White House is entirely up to you."

"What about the kids?" I asked. "How will Abby's and Josh's absences from school be explained?"

"We have already called both institutions to report that the children are suffering with a bout of the flu." He offered a fleeting smile. "That should buy us time until Monday. Let's hope everything is resolved by then."

When he left, Bucky took a long look around the kitchen. "What do we do with all this freedom, Chief?" he asked.

"What say we tackle that massive kitchen project we've always talked about but never found time for?"

Bucky groaned. "That whole top-to-bottom-purge-and-reorganize project that *you've* always talked about?"

"Yep. We've got at least four days ahead of us with nothing to do. Staying busy will help keep my mind off of what's really going on out there."

With a resigned sigh, Bucky pushed up both of his sleeves. "Let's get started."

WE STARTED IN ON THE OVERHEAD CABINETS along the west wall and, working counterclockwise, had managed to sort through the contents of three of them. Standing on a stepladder, Bucky handed me items one at a time. When I took hold of an uncovered plastic bin and stared at its contents, I asked, "How many funnels does one kitchen need?"

He came down from his perch. "I'm guessing there are at least forty in here." Lifting one of the conical utensils from the stash, he blew a hard breath at it.

Dust shot out at me, making me cough. "Thanks a lot."

"Sorry," he said, taking the bin from me and placing it onto the central countertop. "But to answer your implied question, not this many." He and I began pulling all size funnels from the bin, sorting them into sections of large, medium, small, plastic, and metallic. "Can we get rid of them?"

"I suppose." I picked up one of the white plastic versions. It had a huge crack running its length. "This one gets tossed for sure." As we continued to sort, I added, "None of these look as though they have any sort of historical significance. They're all twentieth century or later, I'd guess. Let's start a donate pile. I'm sure there are worthy charities that will be able to use our kitchen castoffs."

Bucky took another look around the kitchen. It wasn't a

large room, but right now, at our slow pace, it seemed to represent a project that might stretch forever. "Can't wait to see how much we come up with," he said with deadpan humor.

"But just think about how much better it will be to have the extra room. And you know how frustrating it gets sometimes when we can't immediately find what we're looking for."

"That doesn't happen often."

"True, but in a perfect world, it wouldn't happen ever."

"Since when is this a perfect world?"

"Ms. Paras?"

Agent Lynch stood in the west doorway. "Yes?" I asked.

"Your presence is requested upstairs, ma'am."

I rubbed my hands together, decided they were too grimy from the cleaning project to ignore and said, "I'll be with you in a second." Stripping off my apron, I went to the sink.

Bucky leaned against the counter next to me and spoke quietly. "You think this is it?" he asked. "You think they've come up with a workable plan?"

"I hope so." I shut off the water, dried my hands, and gave the kitchen a quick once-over. "Listen, this is too big of a job for one person. Wait until I get back to do any more."

"Are you kidding?" he asked. "Keeping busy will help keep me from worrying what's going on with you upstairs." He clapped me on the shoulder. "Go get 'em, Ace."

CHAPTER 15

AGENT LYNCH AND I TOOK THE ELEVATOR UP to the Butler's Pantry. He opened the door that led into the Family Dining Room, and gestured me in. "They're waiting for you."

All conversation ceased when I stepped into the room.

Exactly as he had the night before, Yablonski sat at the center of the room's table. This time, however, he wasn't alone. Six others sat around him, most of whom looked to be in their late thirties. One man and one woman, however, seemed closer to Yablonski's age.

"Come in, Ollie," he said again, much the same way he had last night. "Agent Gavin is on his way."

There were two open seats around the long oval table, one at either end. As I settled myself at the spot at the south end, facing north, I ran my fingers along the shiny tabletop. After so many years in the White House, I should have been able to summon up what kind of wood it was, but my mind blanked and I couldn't remember. It was a lovely reddish brown, with a blond-toned inset trim. Mahogany, probably.

What difference did it make? Why was I fixating on the table right now?

Probably because I was anxious about what I was about to hear.

The agents around the table wore stern expressions and were dressed similarly in gray-toned business attire. I greeted them one at a time as Yablonski made introductions and I was happy to note that little name cards had been tented around the table. What a relief not to have to memorize so many at once. The last person to be introduced was a fifty-something woman, Maryann Morris. "Agent Morris," I said, reaching to shake her hand.

Yablonski cleared his throat. "The team members you're meeting today, along with others who you will most likely never see, have been culled from the Secret Service, the NSA, and from other organizations. Let us dispense with titles. Individual ranks are not material to this endeavor."

"I'm sorry."

"No harm done," he said. "In fact, as we'll be working so closely together, it will be best if you think of these folks as your new best friends."

He'd used that "best friend" descriptor yesterday to pull information from Cutthroat. I knew Yablonski meant well, but the wording chilled me nonetheless.

Except for murmured greetings when each had been introduced, none of the six people surrounding Yablonski had spoken a word since I'd walked in. They all seemed to be waiting for him.

He turned to me. "You've been informed that the First Family left for Camp David this morning?"

"I was thrilled to hear it, yes. I think that was an excellent decision."

"So glad you approve." A corner of his mouth curled up, but no one else reacted. They remained ready, eager, and immobile.

Yablonski's gaze jerked up as the far door opened and Lynch escorted Gav into the room. "Ah, just in time." Yablonski signaled to Lynch. "No interruptions."

The young agent nodded, stepped out, and pulled the door closed. I had no doubt Secret Service agents were stationed outside each of the room's exits.

Gav headed for the end of the table across from me, nodding hello to everyone as he took his seat. No introductions needed, apparently. He shot a quick glance in my direction, but I couldn't read the message it held. All I could tell was that he was angry, and I was pretty sure it wasn't at me.

"Now that we're all here, we may begin," Yablonski said.

It was evident that Gav and I had been positioned at opposite ends of the table on purpose. Yablonski's doing, no doubt, but I wondered why.

The big man glanced at those gathered around the shiny oval tabletop. He nodded, as though pleased.

Gav was anything but. Working his jaw, he glowered at Yablonski. I'd never seen Gav display anything beyond respect and admiration for his mentor. Something had happened. I edged forward on my seat as though doing so would help clear the air faster.

Oblivious to Gav's malevolent stare, Yablonski continued, "Our team has worked through the night to come up with a scenario designed to lure the Armustanians out of hiding and into a controlled environment."

He leaned forward on thick arms, speaking quietly. "We

are only too aware of the fact that these people are ruthless. They had no compunction setting that bomb at Suzette's restaurant." He made eye contact with every person around the table, one by one. "We got lucky," he said. "Innocent bystanders could have been killed." Pointing to the man seated to my left, Yablonski leaned back. "Falduto, where are we on witness statements?"

Falduto, a slim fellow with a wide nose and a rigid demeanor, read from his notes. "The establishment's owner, Jason, said that although several parties had requested seating at the front table window throughout the day, none of them acted suspiciously. We showed him photos of known Armustanian terrorists. Jason did not recognize any of them. He did admit, however, that he was not up front every minute and could have missed these men coming in."

"Agent Gavin?" Yablonski said, turning to Gav. "What do we know about the bomb itself?"

Gav continued to pierce Yablonski with his forceful stare. "As you know, due to the fact that my cover has been compromised, I am no longer conducting field investigations." He indicated the man to his right. "Humphrey will have to debrief us on additional findings. However, I can tell you that, after examining the collected debris, my team back at the lab has been able to make certain determinations."

With a sweeping glance around the table to capture everyone's attention, Gav continued, "Preliminary analysis confirms—with a certainty that nears absolute—that the bomb-maker was an Armustanian who apprenticed under Kern. That helps us because we know who we're dealing with and allows us to anticipate their next move."

"Which is for them to demand Farbod Ansari's release," Yablonski said.

"Right." Gav didn't make eye contact with his mentor.

Continuing to address the group, he said, "We can anticipate escalation—"

"Excuse me." Russo raised her hand. "What was it about the bomb that makes you so certain it was crafted by a member of Kern's faction?"

Gav blinked at the interruption, but moved smoothly to answer the question. "Without getting into too much detail, I can tell you that the style of this particular IED is consistent with that of Kern's men—from its components to its design. They tend to use a particular gauge of wire, and exhibit a preference for using timers. That, in itself, is telling. Many IED makers prefer remote controls—say, using a cell phone to detonate the device—but Kern's team relies on timers. In that sense they're a bit more old-school. But"—Gav held up a finger—"such choices have advantages as well. Kern and his cohorts are highly skilled in creating these particular bombs. They've had great success with them and it's clear they prefer to stay with what works."

"Thank you," Russo said as she scribbled notes on her legal pad.

"What were you saying about escalation?" Yablonski asked.

My husband didn't acknowledge Yablonski, choosing instead to answer the man's question by addressing the table. Yablonski couldn't have missed the subtle slight, but he seemed unperturbed.

"Make no mistake," Gav said, "we are under attack. Unless Farbod Ansari is released—and President Hyden has vowed never to negotiate with terrorists—or until Kern and his team are neutralized, we cannot let down our guard. Not for one minute."

"Which is why we are all gathered here today," Yablonski said. "Everyone at the table, save Ms. Paras, has been advised of the details of our operation going forward."

Every face turned to me. I sat up straighter. Their expressions held a mixture of curiosity, wariness, and compassion. Only in Gav's eyes did I read anger. Not at me, but for me. And in that moment, I felt the first flickers of fear.

Combatting my unease the best way I knew how, I worked up a sassy smile. "From all your expressions I deduce that's about to change." Clapping my hands together, I faced Yablonski. "My turn, then. What *is* the plan?"

The big man leaned forward, catching me with a gaze so sincere, I felt as though I were the only other person in the room. "What you need to understand, Ms. Paras," he said, "is that Kern is driven to succeed. He not only seeks to achieve Ansari's release while discrediting President Hyden's administration, he has it in for you, personally."

No one shifted, no one moved. The only sound in the room was the gentle wash of air, bringing what suddenly felt like too much warmth into the room.

I maintained steady eye contact. "So I've come to understand."

"We've discussed this at length, Ollie." I didn't miss the fact that he'd lapsed into using my first name. "Your actions resulted in Kern's brother's regime being overthrown and his subsequent ignominious murder. Kern won't rest until he avenges his family's honor."

"Yes," I said. "That's been made abundantly clear." I took my time glancing around the table. "I gather from all your solemn expressions that you would like me to play a part in whatever operation you've come up with." My heart beat so vigorously I thought it might start banging against the table's mahogany edge. I breathed in deeply then blew out a breath to steady myself. "What do you need me to do?"

Yablonski shot a smug look at Gav, who stared down at his hands and shook his head.

CHAPTER 16

GAV LIFTED HIS HEAD TO ADDRESS YABLONSKI. My husband's fury hadn't abated; rather, it had intensified. "Before we go any further, I'd like to go on record here to voice my reservations. Again."

He glanced across the table at me oh so briefly, then returned his attention to Yablonski as he continued. "While the plan is sound and I agree with it in concept, I have serious misgivings about requiring Ms. Paras's involvement. As I've reminded you several times, Ms. Paras's safety is paramount. We should have no difficulty enlisting an agent of similar stature and coloring to stand in for her."

"Your reservations have been noted, Agent Gavin. Again." Yablonski maintained a mild-mannered air, but his jaw clenched. "May I remind you that Kern's operatives have shown themselves to be too well-informed about Ms. Paras to be fooled by a stand-in. Additionally, as you and I have discussed, the decision lies with Ms. Paras herself." He turned to me. "It's up to you," he said. "We will lay out the plan and then you can decide whether or not to participate."

Choosing between Gav and Yablonski would, in ordinary circumstances, be a no-brainer. But I knew that Gav's worry for my safety had the potential to cloud his judgment.

I did my best to ignore the sorrow in my husband's eyes. "Well then, it's probably best if you give me the details."

Over the next twenty minutes, Yablonski laid it out, step-by-step. Gav and I were to return to our apartment tonight. Once there, we were to discuss the fact that our lives had been upended lately and that we needed to get away for a romantic night or two.

We would settle on taking a trip to Bill and Erma's winery and discuss staying with them for a couple of days. Yablonski knew and trusted the couple and emphasized how the vineyard's isolated location provided a perfect spot to draw our terrorists out into the open. As soon as the Armustanians made their move, they'd be apprehended.

"And what am I to do during this stakeout, or whatever it's called?" I asked. "Do I have any specific tasks to perform?"

"You will heed direction and follow orders immediately and without question. No matter what they are."

"I can do that," I said.

Gav addressed Yablonski, speaking through tight teeth. "But if something were to go wrong—"

"It's our job to make sure nothing goes wrong," he said. "We will have operatives in the house, including Morris and Del Priore, who will pose as Erma and Bill."

I took another look at Morris, then at Del Priore. They were a little younger than Gav's good friends, but physically not too far off. As long as Kern's people had never met Erma and Bill, these two could pass for the couple.

Yablonski continued to talk to me. "This is assuming

that Kern's people are still listening to your conversations, of course," he said. "Sad to say, we hope that's the case."

Across the long, shiny table, Gav stared, communicating with his eyes. I knew he wanted me to beg off, just as I knew he anticipated my resolve.

"How long do we have to decide?" I asked Yablonski.

"Not long. If you choose to remain behind, we need to settle on your replacement ASAP." He wagged a finger. "The operation is going forward, with or without you. Plans are already in place to evacuate Bill and Erma for the duration. And whether you choose to be part of the strategy or not, you will still need to have that conversation with Agent Gavin in your apartment for the benefit of those listening. Should you decide to remain back, you will be kept under guard, out of sight, until we're clear."

"Gav doesn't have the choice to stay back, does he? He'll participate in this operation, no matter what. Is that right?"

"Yes." From the gleam in Yablonski's eye, I knew he knew what my answer would ultimately be. Still, I couldn't simply shut Gav out, couldn't pretend as though his preferences held no sway.

"Gav?" It was tough to ignore the fact that we were surrounded by silent strangers, but I gave it my best.

He met my eyes but remained silent.

"What do you say?" I asked.

"You know how I feel."

"And you know how I'd feel sending you into danger without me."

"Civilians should never be placed in harm's way."

"I'm not an ordinary civilian," I said. "I'm the target."

"All the more reason for you to stay back."

I really wished the rest of the people in the room would disappear.

"Gav," I said quietly. "We have to do this together. Let's flush these terrorists out. Let's get this done once and for all. Okay?"

Gav and Yablonski exchanged a look I didn't understand.

"Gav?" I asked again. "What do you say?"

Gav's eyes were sad. "Your call."

Yablonski turned to me. "Ollie?"

I nodded.

He rubbed his hands together. "Then let's get to work."

I RETURNED TO THE KITCHEN LATER TO FIND Bucky sitting cross-legged on the floor, surrounded by pans of every shape and size. He had a tablet in one hand and a frying pan in his lap. "Can't think of a better time to do an inventory," he said when he saw me.

I pushed two oversize baking sheets to the side and sat next to him.

"I can tell by the look on your face that there is a plan and you're not thrilled with it," he said. "Can you give any details?"

"Not right now. Maybe in a couple of days."

He arched a brow. "When it's all over, you mean?"

"Something like that." I looked around. "In the meantime, since neither of us is needed here to feed the First Family, why don't you take some time off?"

"Oh." He strung the word out and waved his hand over the top of all the strewn kitchenware. "And leave all this fun?"

"We can finish up what you started today. And tomorrow I'll see how far I can get."

"You're coming in tomorrow?" he asked.

"Yes, but leaving early," I said, knowing that Yablonski wanted us on the road to the winery by five at the latest. "I'll be out all day Saturday. Maybe Sunday. Not sure."

Bucky leaned against the nearest cabinet and crossed his arms. "I don't need days off," he said. "I'll be here tomorrow to work on our cleanup."

"And inventory."

"And inventory," he said. "And I'll come in Saturday and Sunday, too. Brandy's got a commitment with the Egg Board so there's nothing for me at home. Besides, this is the White House. You never know when plans change. The First Family might return sooner than we expect. We wouldn't want them to go hungry, would we?"

I didn't mention that the First Family wouldn't be back from Camp David until after I'd completed my assignment with Yablonski and his team. Before I left the Family Dining Room, I'd asked the powerful man what would happen if the Armustanians weren't listening, or if they sensed a trap and didn't show. What then? He didn't have an answer for me. He admitted that they'd be back to the drawing board.

MID-AFTERNOON, GAV CAME TO VISIT IN THE kitchen. "What are you doing here?" I asked. "I thought you'd be tied up for the rest of the day."

"Change in plan." He turned to my assistant. "Sorry to do this to you, Bucky, but Ollie's on special assignment tonight. She's leaving early." He delivered this announcement with a wink designed to make my assistant think my husband was spiriting me away for a date night.

Bucky wasn't fooled. "Got it," he said with a flimsy salute. To me he said, "See you tomorrow."

"Don't work too hard," I said.

He shook his head. "I'm not worried about me." He pointed his finger like a gun. "You be careful, understand?"

Gav led me across the Center Hall to the Vermeil Room,

where a pile of clothing, including a camel-colored wool coat, lay draped across the Duncan Phyfe sofa.

"What's going on?" I asked.

"Field trip. You'll need to put these on." He crossed the room to the sofa and picked up a pair of black leather boots sitting next to it. "Your height gives you away," he said as he lifted the boots and pointed to their soles. At least two inches thick.

As I sat down to pull the boots on, I glanced around the room. Adjacent to the China Room, this one—sometimes referred to as the Gold Room—featured six portraits of former First Ladies, all of them long since deceased. I thought about how much the world had changed since they'd lived here.

Gav shuffled through the clothing and pulled out a blond wig and fluffy pink knit hat.

"Why is all this necessary?"

"This"—he waved his hand over the garments—"is bare minimum. The best we could come up with on short notice. We're confident that Kern and his men are waiting for an optimal moment to strike. We intend to hand that moment to them on a silver platter tomorrow—but until then, we can't take any chances."

I opened the door to the adjacent ladies lavatory to check out my reflection in the mirror. Using my hip to prop the door open, I adjusted the long blond waves and tucked in errant tresses of my dark bob. Gav watched from over my shoulder.

"I thought you didn't care for me as a blonde," I said, grinning.

He met my eyes in the mirror. "I care that you stay alive."

I hadn't expected such an emotional response to my flippant remark. "I know you don't approve of my participation in the operation tomorrow," I said. "Sorry for making jokes."

"It's who you are," he said. "You get chatty when you're

nervous. Nothing wrong with that. I know that deep down you're taking all this seriously and that's what matters."

As I finished playing with my hair and donning the hat, I asked, "Where did you get this stuff?"

"You can thank Neville," he said. "He wrangled our disguises. The goal is to get you out of the White House without anyone recognizing you. Your height and style choices are probably well-known to the terrorists by now so—if they do have you under surveillance—we're making you taller, blonder . . ."

"And more fashionable?" I asked as I returned to the sofa, lifted the camel-colored coat, and ran a hand along one sleeve. I marveled at the fabric's supple, creamy texture before pulling it on. The hem fell past my knees. "Is this cashmere?"

"Could be. Neville didn't tell me who he borrowed these things from. All we care about, though, is that it's a departure from what you normally wear."

"What kind of clothing do you have? And, more important, what's the point of all this?" I asked. "If they're watching us, the minute we get to our apartment, they'll know we're in disguise."

"We're not going home," he said. "At least, not right away."

"The field trip you mentioned?"

The door opened and two women walked in. It took me a moment to recognize Agent Romero. She wore a long faux-fur coat, matching hat, and shiny black boots. "Good evening, Ms. Paras, Agent Gavin," she said. "I'd like you both to meet Annette."

No title, no last name. Simply: Annette. We exchanged polite greetings. Annette was my height—my height before I'd pulled on the stilt boots, that is—with a build similar to mine. She had on black pants, a White House–emblazoned fall jacket exactly like the one I owned, and she wore a dark-haired wig styled exactly like my standard bob.

"Annette will leave with another agent to embark on a circuitous route around D.C. before returning to the White House," Gav said to me. "Agent Romero will get you to our rendezvous location, where you'll be given further instructions. Remember this code word: Spencer. If at that point we're convinced you and I haven't been followed, I will make contact with you and we'll continue to our destination."

"Which is where, exactly?" I asked. "Aren't we required to return to the apartment tonight?" I asked, alluding to our goal of allowing the terrorists to overhear our plans for visiting the winery this weekend.

"Joe Yablonski has agreed to a small detour," he said cryptically. "I'll explain more later."

A BLACK STRETCH LIMOUSINE—A LIVERY CAR, not a Secret Service vehicle—swung around the south entrance of the White House five minutes later. The chauffeur got out to open the back door for me and Agent Romero. Silently, we eased in. The driver—from a trusted firm the White House occasionally hired to shuttle dignitaries—was to take us to the Thomas, a swank hotel a half mile northwest of my usual Metro station.

Romero and I had been instructed to keep our conversation in the car to a minimum. Even though the driver could not know our real identities or be able to hear us from behind the window that separated his cab from the passenger area, we chose not to talk at all.

Romero and I stared out opposite windows for the quick jaunt. My thoughts were in a crazed rush. Nothing about this made sense. Last I'd spoken to Yablonski, the plan had been to head home like normal and to have our rehearsed-to-sound-spontaneous conversation about the need to get away to the winery. What was going on now?

When we arrived at the Thomas, our limo driver hurried around to open the door for us. Romero hustled me out in front of her, while instructing the driver to return in thirty minutes. The world seemed different from my new height. Not as many people towered over me. Weird.

Inside, Romero wound my arm through hers and broke into a brisk, no-nonsense trot through the bright Beaux Arts lobby, crossing it at such a quick clip that hotel guests couldn't possibly get a good look at either of us even if they'd been paying close attention.

Romero took a sharp left past a shiny grand piano leading me into the hotel's bar, Feathers. Wood-paneled and cozy, the dimly lit establishment was enjoying a surge of business this evening. Almost every chair at the gleaming bar was taken, and most of the tables were occupied. She tugged me to the right, recapturing my attention. "Over there," she said, where a small tented sign on a table read RESERVED. She whispered into my ear. "Keep your head down, okay?"

Seconds after she and I sat, a waiter greeted us, handing us leather-bound menus. I kept my face averted. "Will you be joining us for dinner this evening, or simply enjoying a cocktail?"

"Cocktails only, please," Romero said. "We'll need a few minutes."

"Of course. Take your time."

The moment he was gone, Romero said, "The ladies' washroom is behind you to your left."

"I don't need to—"

"Behind you to your left," she repeated.

"Oh. Sure. Gotcha." I stood.

Guided by elegant signage, I made my way over. Inside the

washroom, a copper-haired woman greeted me. "Good evening." Leaning forward, she whispered, "Spencer," then pointed to the stalls lining the long wall. "They're empty." The facility's main door was equipped with a thumb bolt, which she slid into the locked position. "Let's get this done before anyone comes knocking."

"Oh, yes. Sure," I said, momentarily taken aback. The woman's swift, detached instructions, her no-nonsense approach, and this clandestine meeting set me on edge.

She told me to remove my hat, blond wig, and cashmere coat as she peeled off the wig and clothing she was wearing and placed her items on the marble countertop. The swap took seconds, our transformations only moments longer. I became a redhead with a navy jacquard shawl and blue beret; she became the blonde I'd been two minutes ago. The woman and I had essentially exchanged identities.

My heart went into double-skip mode as adrenaline coursed through my body. It wasn't fear as much as it was that heightened sense of getting caught that made my nerves crackle. I tried to talk myself down from this strange edginess. What was the worst that could happen? A restaurant patron might need to use the facilities? I tried to shake off my old don't-get-in-trouble–schoolgirl mentality. For heaven's sake, I was a full-grown female in a ladies' washroom. Nothing wrong with that.

And yet, jitters zinged like pinballs in my chest. I blew out a breath and fluffed my wavy red hair.

The woman instructed me to remain in the washroom for at least three minutes after she left. She told me to make my way back into the lobby and, if Gav didn't approach, I was to take a seat near one of the pillars near the reception desk to await further instructions. "Good luck," she said, and then ducked out the door.

I didn't recognize myself in the mirror and it wasn't just due to the red wig. The countertop seemed so low. Was this how life was for tall women all the time?

When the door swung open thirty seconds later, I gasped in surprise. Although the fifty-something corporate type barely took notice of me, I coughed my relief when it became obvious she was here for the usual reasons. I was able to keep track of her in the mirror as I ran water in the sink. She pushed the door open to the first stall, peered in, didn't like what she saw, and moved on to repeat the exercise at the second and third stalls before finding one that met her needs. Dousing my hands in the warm cascade before me while counting the seconds on my watch, I waited for another two minutes to elapse.

After lowering my hands into one of those hyper-fast contraptions and triggering the air jets, I drew them upward to dry. Slowly, slowly. Forty seconds is a long time to waste doing nothing, and I wondered if the woman in the stall was waiting for me to depart. With excruciating care, I primped my brand-new copper curls until my three minutes were up. The fourth stall's toilet flushed.

I took a deep breath and headed out the door.

I wasn't surprised to see my doppelganger at the table with Romero as I strode through the cushy bar and back into the hotel's lobby. The woman I'd exchanged disguises with was smiling up at the waiter, who bent at the waist to take her order.

The hotel's reception desk lay across a black-and-white marble floor laid out like a diagonal chess board. I expected my ultra-high boots to click against the hard surface, but was surprised to find myself gliding silently forward. Platform soles this high and still comfortable and quiet? I needed to find out who manufactured these babies and stock up.

I'd only made it about halfway across the shiny expanse in my magic boots when Gav fell into step next to me. He had on a dark gray overcoat and wore a wide-brimmed *Indiana Jones* fedora so low it shadowed his eyes. I recognized him immediately

"My, aren't you dashing?"

That garnered me a quick grin. "One more stop," he said. "You ready?"

"Always."

CHAPTER 17

THE VALET ON DUTY OUTSIDE THE THOMAS
Hotel's other entrance handed me into the passenger side of
an idling SUV. Gav took his place behind the wheel. "Thank
you," he said to the valet as he handed the young man a tip.

"Are we able to talk now?" I asked when we pulled away.
"Can you tell me where we're going?"

"Bombs brought us together, Ollie. I'm determined not to
let them tear us apart." Gav took off his fedora and tossed it
into the backseat. "Beyond that, I don't have much to share at
this point. This is a show-don't-tell field trip if there ever was
one."

"Can I at least get out of this wig?"

"You can get back into all your own things." He reached
behind his seat. "Here," he said as he laid a bag on my lap.

"Bliss," I said as I removed the sweat-inducing wig and
began switching footwear. "But I will miss these awesome
boots. How different the world looks from two inches higher."

A short while later, we pulled up to a gated industrial park, where a sentry checked our IDs against a clipboard list before allowing us to pass.

Low-slung unadorned buildings lay in short, even rows. Sodium-vapor lights gave a pink glow to the structures' corners but did little to illuminate their façades. I scanned them as we passed, looking for labels or logos. I had no doubt these constructions belonged to a government agency, but I couldn't figure out which one.

"Where are we?" I asked.

Gav pulled into a parking space near the front doors of the fourth building on the right. He turned to me with a wry smile. "It doesn't matter. You were never here."

A uniformed guard met us at the door. He neither said hello nor smiled.

Inside, I shivered, though not from fear. The ambient temperature in here had to be at least ten degrees cooler than outside. The next guard, a middle-aged guy with a sturdy build and a robust grimace, led us down a high, cavernous hallway. With minimal illumination, its stark, concrete walls made me feel even colder. Our footstep clicks echoed away almost as quickly as we made them.

About halfway down the hall, the guard stopped and ran his badge through an ID reader. After a promising *click*, the guard pulled a heavy door open and gestured us forward. "They're waiting for you."

Stepping in, I shielded my eyes. After our trek through near darkness, the high-wattage illumination here felt foreign and sharp.

"They" turned out to be two people—one male, one female—wearing white lab coats and purple latex gloves. Standing behind a long, narrow table that held four ominous-looking devices, they glanced up, nodded a greeting, and waited expectantly for us to approach.

With its high, unfinished ceiling and rows of identical boxes stacked on identical metal shelves, the space resembled a mini-warehouse. Roughly thirty feet deep, the room stretched to my right at least double that distance.

I pulled my White House–emblazoned coat closer and wished Gav had brought a heavy jacket along. Didn't the federal government believe in heating their facilities?

Without another word, our escort shut the door behind us.

Gav led me to the table and introduced the two techs as Jane and John. I sent him a skeptical glance and he responded with a "What did you expect?" look of his own. Fine. I probably didn't need to know these individuals' real names anyway.

Willowy and tall, Jane had high cheekbones and a deep brown complexion. Her light eyes were luminous yet charged with energy, like whisky-colored diamonds. John wore charcoal-framed glasses that were too big for his narrow face. With the pallor of a man who never saw the sun, he had a slim build but somehow managed to sport a fleshy double chin.

I had an idea of where we were, or why. The four contraptions on the table before us warped me back to the first time Gav and I had worked together. Back under President Campbell's administration, the White House had suffered a bomb threat. Gav and his team had been brought in to educate the staff on what to look for and how to respond when encountering anything suspicious or unfamiliar.

"John, Jane, and I will be giving you a refresher course on IEDs this evening," Gav said.

"IED is an acronym for improvised explosive device," John said.

"I've learned a little bit about them in the past." I sur-veyed the array of items. "Apparently not enough, otherwise we wouldn't all be here tonight, would we?"

"That's right," Gav said. "And, if all goes according to plan tomorrow, tonight's exercise will have been a colossal waste of time. I don't care. I'm convinced that until the Armustanian threat is neutralized, we should all strive to be overprepared rather than underprepared." He'd said as much on the ride over, but took care to repeat himself for John's and Jane's benefit. "Shall we begin?"

Jane took the lead. "Our goal here tonight is to familiar-ize you with a few of the component elements the Armustan-ian radicals favor when crafting explosive devices. These four prototypes—all of which are inert, of course—represent four designs that have become popular with terrorists from that region of late."

"Let me interrupt here," John said. "I don't want you to think these four items represent the sum total of what these terrorists are capable of producing." He shook his head from side to side, his wobbly double chin following like a pendulum on split-second delay. "Not even remotely close. We can't predict what they'll dream up tomorrow or what deviations they'll scramble to employ when preferred materials are in short supply. We're scratching the surface here. Barely."

Jane cleared her throat. "My colleague is correct in that we can't cover all possibilities." She turned to fix a sharp look at him. "But we can share *probabilities*. That's all we have time for."

"Let's hope it's enough," John said.

Gav touched my arm. "John's point is a good one. Always remember that these are called *improvised* explosive devices because the people who create them have to work with what's available. No two bombs will ever be precisely identical, but we have discovered patterns Armustanians tend to favor."

"You don't really believe I'll ever encounter one of these, do you?" I asked. "I mean, when I'm by myself?" I shot a quick glance to John and Jane to gauge their reactions, but it was Gav's that interested me most. "Until this threat is—as you term it—neutralized, I'm being escorted to and from work, and when I'm not working, I'm with you."

"Today, yes. Tomorrow, sure. What if things don't go as planned tomorrow night? What if the threat lingers? What if Kern disappears completely before he comes roaring back? How long before we become complacent?"

"We won't," I said. "You and I aren't complacent."

"Exactly right. That's why we're here."

"I'm not arguing with you. I'm just curious." After coming to understand the seriousness of our situation as explained by Yablonski, I *wanted* to be here.

"Ollie," Gav continued. "We all hope you never need to utilize the education you're getting tonight. But we also all know that there are no guarantees in life, and our best chance for beating these guys is to prepare for the worst."

"And so we work."

"And so we work," he agreed. "Now, let's look at our first example."

OVER THE NEXT HOUR I LEARNED HOW ITEMS as innocuous as a washing machine timer or a wind-up alarm clock could be used to set off bombs. I learned how these weapons could be made even more deadly with the addition of nails, ball bearings, or razor blades. Jane even showed me a pressure-cooker bomb, a type similar to the one used—with tragic results—at the Boston Marathon terror attack.

I would never be able to understand how any human being could deliberately harm another like that.

By the time we got to the fourth IED, I felt as though I knew everything there was to know about triggers, power sources, fuses, container options, and explosives. I didn't truly know everything, of course, but my brain felt bloated with information, some of which needed time to digest.

The three of them—Jane, John, and Gav—had taken me from the first rudimentary model to this final, sophisticated device, indicating how features could be added to increase the likelihood of detonation.

"To this day," Jane said, "that's one of the bomb-maker's toughest choices. Should he rush the process and create more devices, some of which will turn out to be duds, or should he take his time to ensure optimal results?"

"Optimal results?" I repeated. "You mean explosions that take innocent lives and cause massive destruction? Is that it?"

She gave a brief nod. "I understand how distasteful all this sounds, but to prevent such catastrophes we need to get into the bomb-maker's head."

"I know," I said. "I'm not trying to be difficult. I just need to say it out loud. To remind myself that this isn't a game of one-upsmanship being played online or in an arena full of fans. That this is about human beings with real-life consequences."

Gav laid a hand on my shoulder. "I understand. Because we see this every day, we're consumed by that very one-upsmanship. We're so obsessed with getting ahead of these guys that we have to push past the human cost to stay focused on the goal. You're being hit all at once and it's a lot to take in."

It had been a pounding lesson so far and I'd needed the break that short interchange had provided.

"Okay." Taking a deep breath, I nodded. "I'm ready. Let's do this."

John lifted the fourth IED. The dark gray cylinder looked like a miniature SCUBA tank but without the air hose attachments. "While our field officers have encountered more refined constructions than this one in regions across the globe, the Armustanian faction we're facing hasn't adopted those modifications. This IED is similar to the one that detonated at Suzette's restaurant as well as the one at Cenga Prison."

"How can you be sure?" I asked.

"Fragments recovered from the scene," Jane said.

I pointed to the device. "That's the size of a small fire extinguisher. How did no one notice it had been left there?"

"Good observation," Jane said. "This *is* a fire extinguisher tank we've repurposed for lessons. But to answer your question, we can't know for sure what the one that destroyed Suzette's looked like. Because the bomb-makers were on a tight timeline, they most likely placed one of the less sophisticated devices there." She waved her hand back toward the first example. "A small, easily concealed version, but fully capable of inflicting the damage we witnessed. We believe that they positioned the device beneath the radiator nearest the front door."

"Oh," I said, picturing the location. "How did they manage to do so without anyone seeing? What kind of clearance is there? A couple of inches?"

"More like eight," John said. "But even if there had been less maneuvering room, you're forgetting what we told you at the outset. These prototypes merely scratch the surface of the variety out there. The individuals who create these bombs are constantly changing the devices' appearances, sometimes out of necessity, sometimes by design."

I hadn't forgotten anything; I'd been expressing astonishment. But I held my tongue. The three of them had been more than patient as they educated me on the inner and outer workings of IEDs.

Small steps at lightning speed.

John was still holding the fourth IED. "This one is designed to be detonated remotely."

"Here." Gav pointed to a small rectangular box that sat on the device's exterior. Sizewise, it looked like a one-cup-size plastic container we used to store leftovers. He lifted it.

I reached to touch the cell phone hidden beneath. An older model, the handset had a physical keypad and a tiny display. "I take it they call the number on this phone when they want the bomb to go off?"

"Exactly," John said. "But this method of pulling the trigger has its drawbacks."

"Like a lack of dependable cell reception in some areas?"

John looked taken aback that I'd been able to make that logical leap. "Yes. Yes, exactly," he said. "Very good. Also, equipment failure. I always say that the more intricacies you include, the more trouble you ask for."

Jane tapped the side of the phone. "We've developed methods for jamming such signals. In fact, our colleagues are busy setting up a signal-dampening system for tomorrow night's event."

"You're saying that if they set a bomb at the winery, you'll be able to prevent it from detonating?" I asked.

"Only if it's one of these remote designs," John said, hefting the metal cylinder. "If it's on a timer, you're out of luck."

CHAPTER 18

WHEN WE GOT BACK TO OUR APARTMENT, GAV
hesitated before unlocking the door. "You ready?" he whispered.

I took a deep breath, let it out, and nodded. "Let's do this."

Once inside, Gav tossed his keys in the bowl and
shrugged off his coat. I followed and when he shut the door
behind us, signaling the beginning of our charade, I wondered if I would ever again feel comfortable and safe here.

"Don't you think we eat out a lot?" Gav asked. "I mean,
considering the fact that you're a chef."

"You know what they say about the shoemaker's children," I said.

He laughed. "True enough. The place we went tonight
was amazing. I wonder if they recognized you and that's
why all the courses were served with such panache."

As Gav waxed poetic about an imaginary restaurant, I
recalled the less-than-elegant feast John and Joan had

arranged for. Jane had insisted that we eat there so we wouldn't have to make another stop on the way home. Both of them continued their instruction as Gav and I made short work of the food.

I couldn't remember the last time I'd eaten dinner out of a paper bag, but I didn't complain. The selections had done what was necessary: provide fuel for energy. What more did I need?

Just in case our eavesdroppers were familiar with my work schedule, however, we needed a cover to explain our tardiness arriving home tonight. Gav's goal was to make it sound as though we'd enjoyed a leisurely dinner.

"I doubt they did," I said, "recognize me, that is. They're known for their attention to detail. That's why I chose it for us tonight."

We were both careful to avoid using a real restaurant's name. It would be too easy for someone to double-check our story. Would the terrorists go to such extreme measures? We couldn't be certain they wouldn't.

"Well, then kudos to you for making an awesome choice."

"After our argument the other day, I wanted to do something special for you," I said. "I'm glad you enjoyed it."

Gav continued our script as he finished hanging up our coats. "I did. Very much so."

"Good," I said.

He crossed to join me in the living room, where he kissed me on the forehead with an impossible-to-miss smack.

I withdrew a bottle of wine from our apartment-size wine rack. "Care to continue the celebration?" I asked.

He took the bottle from me and pretended to peruse the label. "You know I love a good cabernet," he said, "but I'm more in the mood for a merlot. We have one from Spencer's Vineyards, don't we?"

I feigned surprise. "Are you sure? We're down to our last

two bottles from them, and I don't know how soon we'll be able to visit there again."

He exchanged the bottles, pulling up the merlot he'd mentioned. "Funny you should say that," he said as he made his way into the kitchen and dug the corkscrew out of the drawer. "I was wondering if you'd be willing to head out to the winery tomorrow night?"

"Tomorrow?" I repeated, hoping to inject a precise combination of wonderment and delight into my voice. "What for?"

"What would you say to a long weekend?" he asked. "And before you ask, I was planning to broach the subject *before* you planned dinner out tonight, so don't imagine that I'm playing copycat here."

I brought two wineglasses to the table. "A whole weekend? Alone? Are you kidding me? Of course. The First Family is away, so I'm clear until Monday. But how can you get away for that long?"

"Well," he said. "There's a little more to the story I haven't told you."

"Uh-oh. Am I going to like this?"

He took his time pouring us each a hefty measure of wine although neither of us planned to drink it. When he finished, we picked up our glasses, clinked them together, and kissed, as was our habit.

After we both sipped, he led me back into the living room. We sat next to each other on the couch. "I've been given new orders that will take me away from home for at least a week. Probably longer."

"No." I elongated the word, this time working to inject disappointment into my tone. "When do you leave?"

"Tuesday morning."

"It's the Armustanians again, isn't it?" I asked.

"I can't tell you that."

"Doesn't matter. It doesn't take a rocket scientist to figure that out." I took a small sip of the deep ruby liquid. "Where are you going?"

"I can't tell you that, either."

I blew out an exasperated breath. "Can you at least tell me if you're staying in the United States or going out of the country?"

"Sorry, no."

I heaved a sigh. "It's not like there's anyone I can tell," I said. "Your secrets are safe with me."

"I know that." Holding his wine in his right hand, he wrapped his left arm around me and drew me close. "But you know I've given my word." He pressed his cheek against my head, but his words stayed clear. "What do you say? Are you willing to go away with me for a couple of days?"

I laid a hand on his leg and squeezed. "I can't think of anything I'd like better. But will it be all right with Bill and Erma? We can't just show up and surprise them."

"I cleared it with them this afternoon. Erma said that you and I are always welcome at Spencer's Vineyards."

"We're staying *with* them?" I asked, knowing the answer. "Won't that get a little awkward?"

Chuckling, he took another sip. "They have a guest cottage a little bit up the hill from the main house," he said. "It'll be just the two of us all weekend, though. Bill and Erma have plans of their own. They'll stay long enough to hand over the keys but then they're taking off for some sort of winegrower's meeting."

"It sounds wonderful, Gav," I said breathily.

"One of the finest vineyards in Loudoun County will be all ours for the entire weekend. If the weather's nice, we can hike. If it's not . . ." He let the thought hang.

Normally I would have picked up on Gav's mild innuendo

and replied with a little suggestive comment of my own. But knowing strangers were listening in on our conversation made me too uncomfortable to enjoy the banter.

"This is a really great idea, Gav," I said. "I can't wait to get away. The last few days have been pretty stressful, what with Margaret's murder and those two men stealing my purse. Not to mention the explosion at Suzette's."

"You and I don't have the opportunity to take vacations too often," he said. "I'm looking forward to it, too."

I sat up. "Should we start packing?"

Gav groaned. "What's there to pack? I can throw a few things in my duffel bag and be good to go."

"I need to prepare a little more than that," I said. "Are we coming back here to the apartment after work tomorrow night before we leave?"

"No, we'll leave straight from work." He made a so-so motion with his head. "But I can't predict what time I'll get out. I'm hopeful it won't be too late."

"What about our Secret Service chaperones?" I asked. "Are they joining us on our romantic retreat?" If we were being followed and recorded, there was no way the terrorists didn't know we had protection. That protection was probably the only reason Gav and I hadn't been sliced to ribbons in our sleep.

Gav laughed. "I struck a deal with the higher-ups on this one. A team will shadow us on the drive out, but once we're tucked in safely at Spencer's, they promise to leave us alone for the weekend."

"I'm surprised," I said. "The Secret Service has been tenacious about guarding us."

"As long as we aren't followed, we'll be fine. You've seen what a remote location it is and no one outside the department knows about my connection to Spencer's. Plus, Loudoun

County isn't exactly the first place a terrorist would think to search for us."

"This will be so great." My entire body trembled, but my voice remained steady and clear. "I think heading out to the country and forgetting about all the terrible things that have happened is going to do us a lot of good."

Gav stood and offered me his hand. "Let's start packing then. Our adventure awaits."

I grabbed his fingers and let him pull me to my feet. "It does indeed."

CHAPTER 19

DEEP INTO OUR REORGANIZATION, BUCKY AND I were again sitting cross-legged on the White House kitchen floor the following morning, surrounded by stacks of bowls, piles of utensils, and an assortment of heavy cookware, when Sargeant dropped by.

"I trust this lack of decorum isn't indicative of new protocols," he said with his customary moue of distaste. He leaned over to pick up one of the smallest metal bowls, using his fingers as a pincer to do so. "And I certainly hope you intend to thoroughly scrub all these items before using them."

"All part of the plan, Peter," I said. "We're using our free time to clean and restructure. Better to get this accomplished now before our new chef is hired. Changing the layout after she starts would cause undue aggravation."

"That's one of the matters I'd like to discuss with you," he said.

"Good, I was hoping that's why you were here." I got to

my feet, rubbing my hands together to clear them of any floor grit I may have picked up. "We haven't lifted the moratorium on hiring, have we?"

"Unfortunately not."

Bucky got up to stand next to me. "What's the holdup? I understand the need for security, but the First Family is out of town until further notice and all the applicants were vetted before this recent crisis began. The longer we wait, the more likely our best candidates will find positions elsewhere."

"Duly noted, Mr. Reed." Sargeant sniffed. "The decision to pursue this matter, however, is out of my hands. In his eagerness to polish the PPD's tarnished reputation, Neville Walker is continuing the suspension on all hiring until the current threat is eliminated, or at least diminished to a great degree."

"No better than being back under a sequester," Bucky said.

"Does grumbling improve the situation?" Sargeant didn't wait for Bucky to reply. "No, it does not." Turning to me, he continued, "The reason I'm here is to inform you that Ms. Catalano's cross-country home purchase has received a green light. She has withdrawn herself from consideration."

I grimaced at the ceiling before returning my attention to Sargeant. "Thanks for letting me know. It's a disappointment, but at least we didn't lose her because we were dragging our feet on a decision."

He nodded. "I understand you're leaving for the weekend?"

"You got my e-mail, I take it," I said.

"Yours and Neville's."

Bucky arched an eyebrow. "Oh, so everyone is in on this covert weekend plan but me," he said. "Is that it?"

Sargeant glared. "The less you know, the better. Trust me."

Bucky held up both hands. "Whoa, didn't mean to touch a nerve. I was just teasing."

Though almost a full head shorter than Bucky, Sargeant took a menacing step forward. "Margaret is dead because of how much she knew about the White House and its staff. The people who killed her think nothing of using and discarding us to further their goals. When I said the less you know the better, I wasn't being funny."

"Of course not," Bucky said, clearly intimidated. "There's been a lot of tension here lately. I was just trying to inject a little levity."

"Didn't you read the memo urging personnel to exercise extra caution in their day-to-day lives outside the White House?" Again, before Bucky could answer, Sargeant went on, "I don't see any room for levity in what we're dealing with here."

Chastised, Bucky's cheeks flamed. "Fair enough."

Sargeant tugged at his collar and straightened his tie. "Speaking of Margaret, I have an update to share."

Bucky pursed his lips but said nothing.

"The reason I asked about your schedule this weekend is because, now that Margaret's remains have been released to the family, funeral arrangements have been made. Margaret will be waked from three to nine on Sunday. Her family is Roman Catholic, so the funeral Monday morning will begin with a mass. I plan to send out an e-mail to everyone on staff, but I wanted to tell you personally because I know it's important to you to attend these things."

It had been a very long time since the day Sargeant and I stood side by side, alone, at a memorial for one of his relatives. Although he'd almost seemed to resent my presence at the time, I knew that deep down he'd appreciated my being there.

"Yes, thank you. I'll definitely attend the funeral, and I hope to be back in time Sunday to make it to the wake. I know how much it means to grieving families to be able to meet and talk with people their loved ones knew."

"Yes," Sargeant said. With a curt nod, he turned and left.

Bucky stopped me from reclaiming my spot on the floor. "Okay, I know you can't share details but—Ollie." He rubbed his hand up his forehead and along his bald head, staring out the direction Sargeant had gone. "That guy is always high-strung, but I've never seen him like this."

"There's a lot of pressure on him right now."

"No, it's more than that." Bucky turned to face me. "You're walking into something big this weekend, aren't you?"

"Bucky . . ." I held my hands out. "I can't."

"I know, I know." His jaw was tight, his eyes blazed. "Just tell me you know what you're doing."

I pulled in a breath. "Other people know what they're doing."

"Do you trust them?"

I thought about Yablonski and the team of people prepared to protect me tonight. "I do."

"That's something, at least," he said. "I don't like this, Ollie. Don't like it one bit."

I fist-bumped his shoulder. "Where's that levity you were talking about? Come on, think about it. I've been in tough situations before. What's one more?"

He didn't smile. "Got a bad feeling this time."

"I'll be fine," I said. The words were a knee-jerk response to allay his fears, but saying them aloud made me feel better, too. "Really."

"I'll hold you to that."

GAV AND I SET OUT FOR SPENCER'S VINEYARDS right on time. The government-issue vehicle he drove wore a thin film of grime and carried an overpowering stench of stale smoke.

"Who used this car last?" I waved a hand in front of my face, for all the good it did me. The smell wasn't going anywhere but up my nose. "Whoever it is I worry for their health."

"This is the car Joe usually takes when he's in the field."

"Joe Yablonski?" I asked, even though there weren't any other Joes we both knew. "You can't be serious."

"He apologized in advance for the car's condition." Gav flicked a glance up at the rearview mirror. "But he insisted we take a secure car and didn't want to pull rank on other agents. He's riding with one of the team members behind us right now, in fact."

"How could I not have known he was a smoker? That's a pretty tough habit to hide."

"Believe it or not, Joe hates everything about cigarettes. Can't stand the things."

"Then how do you explain this?" I asked, wiggling my fingers in the smelly air.

Gav squinted at the windshield. "It's been twenty years, maybe twenty-five since he kicked the habit." He turned to me and smiled at my skeptical look. "No really, he did kick the habit. Ninety-nine percent of the time he won't touch tobacco. But whenever he does, he smokes alone in his car so that no one has to breathe his secondhand smoke." He waved a hand in the air. "Like I said, he apologized profusely for subjecting you to all this."

"Why the one percent, then? I would think that if he hates tobacco so much he'd never risk getting drawn back in."

"Nerves." Gav lifted one hand from the steering wheel as though there could be no other answer. "It's situations like this one—when he puts people's lives in danger—that he turns into a maniac and pulls out a pack. Can't help himself."

"I had no idea. He always comes across so calm and in control."

"That's why he smokes alone. Who would you rather follow? The leader who commands authority and exhibits self-confidence or one who chain-smokes his way through every decision?"

I looked out the window at the city rushing by. "I wish I hadn't asked."

Gav glanced over. "He's human. He experiences self-doubt and anxiety just like the rest of us. The difference is that stakes are much higher in his world than they are in most others. The best decisions can still result in horrific consequences. People can die. Joe lives in a constant state of worry that he's overlooked some key component."

"Are you?" I asked. "Worried, I mean? I know you didn't want me to be part of this."

"Yeah." He flexed his jaw. "If this were any other operation, I wouldn't second-guess a minute of it. But your presence changes everything. I've been trained to see a mission through to the end, regardless of what's going on around me. Life or death is often decided in a split second and the most successful decisions are made objectively. They have to be."

"And you can't be objective while I'm around."

He frowned into the windshield. "Not even a little bit."

"Are you saying you wish I hadn't agreed to take part?"

"Like that would ever happen." He reached over to pat my leg. "No, you made the right choice. This is my issue to deal with. I know I'm being overprotective and trying to shelter you, but Joe has every possible contingency covered. I have faith in him and the team. We're going to be fine."

"What about your objectivity? Won't that be a problem?"

"There should never be a moment where I'll need to make a life-or-death decision." He spoke with confidence, yet grimaced at the road. "Because my judgment could be clouded by concern for your safety, Joe has effectively taken me out of the equation. I'm not running any part of this. I'm not officially on duty. That's why he brought in so many professionals. So that everyone involved—everyone with the capacity to make those life-and-death decisions—*will* do so objectively."

We traveled for some time in silence, my right leg bouncing a nervous rhythm as I crossed and uncrossed my arms. All I could think about was my role in this scenario and wondering when the time would come to play it. Would it be tonight? Tomorrow? Who knew when the would-be assassins planned to strike?

Yablonski had admonished me to obey orders. I'd promised I would, but wondered how hard it would be to blindly follow instructions if conflicting impulses kicked in. I'd found myself in dire situations so often that I'd learned to rely on instinct to guide me through. This time, however, though the stakes were as high as they'd ever been, I needed to suppress my base urges to act out, speak out, flee, or fight.

I reminded myself that, unlike many of my other altercations, professionals were in charge this time. They knew what they were doing. A misstep on my part could have tragic consequences. I hoped for Gav's sake, and for mine, that I had what it took to relinquish control.

Once traffic thinned, I turned around to get a look at the car behind us. Other than the fact that there were two people riding in the boxy, dark vehicle, I couldn't make out much; they were too far back.

"How will we know if we're being followed?"

"Joe has eyes and ears everywhere on this one," he said. "If he has any suspicion that they'll make their move before we get to the winery, Joe will signal and we'll abort."

"Do you really believe the Armustanians picked up enough detail from our conversation last night to know where to find us?"

His face was grim. "Their goal is to eliminate you, for revenge, and to take me down in a blaze of glory to prove they can infiltrate our ranks. If they *were* listening in, they know where we're going. They want us dead. I believe they're going to come."

I shuddered.

"You okay?" he asked.

"I'll be glad when this is over."

"We both will." He reached for my hand and squeezed. "As much as I hate to say it, let's hope they *have* been listening and that they make their move tonight. If they do, then they're attacking on our timeline, when we have home court advantage. This may be our only shot at taking them down."

"And you don't think they'll suspect an ambush?" I asked. "You don't think that they'll find it convenient that we planned this getaway, all alone, in a rural setting? If it were me, I'd smell a trap."

"Let's hope they aren't as smart as you are."

I digested that. "And while we're waiting for them to make their move? What can we—you and I—do?"

He shot me a resigned look. "You heard what Joe said. Our job is to sit and wait."

CHAPTER 20

BY THE TIME WE TURNED ONTO THE GRAVEL driveway for Spencer's Vineyards, even I was convinced we hadn't been followed. Whether that meant that the bad guys were waiting for us to settle in before making their move or whether they were utterly unaware of our plan, I had no idea.

Gav had warned me ahead of time that Joe Yablonski and his driver would abandon us a few miles before our destination, but only if they were sure it was safe. In almost the same breath, he assured me that we would never be out of a team member's sight—we just wouldn't know where our guardian angels might be hiding while they watched.

"This is turning out to be some romantic weekend, isn't it?" I asked, exaggerating my words for effect. "Eavesdroppers at home, voyeurs out here. What more could we want?"

"You're nervous, aren't you?" he asked.

"A little."

He didn't say anything.

The vineyard was set about a mile in from the main road, and I waited a couple of seconds as we bounced and jostled along the uneven drive. "What made you ask?"

"Besides being chatty, you're making jokes. Trying to lighten the mood."

"Is that so unusual? Am I normally not lighthearted?"

He slid a glance my way. "It's going to be okay, I promise. Smooth as silk."

I nodded.

Whenever I'd come here before with Gav, it had been during the day. This was my first time visiting the property at sunset. If it weren't for the apprehension in my heart, I might have taken the time to appreciate the way the waning sunlight stretched over the landscape and shadows patterned the tidy rows.

We usually parked alongside one of the utility buildings nearest the tasting room, but today Gav drove past the single-story whitewashed structures, pulling up in front of Bill and Erma's rustic, two-story home.

When we got out of the car, Gav straightened and stretched in the cool evening air. He flexed his arms, lifting them to the sky before lowering them to his sides. He swiveled his torso right and left. I was close enough to read his expression and knew that he was scoping out the area, seeking evidence of his colleagues' presence, hoping to find none. The better they were hidden, the safer we were.

"Everything okay?" I asked, keeping it vague. Members of Yablonski's team—some of whom I hadn't met—had been on site from the moment the plan had been hatched. There was zero possibility of anyone having planted surveillance equipment here since we hadn't "informed" the terrorists we were coming until late last night, but avoiding specifics was a good habit, regardless.

"All good," he said, reaching into the back for our duffel bags. "You ready for our romantic getaway?"

"Can't imagine anything I'd enjoy more."

As we started up the home's front stairs, the door opened and Maryann Morris stepped outside. "Well, hello, you two," she said, waving us in. "Bill," she called to Louis Del Priore. "They're here."

If anyone happened to be watching from the shadows, they would have seen the two of us greet the older couple warmly, shuffle into the house, and emerge a few minutes later with the key to the guest cottage in Gav's hand.

Del Priore, wearing clothes identical to those I'd seen Bill in plenty of times, accompanied us out onto the porch as he provided helpful suggestions on things to do over the weekend, where to go for dinner if we didn't feel like cooking, and a reminder that the cottage's bathroom door often stuck and we might have to jiggle the knob a bit. If I hadn't met the real Bill as many times as I had, I'd never suspect this guy wasn't genuine.

"Just follow the path." He pointed vaguely north and west up the gentle rise. "Erma stocked the fridge and pantry for you. You know how she is," he said as we headed down the stairs. "And we left you plenty of wine, of course."

Before we made it to the corner of the house where we were to take a right, Gav turned and called back, "You and Erma have a good time at the conference. You leaving tonight or tomorrow?"

"Tonight. Couple hours from now. Will we see you when we get back?"

"We're taking off late Sunday night," Gav said.

"Ah, too bad. We won't be home until Monday." The fake Bill raised his hand as he turned back toward the door. "We'll have to catch up another time. Soon."

"You got it," Gav said.

The path "Bill" had referred to turned out to be a narrow string of flagstones set in a jagged walkway like a kinked ribbon. Not that we needed it to lead us to our destination. Even though dusk had begun to settle, there was no chance of getting lost. Our weekend accommodations—or the target for terrorists, however you wanted to look at it—sat a hundred yards ahead up the hill in the center of a wide horseshoe of low shrubbery.

About the size of a two-car garage, the asymmetrical wood-shingled cottage had a covered porch framed by trellised rosebushes I could smell from twenty paces away. The wide blooms that appeared gray from a distance turned out to be the palest shade of pink close up.

I liked the fact that there was nowhere for anyone to hide. No chance of a crazed Armustanian bursting from knee-high bushes to attack. The nearest trees sat more than a hundred yards behind the tiny cottage. I wondered where Yablonski's team members were stationed, and wondered how close they'd let the Armustanians get before taking them down.

"There's a lot of empty land surrounding this," I said. "Why don't Bill and Erma use more of it for grapevines?"

"I believe they intend to expand in the coming years," Gav said, "but I don't know why they haven't yet. That's part of what they want me to learn before we take ownership, I suppose."

"It's a quaint cottage," I said. "This is where you sleep when you stay here?"

He nodded. "It's nice inside. I think you'll like it."

As he fitted the key in the lock, I placed a hand on his arm. "This feels . . . weird," I said. "I'm jittery."

"I feel it, too." He looked down at me and brushed the hair from my eyes. "And I'm sorry for everything that's brought us here," he said, keeping it vague in case anyone was close enough to listen in. "If we're lucky, this weekend will help us . . ."—he searched for the right words—"find our happiness again."

We were placing ourselves in harm's way, hoping to tempt the bad guys into the open, where they expected to kill us.

"Yes," I said. "I hope we're *very* lucky."

JOE YABLONSKI'S TEAM HAD WIRED THE LOCA-tion before the eavesdroppers heard the first hint about our plans to visit. Gav told me that two team members from the meeting in the Family Dining Room were on surveillance duty. They could see our every move, hear our every word.

When we first arrived, Gav walked me through a couple of important procedures. There were four hot-button stations—emergency alarms—that, when activated, would bring reinforcements running. The first was a kick-plate positioned inside the cottage, to the immediate right of the door. The second, in the kitchen, was attached to the side of the fridge like an uninspired magnet. The bedroom alarm sat slightly below the light switch and was labeled "fan," even though there was no such device in the room. The final button had been secreted in the narrow space behind the toilet tank and the back wall in the bathroom. Except for the kick-plate, which resembled an oversize length of baseboard molding, all the alarms were plastic, white, about the size of a nickel, and set inside a square metal frame.

"We need to be careful not to set these off accidentally." Gav led me back into the kitchen, where he opened the upper cabinet to the right of the sink. He moved two drinking glasses aside and pulled out a small black case that sat behind them. With three backlit buttons and a hook on its back, it resembled a garage door opener. "If we need to get out of the cottage quickly, we'll be alerted here." He pressed the widest of the three buttons. "We're in," he said. "You copy?"

A moment later, a voice said, "Affirmative. We are live. No company yet."

Gav pressed the button again. "We're ready for the test."

"Stand by. Ten seconds."

Gav held up a finger and I waited. Ten seconds later, a shrill whistle sounded. By the time I blinked, it was over.

"Yikes, that's harsh," I said.

"It's effective. If we hear that, we leave. Immediately."

"Understood," I said.

Pressing the Talk button again, Gav said, "We are in for the night."

"Copy that," the disembodied voice responded. "Out."

He pointed to the button he'd been accessing. "If I slide this latch over the control to hold it down, I can keep an open com link."

"What are the other buttons for?" I asked.

"This one," he pointed to the small one on the left, "allows us to listen in on the team, to hear what's going on at the main location. When we do, they're alerted that we're listening in. When I press it, I need to immediately provide a code word, 'Storm,' otherwise they will assume the device has fallen into enemy hands and react accordingly."

"Great." I didn't know whether to be happy or terrified that Yablonski had planned for such a contingency. "What about the last one?"

"The likelihood of our having to run is slim, but if we do, we take this with us. It's a form of GPS. The third button is one we don't want to have to need. Remember the jamming technology John and Joan talked about last night?"

"The method to prevent cell signals from getting through so that remote-controlled bombs can't be detonated?"

He nodded. "That's the one. If we find ourselves facing a bomb situation, we need to hit this button to engage that dampening field. But the moment we do, we no longer transmit our location. This effectively shuts down all signals within about a half mile."

"Wow," I said.

Reacting, perhaps, to the look on my face, Gav said. "Overwhelming, isn't it?"

"Feels like something out of James Bond or *Mission: Impossible* but this setup, this type of scenario, is all in a day's work for you. Isn't it?" I asked.

He nodded.

"I'm always worried when you're out on a mission," I said. "My worry level for you is skyrocketing right about now."

TWO HOURS LATER, WE SAT NEXT TO ONE another on the compact love seat in front of the droning television, two untouched glasses of wine on the coffee table before us. I had no complaints about the cottage. Though small, it was cozy, with a stone fireplace in the corner of this snug living room, a galley kitchen—abundantly stocked exactly as "Bill" had foretold—and a sleeping area so small I needed to scoot sideways around the bed to get around it.

"Well, this is nice," Gav said after a prolonged period of silence.

I shot him a look. "Would you rather have me chatty, making jokes?"

"I'd rather we both were home and safe."

"Yeah." I couldn't see anything out either of the windows

flanking the television, but I found myself glancing over at the dark panes every few seconds nonetheless.

After we'd prepared and consumed a light dinner of roast beef sandwiches and vegetable soup, we'd unpacked our few belongings and toiletries. Now we had nothing left to do but wait. And I couldn't help but think that every passing moment brought the murderous Armustanians closer.

Although we'd turned on the television, we kept the sound low lest we miss an important alert from the garage door–opener communication device. Not that it mattered. I couldn't concentrate on the broadcast anyway.

"We brought books," I said. "Would you rather read?"

He rested his elbows on his knees, one of which bounced exactly the way mine had on our car ride over. He glanced at his watch. "You tired?"

With tension gnawing at every nerve in my body I didn't think I'd fall asleep for a month. "Not in the least."

He frowned into some middle distance. "It's probably a good idea for us to make it look as though we're turning in for the night. If anything happens, they'll want to believe they have the element of surprise."

"Sounds good," I said without conviction.

We got up from the tiny sofa and made our way to the bedroom, turning off the cottage lights along the way. When I scooched behind Gav to get past him in a particularly narrow passage between the bedroom and bath, he turned and grabbed me by both shoulders. "We're going to be okay," he said. "Really, we will."

Though reassured by the words, I was more warmed by the depth of emotion in his eyes. "I know," I said. And in that moment, I believed it. "But . . . is it supposed to be like this? My nerves feel like they've been doused in jalapeño pepper juice. Is this . . . normal?" I asked. "I want to *do* something. Not sit and wait for strangers to decide my fate for me."

"Come on, let's talk." Gav went ahead of me into the bedroom. He pulled back the red-and-sage-plaid coverlet and sat down. "I'll take this side, nearer to the door. You take the wall." He chanced a look directly above the headboard at the room's lone window, then got up to lower its shade. "Climb in," he said as he patted the mattress. "Let's get comfortable; we may be here a while."

Still fully clothed, I eased between the covers while he shut off the remaining lights. This charade—this pretending to be blissfully unaware of a plot to assassinate us—was far more difficult than I'd expected it to be. I blinked up into the darkness, wondering when we would have our lives back.

Gav eased an arm around me. "Yes, this is normal." He gave a quick chuckle. "Well, to an extent. Most operations involve me with a partner but we're usually on our feet, not snuggled up in bed together." He pulled me closer. "I agree. It's aggravating. Being in the dark—quite literally in this instance—isn't a happy place to be. This is tough work, and even those of us who've trained for years have a difficult time sitting still for hours on end. What you're going through is completely normal. I'd be worried if you weren't feeling the strain."

"That's good to know."

"Good people—even strong people—crack under stress. We're at the very start of this mission, and it could go on for half a day before we get any word of movement. And the possibility exists that nothing will happen at all."

"Which would be worse," I said. "Because then we'll never know when they might strike."

He didn't answer, but I felt his body tense. "Why don't you try to sleep? I'll wake you if there's any news."

My eyes had adjusted to the dark. I propped myself up on one arm to glare at him. "You have to be joking," I said. "Do you really believe I could sleep?"

He pulled his arm back out from under me and shrugged. "No, but it was worth a try."

I settled back against the pillow to resume staring into the shadows. "If they do plan to strike tonight, how long do you suppose they'll wait?"

"It's anybody's guess."

CHAPTER 21

RESTLESSNESS KEPT ME FIDGETING FOR THE next hour or so. "Does it bother you?" I asked Gav. "To have me talking constantly? Asking questions?"

He lay with his fingers laced behind his head, staring upward. "Helps pass the time, actually," he said. "These things can get mind-numbingly boring. You're keeping me alert."

Sitting up, I propped my pillow against the headboard in a new attempt to find a comfortable spot. "If it were me," I said, "I'd strike now." I pulled up my cell phone and checked the time. "I'd assume my targets were asleep. What more do they want?" I asked rhetorically. "Plus, I'm impatient."

"Let's hope they are, too."

"So we can get this over with?" I asked.

"Exactly."

Although scant light streamed around the window shade's edges, and the rest of the small house was dark, I could see clearly. "Using the washroom would probably be a bad idea right now, wouldn't it?" I asked. "If they're watching, that would alert them that we're awake."

Gav sat up. "Go ahead. Just don't turn on any lights and don't flush."

"Don't flush?"

"This is a small structure. Who knows what can be heard from outside?"

I scooched forward all the way to the foot of the bed and lowered my feet to the floor. We both still wore shoes. A necessary precaution in case we needed to flee, but keeping our footwear on had an added benefit I hadn't anticipated. Even if I weren't too stressed to relax, wearing shoes in bed made it next to impossible to fall asleep.

I'd taken two steps toward the lavatory when a low voice stopped me cold. "Movement detected within the perimeter. Do you copy?"

Gav was on his feet before I could react. Grabbing me with his right hand, he pulled up the remote with his left. He pressed the Talk button and answered with a whispered affirmative.

"Unidentified persons closing in." I thought the voice spoke far more calmly than the situation warranted.

"How many?" Gav asked.

"Stand by."

"Gav?" I whispered.

"Stay behind me. No matter what."

He stood in the bedroom doorway facing out. I positioned myself behind him, keeping one hand on his back so that he'd know I was there.

The disembodied voice came through very softly. "One hostile at the northwest window. Two more hostiles circling, approaching front door."

"Understood." Gav growled his response. "Out."

From behind, I watched him finger the latch over the Talk button to maintain the open com link. He then slid the device into his pants pocket and used his other hand to gesture. "Get into the bathroom," he said. "Hide in the tub."

Holding my breath, I inched around him, stepping quickly but quietly. In one synchronistic second, as I bumped against the doorjamb, glass shattered behind us. Instinctively, I spun. Gav grabbed my arm to shove me into the bathroom, but he was too late.

In the time it took for me to comprehend that the sound had come from the window over our bed, a figure had hurdled through the opening. Yelling in a language I couldn't understand, he bounded off the bed and straight at us.

Though the cottage was dark, I couldn't miss the silhouette of the handgun the man pointed at us. Strapped across his back, he wore a giant rifle that looked exactly like the ones used by White House rooftop snipers.

Gav pushed me back to shield me with his body while shouting at the man in the same foreign language. I stumbled backward, catching myself against a small table, sending its lamp tumbling to the floor. Gav turned at the sound. "Go," he said to me. "Get into the bathtub. Now."

Still doing his best to shield me, he held his hands up as he spoke to the man with the gun. Though I couldn't understand a word of what was being said, I could tell that Gav's rational, conciliatory tone was having no effect on the intruder's state of mind.

Ignoring the man's shouts, following only what Gav had instructed me to do, I hurtled myself away, seeking shelter. One second later, the front door broke open with a resounding *bang*.

Two more men raced in, carrying similarly huge weapons.

Again, I stumbled backward, this time landing on my rump.

The first man—I assumed he was the leader—pushed Gav into the living room, using the muzzle of his gun. "Get up," he said to me in heavily accented English. His two comrades barricading the front door remained silent, looking to him for direction. "Go stand. By *mafalar.*" He jammed the gun into Gav's chest. "You, too."

I'd never heard the word *mafalar* but there was no doubt he wanted us in front of the fireplace. I pushed myself off the floor, expecting Yablonski and his team to move in any second.

Though the cottage's lamps remained off, there was enough ambient light to know that we were surrounded by angry men with giant guns. The trigger-happy gleams in their eyes made it clear that one word from the guy in charge and we'd be shot. Point-blank range. In cold blood.

Any time now, Yablonski. One second from now we could be dead.

Gav came to stand next to me. He lowered his hands and shifted to English as he continued to reason with the leader.

"Who are you?" he asked. "What do you want?"

Though the leader backed up, his aim never wavered. "You speak my language, you must know who I represent."

"Kern?" Gav asked.

The man's lips spread in a wide smile. "See," he said to the other two, "the arrogant American is not as stupid as he looks."

Gav gave a deferential nod. "We know you seek the release of Farbod Ansari," he began soberly, calmly, without any indication of panic or fear. "Our government has expressed willingness to discuss your concerns, but only if you work through diplomatic channels. This"—Gav waved his hands to encompass the room. The three men tightened their grips on their guns, but Gav didn't flinch—"isn't the way to achieve your goals."

"You know nothing of our goals."

"Then tell me." Had I not known better, I might have been convinced by the sincerity in Gav's voice. "Maybe I can help. I work for—"

The shorter of the two men at the door spoke up. "We know who you are. That is why we have come here. You are our instrument of success."

"How can I be?" Gav feigned confusion. "I can do nothing from here." Again he gestured into the air. Again, the three men reacted—this time, though, with a little less alarm. He made eye contact with each of them in turn. "We are at your mercy. Tell me what you want from me, but please, let my wife go." He gestured again, toward me this time. No reaction. "She's not a part of this."

"You know nothing." The third man spoke with such undisguised anger I was afraid he'd pull the trigger if I so much as blinked. "She is the reason we are here."

Gav ignored the man, directing his attention to the leader. "Tell me what you want from us."

"You were to die at your favorite restaurant," he said, arching the words *favorite restaurant* into a high, mocking falsetto.

"That was you?" Gav brought a hand to his forehead, simulating incredulity. "But you couldn't have known we would be there."

The three men exchanged a triumphant glance. "We are no longer content to kill you both," the leader said. "You and the female will be our hostages. These are *our* diplomatic channels to secure Farbod's release. Let us see how eager your president negotiates now." He made eye contact with the men at the door then nodded toward us. "Restrain them."

"Wait." Gav held up both hands. "Where are we going? You know you can't get away with this. Your best move is to give up now."

The leader laughed. "You think we are foolish. You think

Kern has no plan. He knows that on American soil we cannot hope to achieve our objective. But if our hostages are held in Armustan, we maintain control. Our country is beautiful this time of year," he said with a laugh. "You will love it."

"You plan to fly us there?" The question tumbled out of my mouth before I could stop myself. "There's no way. The minute we're reported missing, all flights will be halted."

He gave a throaty chuckle. "By the time you are missed, our private jet will have transported all of us to Armustan and Kern will open negotiations for your release." He swung the muzzle of the gun toward me. "Kern is eager to meet you face-to-face," he said. "He has been waiting a long time to exact his revenge on you."

"On me?" I asked, doing my best to feign innocence and hoping my outbursts weren't throwing off Yablonski's plan. *Where were they, anyway?* "Who is this Kern? What revenge are you talking about?"

"Enough for now. We have plenty of hours to explain exactly how difficult your situation is," he said. "The agent is of value to us alive. You are not. You will be brought to our circle and—if Kern is in a generous mood—granted a quick, merciful death. But only if he is in a generous mood." At that he chuckled.

One of the two other men laid his gun on the floor and made his way over. Intent on handcuffing us with Velcro-style restraints, he gestured for me to put my hands out. I inched closer to Gav. The man growled what sounded like an order, but I kept my hands behind my back.

"Wait," the leader said. Eyes wide, he backed away as though seeing us for the first time. "Why are you wearing day clothing?" Turning to his men he shouted in Armustanian. Though I couldn't understand the words, I knew he'd ordered them to run.

They didn't stand a chance.

One breath later, black-clad figures swarmed the three Armustanians. In a precisely orchestrated advance, they grabbed the men's guns, disarmed the terrorists, and tackled them to the floor.

The Armustanians cried out and struggled for control, but the stealth warriors were too strong and in too great a number to combat. The attack took less than thirty seconds, but in that short time, five team members managed to hand-cuff the Armustanians with the same Velcro restraints they'd intended to use on us.

I hadn't had time to utter a word. Hadn't had a chance to react, so when one of the team members came over to ask if I was okay, I stammered a lot of nothing.

Gav gave me a quick squeeze and kissed the top of my head. "Have a seat," he said, leading me to the table where we'd eaten dinner. "We're okay."

"I know," I said, finally finding my voice. "How did it happen so fast? I thought—"

"We'll talk about it later," he said. "Right now I need to help question these men. Will you be okay sitting here awhile?"

I nodded.

Yablonski showed up at the front door. Arms crossed, he surveyed the scene.

Gav strode past me. Although he spoke quietly to Yablonski, I heard angry tension in his voice. "What took you so long?"

"I'll explain. But for now, let's get some lights on in here."

CHAPTER 22

I'D BEEN THROUGH FAR MORE HARROWING predicaments in the past, some that had left me battered and trembling. As I sat at the table, watching the team take control of the scene, I realized I was suffering none of the residual terror I usually experienced after an altercation. I had no compulsion to collapse in post-traumatic relief. Sure, having high-powered weapons aimed at our chests had shaken me up a bit, but I'd always expected to come through this one unscathed. And now that I had, I felt odd, as though I'd missed a step along the way.

Louis and Maryann—the fake Bill and Erma—joined the crew in the increasingly crowded cottage. Maryann came to sit with me. She asked if I was all right and if I needed anything. I assured her I was fine.

"But . . . what took them so long?" I asked her. "Why did Yablonski wait to take them down? We could have been killed."

"The situation was under control," she said. "Team members

around the perimeter caught some chatter before the terrorists made their move. That's when we learned they were here to capture, not kill you." Her eyes clouded. "It was a last-minute decision to allow them into the cottage, but a good one."

"You didn't think it might be important to tell us?"

"No time," she said. "That's exactly why your husband was taken out of the equation, why he wasn't even allowed to carry his gun tonight—in case plans changed. Gav would have protected you, possibly compromising the operation. Joe Yablonski couldn't allow that."

"Even though we were in danger?"

"The situation was under control," she said again.

Near us, Louis shoved the sofa and side tables to one side of the living room, clearing space to settle the Armustanians facedown in the center of the floor.

Other team members secured the perimeter and still others were sent to locate the getaway car and driver, which were, no doubt, nearby. The attackers, lying prone, were frisked and stripped of all weapons. No bombs detected, no remote-control devices anywhere to be found. I breathed a sigh of relief.

With their hands bound behind their backs and their ankles tightly trussed, the men weren't going anywhere on their own. I came to understand that another team had been dispatched to ensure that no backup Armustanians waited in the wings—or the vineyard, as it were.

The leader lifted his head high enough to make eye contact with me. His upper lip curled as he bared his teeth. I knew he meant to intimidate, but surrounded as I was, by some of the best and brightest guardians of American freedom, I felt no fear. I gazed back at him and slowly shook my head. He growled.

Twisting his head toward his cohorts, he barked out what

sounded like imperatives, wriggling against his bonds as he did so. He looked like a wannabe break-dancer trying, and failing, to do the worm maneuver.

I caught Gav's attention and sent him a questioning look. "He's warning the other two not to speak to us, not to admit to anything."

Moments later, I heard the unmistakable sound of a helicopter arriving and then landing nearby. I tilted my head and reconsidered. Multiple helicopters. No one, except me, seemed the least bit surprised by their arrival.

The angry Armustanians were removed from the scene one by one, each accompanied by four team members. I had no idea where the terrorists were being taken, but weariness had begun to settle over me and I realized I didn't care. Gav and I were safe. Mission accomplished.

Eventually only four of us remained in the cottage: Yablonski and Gav returning the furniture to its proper arrangement, and Maryann and I at the table. I stood. She did, too.

Yablonski replaced the coffee table in front of the sofa and slapped his hands together. His eyes were sharp things, razor-edged with impatience. "Let's go."

"Go?" I repeated. "What happens now?"

I watched dismay cross Yablonski's features. I had no idea how he could have forgotten I was there, but the realization that he still had me to deal with dimmed his sparking anticipation. "Tonight," he said with exaggerated exuberance, "we keep *you* under surveillance at the main house." He pointed in the direction of Bill and Erma's dwelling. "It's an extra precaution, you understand. We don't anticipate any further incursions."

Reading his expression and tone, I sought clarification. "Keep *me* under surveillance?" I hoped I was wrong. "By myself?"

Yablonski winced. Gav eased an arm around me, and I had my answer.

"You're taking Gav, aren't you?"

"Ollie, I apologize," Yablonski said. "I'm bringing Gav back in to debrief the assassins. I promise to bring him back safe and sound as soon as humanly possible. Maryann will stay with you, and we'll have armed agents surrounding the house all night. You'll be perfectly safe."

There were times when being married to a special agent tried my patience. This was one of them. "I'm not worried about being safe."

Gav gave my sloping shoulders a squeeze. "I'm sorry," he said. "When Joe relieved me of duty, I assumed I wouldn't be invited in on this."

"Again, my fault." Yablonski tried, unsuccessfully, to curb his eagerness to get away. "We have an extraordinary opportunity here. Once the team gets our detainees settled, we will rely on your husband's fluency with the language and his expertise with this culture to extract the answers we need."

I understood, but wished I didn't.

Yablonski took my nonresponse as an opening to continue. "All that just took place here, coupled with the intelligence we've received thus far, supports what we've suspected all along: Kern is on the attack. He's targeted the administration to bring about Farbod's release, and he's targeted you, personally. Although we thwarted him here tonight, he isn't going away."

Gav gave my shoulders another squeeze. "We have a day, maybe two at the outside, before Kern gets wind of all this. After that, we estimate it will be less than a week before he sends another squad to accomplish what these men failed to achieve. If Joe and I can persuade these prisoners to cooperate, it will be our best chance at stopping Kern permanently."

"I understand," I said.

Gav shot Yablonski and Maryann a "Do you mind?" look. They trotted out of the cottage, giving the two of us a moment alone.

"What kind of 'persuasion' do you and Yablonski plan to offer the prisoners?" I asked.

Placing his hands on my shoulders, Gav turned me to face him. "Nothing you wouldn't approve of," he said. "I'm surprised you'd even ask such a thing."

"I have no doubt about *you*." I flicked a glance toward the open door. "It's Yablonski I worry about. Sometimes he scares me."

"I'm sure he'll be happy to hear it." A smile played at Gav's lips as he raced his gaze around the room. "We're probably still being recorded, you know."

I'd forgotten. Totally. With a groan, I let my head drop.

Gav lifted my chin, placed a soft kiss on my lips, and grinned. "Don't worry," he whispered, "sometimes you scare him, too."

SPENDING THE REST OF FRIDAY NIGHT ALONE in Erma and Bill's guest bedroom wasn't terrible. I slept fitfully, but at least I slept. Spending half of Saturday knocking around the house while waiting for word from Gav, however, stretched my nerves to the breaking point. Yablonski, Gav, and the prisoners were no longer on property, and Maryann couldn't—or wouldn't—tell me where they'd gone.

My belongings had been shuttled over from the cottage to the house, which meant that at least I had books to read. And if I became bored with the titles I'd packed, the home's jampacked shelves offered plenty of alternatives, plus a plethora of magazines. Erma subscribed to dozens of them, it seemed.

Bill and Erma's house was comfortably lived in and chock-full of cozy corners to snuggle into. But, whether it was Mary-ann's presence or the events of the night finally taking their toll, I was too restless to do more than pace and sit.

Settling myself at the kitchen table after a prolonged period of trekking between the living room and the back porch, I stared into one of Erma's cooking journals for an extended period of time before realizing I had no idea what the article was about. I pushed the glossy magazine to the side and stood up.

Across from me, Maryann looked up from her laptop. "Are you hungry?"

"Not in the least."

We'd eaten when I'd first gotten up. Eggs, toast, coffee, bacon. Simple stuff from the cottage cupboard's bounty. Maryann had offered to cook, but I took over, claiming it would help settle me, help clear my brain. That was true. I insisted on cleaning up afterward, for the exact same reasons. Although breakfast had taken place hours ago, I had no fresh appetite. I was, however, antsy.

"Am I allowed outside?"

Maryann laughed. "You're not a prisoner."

"Good to know," I said, striving for levity. "And I'm not trying to be difficult. I just feel as though it would help if I could stretch my legs a little. Do something."

"Not a problem. Until we get the all-clear, we have the entire property covered. Don't be alarmed if you notice you're being followed. It's only to ensure you stay safe." She reached for a nearby cardigan. Hardly government issue. I assumed it was one of Erma's—or at least one provided to look like it belonged to Erma. "I can come along if you'd like."

"No, thanks," I said. "I appreciate the offer, but I'm feel-ing a little claustrophobic."

A glance around the spacious house made my words sound silly, but I could tell she knew exactly what I meant. Reclaiming her seat, she resumed working at her laptop. "I'll be here if you need me."

The early afternoon air hit me with a burst of unexpected joy. I loved the fall season with its crispy leaves and tickling chill. Standing on the front porch, I closed my eyes for a moment to take in the sunshine on my face and the brisk breeze through my hair.

With one hand on the wooden rail, I decided to take my time to enjoy the moment before setting off. Keeping my eyes shut, I breathed in slowly, allowing the smells of wet dirt, green leaves, and sun-warmed porch paint to settle my nerves.

Gav had been gone for less than twelve hours, but it felt like much longer than that. I wanted him to return, of course. But if I were being truthful, I wanted more. I needed to know what the Armustanians were up to, what their boss, Kern, had planned for us. Yablonski had alluded to the fact that this revenge war Kern had declared on me wouldn't be over until Kern was taken down or I was dead. Given the choice, I hoped to heaven that the Armustanian prisoners had chosen to cooperate.

I didn't want to live the rest of my life in fear. But worse, I didn't want Gav and I to have to give up our lives the way Yablonski had hinted we might have to do until the Kern situation was fully resolved.

They had to have gotten answers. They had to. I tilted my face toward the sun and breathed deeply, determined to quell this temporary impatience and even more adamant to permanently reclaim my life.

Tires crunched gravel. My eyes flew open as a government-issue sedan pulled up and parked near the property's entrance. Gav stepped out one side of the backseat and Yablonski emerged from the other. I ran down the porch stairs to greet them.

The older man rubbed his palm against his stubbly cheek. "Good morning, Ollie," he said. "As promised, I brought him back to you safe and sound." With that, he gave a giant yawn and lifted his elbows high to stretch.

Gav's eyes were small. The tiny wrinkles at their corners seemed deeper than usual. "Sorry it took so long," he said, giving a stretchy yawn of his own, "but we got him."

"You got . . . him?"

"Kern," he said. "He's in custody."

"He was here in the United States?"

Gav pulled me into a tight hug. "We got him. You're safe."

"We're safe," I corrected.

Gav chuckled.

"Break it up, you two." Yablonski waved as though shooing us apart. "We need sleep now. We'll fill you in later." He pointed to the house. "They've got an empty couch or two in there, don't they?"

Even though Gav looked ready to fall asleep standing up, he raised a hand. "Thanks, but I think Ollie and I would prefer to head back to the apartment." He turned to me. "You don't mind driving, do you?"

Thrilled to be able to go home, I shook my head and started for the stairs. "Get in, I'll pack up our stuff and be right out."

CHAPTER 23

GAV DOZED IN THE CAR ON THE WAY BACK and, once home, went straight to bed. I didn't mind. Content beyond belief, I read a little and puttered in the kitchen, humming as I prepared dinner.

Life had returned to normal and I intended to enjoy every moment I could. Especially cheery was knowing that all listening devices had been removed from the apartment. The minute the Armustanians were in custody, Yablonski had given the go-ahead to a group of agents. They'd swept through the place, restoring our cherished privacy. On top of that, our Secret Service bodyguards had been relieved of duty.

I wondered if Mrs. Wentworth had been around when the surveillance team had let themselves in to clear the apartment. I had no doubt that if she had, she'd hit me up with hard questions about it soon.

Gav emerged from the bedroom around seven in the evening, looking adorably rumpled in his T-shirt and pajama pants, with half his hair sticking straight up. Scratching at the top of his head, he tried to flatten it down but that only made it worse.

"Good morning, sunshine," I said.

"Morning?" He gave a low chuckle and pointed to the balcony doors. "It's dark out."

I shrugged. "Close enough. You hungry? I'm making those grilled chicken breasts you like."

"Starved." For the second time, he pointed toward the balcony. "Do you need me to light the grill?"

"Already done. I heard your alarm go off a few minutes ago, so I knew you'd be up soon. Everything should be ready in less than twenty minutes."

He sat at the kitchen table, still trying to tame his hair with one hand, holding his cell phone with the other. "Wasn't my alarm," he said, holding the device aloft. "It was Joe."

"I thought he'd still be sleeping, too." I lowered the flame under one of my simmering saucepans. "You guys had a busy night."

"Yeah." Gav grimaced and looked away.

I lifted the pan of marinating chicken from the counter, intent on taking it out to the grill but something in his mood stopped me. "Are you ready to bring me up to date on everything you guys learned from our visitors last night?"

He sat back, plunked the phone on the table, and used a fingertip to spin it. "Yeah," he said again with just as little enthusiasm.

I put the chicken back down and sat across from him. "What's wrong? Did Yablonski change his mind about sharing information with me? Did he issue some sort of gag order?"

"Not at all. The big news you already know—we got Kern. That's better than we were hoping for."

"You thought he was still in Armustan."

"So much for recent intelligence reports." Gav grimaced. "We caught up with Kern about a half mile away from the winery. He was waiting in a cargo van that was meant to whisk the two of us away. In addition to apprehending Kern, you'll be happy to know that we got Cutthroat to identify two of the men as the ones who killed his friends. They were the same two responsible for Margaret's murder."

"They admitted it?"

"Initially, the captives refused to cooperate, but once we got the first one to break—he's the one who gave up Kern—the rest followed suit. And once they let loose, they let us have it, spewing platitudes and vitriol . . ." He leaned back and rubbed his temples. "Got ugly. Kern and his men are furious to have failed at their objective—killing you and securing Ansari's release—but they are arrogant and inordinately proud of what they have accomplished. Their sick satisfaction at the amount of damage done . . ." He shook his head. "Tough to listen to but we learned a lot."

"Wow," I said, at a loss for words.

He held up a finger. "We won this time. No question about it. Kern is going away for good, but that doesn't mean there isn't some eager Armustanian warmonger out there waiting to have a go at us next. In fact, I'd count on that."

"So we can't relax?"

"The United States government can't relax," he said. "As long as we have Farbod Ansari incarcerated, the Armustanians won't let up. But you, on the other hand . . ." There was a twinkle in his eyes I hadn't seen in a long time. "You've sailed through another life-threatening circumstance unharmed. Kern's failure is your ticket to freedom."

"And that's it?" I said. "There are no other avengers in that family—no cousins or other relatives ready to take up the cause?"

Gav shook his head, not even bothering to tamp down his smile. "We've done extensive homework on Kern's faction. Under the brother, they were a fractured group, but one feared by other factions. Kern offered his followers hope and, from our perspective, presented a real and credible threat. Armustan is not a forgiving culture. Now that Kern has been defeated, they'll find someone else to follow."

"And because it won't be one of Kern's relatives . . ."

"You are almost certainly safe."

I found myself grinning. "That's wonderful news. Absolutely the best."

He nodded.

"So, what's bothering you? Isn't all this finished?"

"Not for me. Not yet, at least. As you know, Joe took me off duty because my cover had been compromised—because Kern and his men knew who I was." He glanced up and waited for me to acknowledge that I remembered. I did. "Now that the Armustanian attack has been defeated, now that we have these men in custody, now that we've been presented a weeklong window of opportunity, he wants me back in."

"To find the next leader waiting in the wings?" I finished, seeing the big picture come into focus.

Gav gave a slow nod.

"We have a chance to make a difference right now. Until the other factions in Armustan learn of what went down here with Kern, we have the opportunity to get in there and influence changes. And until this window of safety closes, Joe wants me to lead the strategic sessions. I've been to Armustan enough to be considered the resident expert."

"He wants you to go there? Isn't there a risk that your cover was compromised beyond Kern's people?"

"I won't enter Armustan." Gav drew in a long breath. "You're right; it's too big of a risk. I will, however, be invaluable as a consultant. We have a number of safe houses in nearby countries. Allied countries."

"Which ally?"

"That hasn't been determined yet. Even if it were, I couldn't tell you. Joe believes that between the two of us and the team we've assembled, we should be able to mount and implement a mission before anyone takes another swing at us."

I blew out a breath. "When do you leave?"

He nodded. "Tonight."

Moments ago, my heart was light. Not anymore. Stiff and solid, it sat like an angry brick in my chest. And yet, I understood. "You want to do this, don't you?" I asked rhetorically. "You want to determine for yourself that we're safe from future attacks."

"I'm going there to ensure the safety of all the citizens of the United States," he said. "But yes. Even though there is no one in Armustan who would want to target you, I won't be able to relax until I can ascertain for myself that the threat against you has been eliminated completely."

He stared as though to press the weight of his words into me.

"We don't negotiate with terrorists. That's why there will never be room for discussion where Farbod Ansari's release is concerned. But right now, before news of Kern's failure makes it to his remaining followers, we have the rare opportunity to help influence who becomes that country's next leader. We have to take advantage of this window and put our people in motion before a more aggressive faction assumes control."

"I understand."

"I knew you would."

I stood up to get back to preparing dinner. "Let's at least get you fed before you take off."

When I picked up the pan of chicken and turned, I was surprised to see Gav blocking my way. "Ollie," he said with such gravity I felt my stomach drop. "You need to know that if we weren't successful this weekend—if we hadn't managed to capture Kern—you and I would have had a serious talk about our future."

"I know," I said. "Yablonski danced around that topic."

"He was concerned. He *is* concerned."

"I know he believed I didn't understand what he was hinting at," I said. "I understood perfectly, but I preferred not to hear." I met Gav's eyes with no apology, no regret. "I chose to ignore the warnings for as long as possible."

Gav smiled again. "That's what I told Joe."

"And this time it paid off, didn't it?"

"We were talking about your life, Ollie."

"Yours, too," I said.

"You know as well as I do that I was always a bonus. You were the target. They get you, they get me, too. If you're safe, out of the picture where no one can find you, then we both survive."

"But Yablonski meant he wanted us gone." I put the chicken pan back on the counter and laid both hands on Gav's arms. "I know he wasn't being heartless or cold. He cares about us. About you especially. I realize that. But I also know that he has a job to do and that my very existence made his job harder. I can't blame him for wanting us out of the picture."

"He never intended for us to be gone for good."

"But he did want us to disappear, didn't he? To leave D.C. and start anew across the country. Maybe even take on new identities. Was that it?"

Gav nodded.

"Like the Witness Protection Program?" I asked.

He nodded again. "It would have only been temporary. Until Kern was apprehended."

"And now he has been," I said. "Which means we don't have to worry about leaving our home, our families, our lives. So let's be grateful that this drama is at an end."

"I am grateful. For you."

I stared up at him. "I'm safe now, but until the entire Armustanian threat is eliminated, other Americans are at risk, aren't they?"

"We have a chance to make this right, Ollie."

"Then go," I said over a lump in my throat. "Go study, infiltrate, influence, whatever you need to do to keep our country safe."

CHAPTER 24

"BOY, IT'S GREAT TO BE BACK," I SAID TO BUCKY Sunday morning.

My assistant looked up from a cookbook he'd been reading. "You're here."

"I am."

"How did it go? Or can't you tell me?"

"Very well. So well that I'm free to tell you that the Armustanians are no longer a threat to me." I tucked my tote onto my shelf next to my purse and peeled off my coat. "That's not exactly right. The current regime is no longer a threat, and there's hope that this détente continues."

"Wow," he said, eyes wide. "Details?"

"Let's just say that we accomplished everything we set out to do. And as our reward? Gav has been spirited out of the country again."

"You're joking."

"If I were joking, would I be here right now?"

"Sorry to hear it. When do you expect him back?"

I gave an exaggerated shrug. "The wife is always the last to know."

Marshaling a chastising air, he pointed to the clock. "And I got in early today planning on a nice quiet, lazy day on my own."

I reached to pull out a smock and accidentally grabbed an apron. "You switched these," I said. Before he had a chance to answer, I kept talking. "Sorry to mess with your plans, but if you'd been paying attention, you'd remember I always hoped to be back today."

His cheerful expression faded. "That's right. You wanted to be back in time for Margaret's wake."

"I packed a change of clothes," I said, gesturing vaguely. "I plan to go right after work. Are you going?"

"I'll stop by this afternoon," he said. "That is, if you don't mind me taking off early. I'm taking Brandy dancing tonight."

"Dancing?" I asked. "You?"

He folded his arms. "What's wrong with that?"

Grateful for the upbeat turn our conversation had taken, I stepped back as though sizing him up. "Nothing at all. Hmm . . . What kind of dancing? John Travolta? Patrick Swayze? Michael Jackson?"

"More like Fred Astaire," he said. "We're taking ballroom dance lessons. It's my birthday gift to her this year."

"That's awesome," I said. "Whatever made you think of it?"

"I ran around like an idiot shopping in every store I could think of. All the while I knew she didn't want things. She never wants *things*." Shrugging, he held up both hands. "All she ever wants is for us to spend time together. And you know how tough that can be for those of us in service to the White House."

I thought about Gav, probably landed in the unnamed allied country by now. "I do."

"My gift to her was to choose an experience we could enjoy together. I thought she might want to go hiking or take up tennis." He gave a wry frown, but I could tell he was far less disappointed than he pretended to be. "She chose dancing."

"Good for you. Enjoy yourself."

"I plan on it." He clapped his hands together. "In the meantime, I want to show you what I got done yesterday."

Bucky took me on a tour of our newly organized kitchen, and—in between my appreciative comments—explained why he moved our mixing bowls here and measuring utensils there. Why the aprons were stacked to the left and the smocks to the right.

"Efficiency," he said for the fourth time. "I thought about how often we use these items and tried to come up with a better pattern for those of us working in the kitchen."

By this point, we'd opened all the cabinets, both above and below our work areas, giving me a panoramic view of the kitchen's contents. Bucky's hands flew about as he described all the changes and provided reasoning for his decisions. He spoke quickly as he bounced from one end of the kitchen to the other, gesticulating and babbling.

I stood as far back as I could, leaning against the far counter, taking it all in, saying nothing.

Eventually, when Bucky began repeating himself, I waved him down. "I got it."

"And?"

"I like it."

"Do you really?" he asked, "Or are you just saying that?"

"I wouldn't lie to you, Bucky, you know that. I like it a lot. I can see you've put a great deal of effort into this. What amazes me is how much you got accomplished in so short a period of time."

"It's amazing how quiet this place is when the entire First Family is out of town."

I chuckled at that. "They're coming back tonight."

"They are?" Bucky blinked as he took in the news. "I didn't think about that. Didn't put it together. I guess if the Armustanians are out of the picture, it's safe for them to return."

"That's about right. At least for now." Thinking about Josh's difficulties at school and his reluctance to share any of it with his parents, I added, "I hope things went well for them at Camp David."

"Why wouldn't they?" When I hedged, he glared. "What aren't you telling me?"

Peter Sargeant walked into the kitchen at that moment. "Whatever it is, Mr. Reed, is likely not your concern." To me, he said, "I've been quite pleased by the reports forwarded to me. While they are understandably short on detail, they are exceedingly clear on one point: You have had a very productive weekend."

"I have," I said.

"And you're aware that the First Family intends to return to the White House this afternoon?"

"I didn't realize they'd be back so early. I thought it would be later tonight. But that's fine."

Bucky touched my arm. "If you need me to stay . . ."

"No, I'll be fine here alone," I said. "Go ahead and leave when you need to. Celebrate Brandy's birthday. Enjoy yourself."

Sargeant rolled his lips but said nothing. Before he could inject his opinion as to whether or not Bucky ought to leave me alone in the kitchen, I turned to him. "Is there something I can do for you, Peter?"

"Two things." He sniffed. "First of all, the president and

his family will be making a special stop to visit with Margaret's family before they return to the residence."

"That's very nice of them."

"They believe it's the least they can do to show support. The Secret Service has arranged for the president to have a private conversation with Margaret's family before visitation officially begins. He recognizes that wherever he goes the press follows, and he wants to afford the family as much privacy as possible. So we're keeping everything low-key."

"A sound plan," I said. "What's the second thing?"

Sargeant's mouth twisted downward. "I was coming to that, thank you. In addition to informing you about the First Family's imminent return to the residence, I wanted to let you know that the Secret Service has given us the go-ahead to resume interviewing chefs."

"Good." Bucky had his arms crossed. "The sooner we fill Cyan's job, the better."

Sargeant wrinkled his nose then sniffed again. "I believe we would be better served to cease referring to it as 'Cyan's job' and to begin calling the position by its proper title. We are seeking a *chef de partie*, are we not?"

"Technically, yes. However, I would hope that the person who joins our kitchen is not prone to standing on ceremony." I didn't add: *Like you.*

"Perhaps, going forward, you should consider taking a page from Neville Walker's playbook," he said.

"I don't understand."

On his best days, Sargeant's smiles came off as condescending. Today was clearly not a good day. "Agent Walker is in the process of restoring the PPD to its full glory. He has taken what had become a broken, dilapidated version of what is arguably the most important arm of the Secret

Service and made it new again. How did he do that? By
instituting order. By bringing in professionals who understand the chain of command and who don't confuse cowork-
ers with friends."

"Peter—"

He *tut-tutted* me silent. "I know you prefer to maintain
a casual atmosphere in your kitchen because you believe it
promotes a sense of camaraderie. I would suggest that you,
as executive chef, consider adopting a new order. What better timing to institute structure than right before you bring
on new personnel?"

I opened my mouth, but closed it again before I said something I might regret later. In the short while Sargeant had been
talking, I realized what was really at stake: He had let his
guard down—albeit slightly—with Margaret, and he was paying for that now. Her death had hurt him and he didn't know
how to cope. So he retreated to what he knew best: imposing
rules and structure. It helped him feel safe.

Sargeant continued to pontificate, advising us on the best
practices we ought to consider establishing in our kitchen.
I contemplated ways to cut him off but found I couldn't bring
myself to do it.

"It seems to me that your staff should never address you
as 'Ollie,'" he was saying. "When the new person starts, I
believe you should insist that he or she address you as 'Chef
Paras' at all times." He pointed over his shoulder to indicate
Bucky. "And Mr. Reed, as your sous chef, should be addressed
with similar respect."

In a close-quarters kitchen like this one where success
depended on our being able to call upon one another at a
moment's notice, having multiple individuals referred to as
"Chef" would get confusing fast.

I knew, Bucky knew, and I suspected even Sargeant knew

that I would continue to run my kitchen the way I saw fit. This was not the time or the place, however, to drive that point home.

Doing my best to ignore Bucky's exaggerated eye rolls, I said, "I'll take it under advisement."

"See that you do."

Behind him, Bucky sucked in his lips and glared. Over the years I'd learned how to manage Sargeant—or, at least, how to manage my reactions to him. Bucky still had a way to go.

"Anything else?" I asked.

"Not at the moment," he said. "Once the Secret Service and I come up with a new list of viable candidates, I will contact you about scheduling interviews."

"Let's hope we find a good fit," I said. "Someone who can both respect authority *and* enjoy the camaraderie."

Sargeant pursed his lips.

"Hey, I know the perfect candidate," Bucky said before Sargeant could come back with a retort. "This person has successfully worked with us in the past, understands the requirements of the job, and possesses solid skills and abundance of energy. To top it off, this person would have no trouble being cleared by the Secret Service." His mischievous grin grew. "And you know how it can be difficult to win over the First Lady."

I nodded.

"This candidate would be a shoo-in. Guaranteed."

"I'd like to meet this impressive chef." Sargeant folded his arms. "Where, pray tell, is this individual currently employed?"

"He's not." Bucky's pink cheeks and bright eyes were nothing compared to the giggle he tried to tamp down. "Employed at the moment, that is."

With a sense of what was coming, I covered my mouth with one hand, struggling to contain my own mirth. "Bucky . . ." My voice was a warning.

Sargeant flipped glances between the two of us. "What is so funny?"

Bucky's joke wasn't really funny at all, but the pressures from the past week had bubbled up, making silliness irresistible.

"Who is it?" Sargeant demanded. "Enough with the games. Who is this ideal candidate you have in mind?"

"Can't you guess?" Bucky asked, trying his best to sober up. Failing. I swore he would burst if he wasn't allowed to laugh out loud. Time to get our chief usher out of here.

"Peter, it's fine." I took him by the arm with one hand on his shoulder and led him out of the kitchen. "We're just enjoying a bit of that familiarity you warned us against. Forget it."

"You want me to forget this perfect candidate?" Indignantly, he turned to look over his shoulder. I twisted to see Bucky bent in half, holding his stomach. Sargeant raised his voice to be heard. "Why on earth won't you tell me who it is?"

Bucky turned his back to us, waving us away.

Five steps outside the kitchen Sargeant stopped walking. "The familiarity I warned you against?" he asked, pointing back the way we'd come. "*This* is what you want for your kitchen?"

I bit my lower lip trying not to laugh. "It really isn't all that funny. Bucky just took a goofy idea and ran with it." I'd been certain Sargeant knew what Bucky had been hinting at, but facing the man's dour expression now, I couldn't be sure.

He blinked several times, giving me that alert-squirrel look he was so partial to. "Mr. Reed suggested someone who has worked in the kitchen, yes? Someone you *know* the First Lady will love? A person with energy, vitality, and one who would be instantly cleared by the Secret Service?"

"Yes . . ."

"Ms. Paras, really." He shook his head, said *"Tsk, tsk,"*

a couple of times, then walked past me to the elevator. He pushed the button, then turned to face me. "You might want to inform your sous chef that the White House has no intention of disregarding child labor laws. If Mr. Reed wants us to hire the president's son, he'll have to wait until the lad is a few years older."

I laughed out loud.

Sargeant whispered, "Does he honestly believe I'm that dense?"

"No, of course not," I said, laughing.

He arched a brow.

"Okay, maybe a teensy bit." I held up my thumb and forefinger in emphasis.

"People underestimate me at their peril." The elevator dinged its arrival. Sargeant boarded, leaned out, and placed his finger in front of his lips. "But let's keep that our secret, shall we?"

CHAPTER 25

AS EXECUTIVE CHEF, I WAS RESPONSIBLE FOR every one of the First Family's meals whenever they were in residence. Generally, I sent two weeks' worth of menus to the First Lady every Monday morning, seeking her input. The first week's menu served as a reminder of what she'd approved and it gave her the opportunity to make last-minute changes. The second week's menu—presented as a work in progress—often included new recipes I thought the family might enjoy, special requests, and reliable favorites. Mrs. Hyden might scribble a helpful note now and then, but rarely made substantive changes to the plan.

Thus, though I knew the family wouldn't complain if I served them exactly what had originally been scheduled for today, I thought their return to the White House called for a bit more celebration than their typical Sunday night soup and salad. I sent a note up to Mrs. Hyden's assistant outlining my plans for a more substantive meal and asking her to let me know how to proceed.

"You have that rib roast-with-all-the-trimmings gleam in your eye," Bucky said when I told him what I'd done. "But you'll be here by yourself. Are you sure you want to open that door?"

"Too late. Already sent," I said. "Plus, I'm feeding only four people. Even if I had a five-course dinner planned, I should be able to handle that on my own."

He gave me a cranky look. "Thanks for that vote of confidence, boss. Don't need me at all, do you? Yeah, I'm feelin' the love."

I picked up a dish towel sitting on the counter next to me and threw it at him. "Don't joke about that. I don't know what I'd do if I lost you. But one day, one meal? I can handle it."

He folded the towel and then tossed it into the nearby laundry bin. "I know, and I'm glad, really. It'll be nice to enjoy a night out with Brandy for a change. If you don't mind me asking, what exactly do you envision as your entrée for this evening? I wasn't kidding when I said you looked like you were planning something big."

"Comfort food, for sure," I said from my seat at the computer. "This sudden trip to Camp David had to put an enormous kink in their plans." I thought about Josh being pulled from school—and his bullies—for that amount of time and tried to decide whether his absence would make it easier or harder to return to class tomorrow. "I want to do everything in my power to make them feel good."

"I have no doubt they'll take you up on it."

"I'll let Dennis know that we may be relying on his expertise tonight." As I turned to compose a fresh e-mail to our sommelier, a new message pinged in. "Wow, that was quick."

"What was?" Bucky asked, coming to look over my shoulder.

"Mrs. Hyden's assistant replied." I opened the message and paraphrased as I read. "She says that she'd been about to e-mail me on the same topic when mine arrived."

"Great minds thinking alike?"

I half-laughed. "Yes and no." Tapping the screen, I said, "According to this, Mrs. Hyden is requesting a special dinner tonight. I was right about one thing. They do want comfort food."

Bucky leaned forward, squinting at the screen. "Ha," he said. "Who'd'a thunk?"

"Breakfast for dinner," I said, reading aloud.

He smirked. "The wine may be overkill."

"You think?" I kept reading. "Dinner at five; we can do that. And apparently Josh wants to come down to help prepare it." I turned to my assistant. "How perfect is that?"

"I'm telling you . . ."—he pointed to the ceiling— "Sargeant needs to look into hiring that kid."

JOSH ARRIVED IN THE KITCHEN ABOUT FIFTEEN minutes after Bucky left for the day.

"It's good to have you back," I said when his Secret Service escort departed. "How was Camp David?"

Before I'd gotten to know Josh, I would have scoffed at the notion of an eleven-year-old being stressed. Especially one who lived a comfortable life with parents who loved and supported him. But kids, it turned out, were more complex beings than I'd ever imagined. He'd been wound terribly tight before they'd left, and I was delighted to see the president's son back to his more-relaxed self.

"The big shots who came to talk to Dad thought they were

being so clever. They kept telling us how this was just an unscheduled vacation, just a change in plans." He rolled his eyes good-naturedly. "Do they really think we're that stupid? I mean seriously. A bunch of bad stuff happens to people who work in the White House and then the president of the United States and his family gets sent away for a vacation?" He laughed.

I pulled out a large bowl of fingerling potatoes, three zucchini, and a yellow squash and placed them on the center countertop. "That obvious?"

"Even if Abby and I didn't know everything that had happened, you know, like, to Margaret and to you, it was still crazy down there. Dad had meetings with advisors and military people every few hours."

"Sounds stressful," I said as I started peeling the potatoes.

He gave a can-you-believe-it shrug. "Actually, we wound up having a lot of family time in between the meetings. More than we usually do." He picked up the vegetables and took them over to the sink to wash. Talking over his shoulder, he continued, "We played board games and hung out together. It was, you know, cool."

"Glad to hear it." I retrieved onions and portabella mushrooms from a nearby container. "Were you . . ." I hesitated.

He brought the wet vegetables to the counter and laid them down. His brows arched as he waited for me to finish my question.

"Were you able to talk with your folks about what's going on at school?"

"I knew that's what you were going to ask." His shoulders shifted. Kind of a shrug, kind of a shiver. But as he grabbed a few potatoes to help me peel, he met my eyes. I took that as a good sign. "Yeah. We talked about that, actually a lot. Mom was all ready to call up Seth's parents and ream them out, but

Dad talked her out of it. By the time we got the okay to come back, she'd calmed down. A lot."

"I'm glad to hear it."

"I told them what you said about my dad being a good man and a strong leader and that no matter how much he accomplishes, people will disagree with him and how you said that's okay because it's how the system works."

Yikes. Though I didn't regret a word of what I'd said to Josh, I hadn't expected him to share it with the president and First Lady, either. "I hope they didn't mind me poking my nose in on that."

He shook his head. "They both said it was the best way to look at things and that you are a really good role model."

His words warmed me. "Thank you," I said. "That's one of the nicest things I've ever heard."

He looked up from what he was doing. "I told them what else you said."

"What's that?"

"That Seth is a jerk."

A laugh leaped out of me. I covered my mouth with the back of my hand. "You told them I said that?"

He gave me one of those "You've got to be kidding me" stares teens and preteens are supremely capable of pulling off. "People are always acting so polite around my parents. I mean, I get that, but what's wrong with saying what you really think?" He went back to his potatoes, but glanced up briefly. "They agreed with you, by the way."

We worked quietly until all the potatoes were peeled and properly sliced. I used my knife to point at the onion and mushrooms waiting to meet their fate. "Breakfast for dinner tonight. You think the veggie egg scramble with a side of home fries will do?"

"Sounds great." He crossed to a cabinet, opened its door,

and looked over to me, puzzled. "What happened to the ingredient bowls?"

"Forgot to tell you, Bucky rearranged the kitchen while we were gone."

"You were gone, too?"

Clearly, Josh hadn't been told of the part I played in eliminating the Armustanian threat. "Just for a day," I said. "Bucky did a complete reorganization."

"Wow," he said as he did a brief survey of the room. "This could get confusing."

"I'm sure it will, for a while. But like with anything, the more you work with it the easier it gets."

"That's kind of what Dad said, too."

I perked up. "You mean about Seth?"

He found the bowls he was looking for and brought two back to the counter, where we began chopping our vegetables. "Dad said that it's extra tough for me right now because I'm the newest kid and before I could find my bearings, Seth started attacking. He said that it'll get better, as long as I remember that Seth is the one with the problem, not me."

"That's good advice."

"Doesn't make it easier to deal with right now, though," Josh said with an emphatic frown. "I mean, I'm not looking forward to going back tomorrow. I know they're all going to say that my dad shouldn't be taking vacation."

"They don't realize that it isn't a vacation," I said.

He gave a resigned nod. "And I can't tell them why they're wrong."

Once our ingredients were ready, I settled a large skillet on one of the cooktop burners and gestured with my eyes. "You see that grapeseed oil? Let's have a little here."

Josh complied. "How much?"

"Look at the potatoes and decide how much you think they

need," I said. Before he could ask, I answered, "Eyeball it. You've gotten good at that. Trust yourself."

He dribbled the oil into the pan, and I set the heat to medium-high.

"That's another thing both Mom and Dad said this weekend."

"What?"

"To trust myself. They say I have good instincts."

"You do."

His bright-eyed reaction told me that he'd been hoping I'd concur. "I only wish I knew the best way to come back at Seth when he criticizes Dad."

"That's a tough one." When the oil grew shimmery, I had Josh add the potatoes, season them, then toss to coat evenly. We'd have time to work on the eggs while they cooked. I pulled up another skillet and had Josh set us up with oil again.

"It seems to me that people are far more likely to criticize when they don't have all the facts," I said.

He gave me a skeptical look.

"Listen," I began. "Your dad has a lot going on all the time. Running the country is no small feat. And because of security concerns or other confidential situations, the public can't know every detail behind every decision. Because if the public knows, then our enemies know. You and I both see what goes on behind the scenes because we're part of it, but even we can't know the whole story. Your dad could make the best decision possible every single time and things could still go wrong."

Josh nodded. "Nobody's perfect."

"Exactly. And it seems to me—from watching the goings-on around here, and even in everyday life—that the more people truly understand situations and the more they remain open to one another's viewpoint, the closer they come to agreement on how to handle things."

"You're not just talking about Seth, are you?"

I shook my head. "Your dad faces harsh criticism from his political foes every single day. He knows that if he fails, they'll descend on him like vultures ready to rip him to shreds. It isn't constructive criticism they're offering. They seek to destroy because they mistakenly believe that that's the only way to build themselves up." Pointing to the second skillet, I said, "Let's add the onions and mushrooms."

Josh did, then stirred them around with a wooden spoon.

"The thing is," I said, "trying and failing is part of life. And failing, for all the bad rap it gets, is a good thing. It's where we do our best learning."

"You really believe that? About failing being good, I mean?"

"Absolutely," I said, turning the heat down a little bit. "Those who aren't afraid to fail are the ones who change the world because they're the ones who create. They dream. They grow. Those who are content to criticize from the sidelines bring nothing to the table. You won't see their names in history books or on marquees. They're *afraid* to create, and so they criticize those who do."

When the onions and mushrooms began to brown, I had Josh add the zucchini and squash. "I'll bet you're wondering what all this has to do with your situation with Seth," I said with a self-effacing chuckle. "I really went off on a rant, didn't I?"

"I kind of get it," he said. "You're trying to tell me that I'm a creator and Seth's a destroyer and that in the long run, I'm going to win."

Simply put, but accurate. "That about sums it up," I said.

"That's pretty close to what my parents tried to tell me, too," he said. "I know they're right, and you're right." He wrinkled his nose. "It's just tough waiting for the day when everybody else knows it, too."

CHAPTER 26

I SENT DINNER—AND JOSH—UP TO THE RESI-
dence shortly before five o'clock and turned my efforts toward
restoring order in the kitchen. Josh had offered to stay back
and help clean, but I'd shooed him upstairs so he could enjoy
dinner—such that it was—with his family. I was very glad
to have been able to connect with him and find out that he'd
talked about Seth with his parents. The advice I'd given him
about how to deal with the bully had been the same tactics
I'd employed when I'd had difficulties with Margaret.

I glanced up at the clock and wrinkled my nose, redoubling
my efforts to get the place spruced up so that I could leave in
enough time to make an appearance at her wake. While she
was alive, I'd been holding out, trying my best to take the
high road, convinced that the "long run win" I'd talked about
with Josh would eventually come to pass and that Margaret
and I—though we might never have been friends—would at

least come to an understanding and achieve a level of mutual respect. That was the "win" I'd been hoping for.

But now there would never be a win. For either of us. Kern's men had stolen that from us and had stolen far more than that from her.

I had to stop myself from recleaning and double-checking every single spot in the kitchen. It was time to retrieve my tote so that I could change clothes. I knew that my subconscious was slowing me down.

I didn't want to go to Margaret's wake tonight—not from any sort of selfishness, but because I didn't want it to be true. There was no disputing facts, however, so I lugged the bag to the ladies' washroom and made the quick change from comfortable work clothes to dressier slacks, jacket, and top.

From talking with other staff members, I knew that few others planned to attend the wake. Peter Sargeant and Neville Walker would make an effort to stop by, but Margaret hadn't developed any close friendships at the White House. Or, perhaps more accurately, Margaret had kept everyone at arm's length.

When I stepped outside the White House gates a little while later, sunset was still an hour off. The late-day sunshine warmed me more than I would have expected as I made my way to the Metro Center station. I needed to board a red line train to Glenmont, switch to a bus, and then walk less than a half mile to the Altergott Funeral Home that boasted on its website to have been in business for more than thirty years.

From the photos on the site, the stately establishment gave off a warm and welcoming air, but I suppose that would be a minimum requirement in that line of business.

Dusk began to settle as I walked the final few blocks to Altergott's funeral home. I felt myself dragging, reluctant to face Margaret's family and fearful that I might break down. I wasn't a woman who cried very often, but once the tears started I found myself unable to rein them in. I hoped I'd be able to keep my composure.

As I rounded the final turn, I caught sight of the funeral home ahead of me. It looked exactly like its photograph. Two-story redbrick, it was an imposing structure, with white pillars running its length and a solemn brick sign out front with ALTERGOTT in tasteful illumination.

I approached from the east, crossing in front of the property's expansive parking lot and its adjacent covered drive. No doubt that was where the hearse would pull up in the morning, allowing the funeral cortege to assemble in line behind it. Right now, the wide driveway was quiet, the glass doors beyond it dark.

Maintaining a brisk pace on my way to the building's front doors, I thought about my cell phone. I'd be morose if I missed a call from Gav, but having it ring while attending a wake would be a mortifying breach of etiquette.

I started to reach for my back pocket, belatedly remembering that when I changed clothes I'd stuffed the device into my purse so I wouldn't accidentally leave it behind. I finger-walked through the contents of my cross-body bag before encountering the cell's smooth case. Pulling it up, I switched it to silent and returned it to my purse.

There weren't many cars in the lot, but maybe I shouldn't have been surprised. Sargeant had explained that Margaret came from a relatively small family and that she didn't belong to any community or social groups that he knew of. Even so, I would have anticipated more than the half-dozen vehicles that sat there.

The building itself was beautifully landscaped. Set back from the street, its evergreens and trees softened the brick façade. The long row of waist-high hedges to my right blocked the street view of the wide asphalt parking lot.

A dark-haired man wearing a gray pea coat stood about ten feet outside the building's verandah smoking a cigarette. He leaned against one of two facing stone benches. If he noticed my approach, he made no show of it.

I turned at the sound of a car door slam, hoping to see either Sargeant or Neville, but was disappointed when the newcomer turned out to be a stranger. Even though we were in the middle of an upscale residential neighborhood and another human— taking a smoke break—hovered nearby, I felt my pulse quicken. There was no doubt the man was simply another mourner coming to pay his respects, but events of late made me hyperaware of my surroundings.

The man who emerged from the car had wavy white hair that came to the nape of his neck. He carried a messenger bag and although he walked hunched over the way aged people sometimes do, he moved quickly along the far side of the hedge. It was clear he and I were headed in the same direction.

I slowed my pace to allow him to keep a few feet in front of me, but he seemed not to pay me any attention. In fact, when he was forced to survey the area to find the path through the bushes to the sidewalk, he straightened as though surprised to see anyone else around.

"Hello," he said, regaining his composure. "Are you here for Margaret?"

"I am," I said a second too slowly. The forthright question hadn't startled me; his clerical collar had. Likewise, the priest's white hair had thrown me off; I realized he was younger than I'd first assumed. Close to my age. "I take it you are, too?"

His pale hair and ashen complexion gave him a sickly appearance. Lines around his eyes could have come from sun damage or pain.

"May I walk with you?" he asked.

With no polite way to decline, I nodded. He fell into step next to me as we made our way the final fifty or so yards to the front door.

"Margaret was one of my parishioners," he said. He had an odd accent. I'd describe it as a cross between South African and Italian. "Even after she moved away, we remained friends. The world has lost a good woman."

I didn't know what to say to that, so I asked, "Will you be saying mass for her tomorrow?"

The priest shook his head. "No, unfortunately. The family called in someone else. An uncle or cousin, I am told. I am simply here to pay my respects."

We turned right onto the walkway that led to the funeral home's front doors. Ahead of us, the building glowed in the rapidly descending dusk. Low evergreens lined the wide walkway.

The man in gray by the bench shook out a fresh cigarette and lighted it. As we approached, I got a better look at him. Mid-thirties, he had a jerky, unsettled air. He held his cigarette with the tips of his fingers and drew deeply with each drag. As we approached, he huffed loudly then strode off down the walkway.

The priest nodded at the man's departing figure and whispered. "Somebody is having a bad day."

The man made a right at the sidewalk and disappeared behind the trees.

"Margaret's death may be hitting him especially hard," I said, "and we interrupted his time alone."

"That's a very compassionate way to look at it. I am Father Waters, by the way," the priest said. "But you can call me Greg."

"I'm . . . Olivia," I said.

He stopped walking. Faced me. "Olivia Paras? The chef of the White House?"

After the week I'd had, the question sent alarm bells clanging in my heart and sounding in my ears. I took a step back. But Father Waters made no aggressive moves. He didn't suddenly adopt a threatening air. No, he simply stood patiently and waited for my answer.

I gauged the distance to the funeral home's front doors. Less than fifteen yards. I inched farther away from him. "How would you know that?"

He gave a sad smile. "Margaret talked about you."

"She did? I'm surprised." I started for the door.

Father Waters didn't move. "Margaret said you were compassionate."

I stopped in my tracks, weighing my words before responding. "Margaret wouldn't have said that about me."

The priest smiled gently, arms folded across his chest. "But she did."

"You don't understand. She didn't like me very much."

"You would be surprised by how often your name came up in our conversations."

Torn between wanting to get into the building to pay my respects and go home, and knowing more of Margaret's thoughts on our relationship, I hesitated. Could this Father Waters help provide the closure I'd been seeking?

As though answering my unasked question, he said, "She felt very guilty."

"About what?"

We were facing each other between the stone benches. My view was east over the parking lot, his was west, toward the neighborhood. He seemed to be weighing his words as he stared off into the distance. "There are some details I'm not comfortable divulging," he said.

"Because she shared her thoughts during confession?"

The question seemed to take him aback. Instead of answering, he said, "She wronged you. I know that if she were here, she'd ask forgiveness."

"Margaret?" I nearly choked her name out. "Not to speak ill of the dead, but that doesn't fit her personality in the least."

One of the home's double doors opened and a large man stepped outside. Six feet tall and at least three hundred pounds, he wore a perfectly tailored black suit, navy tie, and a look of impatience. I recognized him from the website as Mr. Altergott, the funeral director.

Spotting us on the walkway, he lumbered down the two steps to the walkway. "Father, I'm so glad you're here. We're waiting inside for you to lead prayers."

Father Waters blinked, looking puzzled. "I believe you have me confused with the family priest," he said.

"You're not Father O'Neill?"

Waters shook his head. He tapped his messenger bag. "I'm here to deliver some mementos."

Altergott rubbed his receding hairline. "The deceased's grandmother needs to be taken back to her nursing home, but she's insisting on staying until she talks to a priest."

Waters glanced back toward the parking lot. "I wouldn't want to overstep."

The funeral director grimaced. "The grandmother is really old and there are some medications she needs back in her room. If you could spare a little bit of time?"

Waters scratched his head, but then gave a crisp nod. "Of course. I'll be in momentarily."

Altergott beamed. "Thank you. I'll let the family know."

As soon as the door closed behind him, Waters turned to me again. This time he was smiling broadly. "What I wanted you to know about Margaret was that she told us everything . . .”

In the heartbeat it took me to process the incongruous use of the word *us* and Water's strangely inappropriate expression, I became aware of movement behind me.

I didn't waste time turning to see who was there. Instinct thrust me into motion. I heeded the imperative bellowing from my gut and bolted for the door.

An arm sliced forward, clotheslining me at the throat before I could take a single step. Coughing, I fell to the ground, my hands groping at my neck, pulling at my collar as though doing so might reopen my airway. I couldn't scream. My breath was gone.

Five seconds, I thought. Five seconds earlier I could have walked in with the funeral director. Why hadn't I?

CHAPTER 27

SPARKLES DANCED BEFORE MY EYES. I STRUG-
gled to regain control of my breathing as the smoking man—
the man in the gray pea coat—stepped into my view. He'd
been the one to incapacitate me, and now he and the priest
yanked me to my feet as they jabbered in a foreign language.

Wheezing, I strained for breath even as I fought to break
free from their hold. But, like that day in the park a week
ago—had it been only a week?—there were two of them
and both were bigger and stronger than the one of me.

I gurgled incoherently. Pain seared my throat—the
sharpest I'd ever felt. Or so I thought until Gray Pea Coat
jammed a needle into the soft flesh just above my collarbone.
I felt myself try to scream, but all I could do was bleat.

My strangled moans intensified, my brain raced, but I
couldn't figure a way out. Not this time. As the smoker guy
injected a substance into my neck—a drug I knew would kill
me—I thought of Gav.

My husband would blame himself for not being here.

At that moment, the front door of the building opened again and Altergott came back out. "How much longer will you be?" he asked. Then, one second later, "Hey, what's going on here?"

Waters—or whatever his real name was—shouted to the other guy. I'd begun to lose control of my legs and felt myself slump toward the ground.

The funeral director clumped down the two steps. "Is she all right?"

My attacker wrenched the needle from my neck and launched himself at Altergott, jamming the same needle into the large man's neck. Stunned and surprised, the funeral director was slow to react. When he did, he backed up fast, losing his footing. His eyes went wide and his thick arms pinwheeled. His slack lips moved, but no more than a whimper came out.

Through it all, the smoker guy never lost control of the needle, and I watched as he wedged himself up against Altergott's back to keep the man upright while plunging the remaining liquid into his body. Why wasn't he fighting? Why wasn't he calling for help?

My breathing had begun to even out. Why wasn't *I* fighting? Why wasn't *I* calling for help?

It took a long three seconds for me to realize I couldn't move. Whatever they'd injected me with had completely immobilized my limbs. A quick glance at the funeral director confirmed he was paralyzed as well.

The fake priest held me with both hands, bracing me from behind. I had no feeling, no sense of my own body. I could see, I could hear, but I couldn't move any of my extremities. And I couldn't conjure a sound.

The only control I retained was my eyes. I stared across

the six feet separating me from the slack-jawed funeral director. His head had lolled to one side, but his eyes met mine, conveying the same fear and helplessness that twisted my gut.

The two Armustanians—I had no doubt at this point—never stopped moving. From the moment they'd sent me sprawling, it was clear they had a plan and intended to see it through.

The fake priest deftly twisted me around, bent at the knees, and hoisted me into his arms, my feet dangling at his left side, my head drooping backward like a rag doll's on his right. He took off at a brisk pace the opposite way I'd come.

I couldn't see anything but the dark sky above, but I could hear Gray Pea Coat grunting and muttering and could imagine he was doing his best to get the funeral director's body out of sight.

The fake priest turned right; above me, the stars spun. He whisper-shouted to his partner and twisted back, resettling me in his grip like one would a sack of mulch. As we rounded the building—or so I deduced from my view of its top corner, I caught sight of the pointy evergreen tree tops lining the property.

I'd admired them earlier. Now I wished I'd never seen them, that I'd never come here tonight. There were no floodlights in this area of the property and the tall trees provided my captor ample cover. I stared up at the sky and tried to focus on a star. One star. The first star of the night.

Like I had when I was little, I wished with all my might.

As my captor quickened his pace, my body bounced and my head jerked side to side. I lost sight of my wishing star before I could complete the poem in my head. I wondered if the drug they'd administered was affecting my mind. I knew I should be coming up with a plan or figuring out how to escape, but I didn't know where to begin.

Whatever had stilled my limbs had probably slowed my brain. Either that or the shock and loss of hope had strangled my will.

The priest dropped me to the ground. My back hit a wall that made a hollow sound when I was slammed into it, and his messenger bag whacked me in the face. As soon as I'd been unceremoniously dumped, he took off again.

I rolled my eyes around looking right, left, up, down. Below me, asphalt. Behind me? No idea. I seemed to be at an annex of sorts because the funeral home's main structure sat to my left. A driveway and more tall trees were to my right.

The priest had been gone for no more than ten seconds when gravity flexed its muscle. My torso shifted and I began to slide sideways along the wall to my left. With no power to control anything but my eyes, I could do nothing to halt my movement or brace myself for impact.

Friction between my jacket and the wall behind me slowed the process some but I continued to slide sideways. On my way down, my torso swiveled enough to lose its connection with the wall, and I slammed to the ground, taking the brunt of the hit with my face and left shoulder. I imagined it was a solid collision, but I couldn't feel a thing.

Panic skewered my insides, drilling curlicues of fear up from my stomach into my heart. Now *that* I felt. Or at least imagined I did. For as many close calls as I'd endured these past few years, I'd never been faced with a predicament like this where I was unable to lift a finger—literally—to help myself.

Sluggish or not, I forced myself to engage the logical part of my brain. I couldn't just lie here and do nothing. Though my fear didn't abate, I couldn't let it consume me. I had to dig deep to find that spark of ingenuity that might keep me alive.

I strove to take in as much as I could. *You never know*, a

familiar corner of my brain reminded me. *Think, plan, hope. Don't give up.*

Swinging my gaze upward to my right, I realized that the wall I'd been propped against was actually a vinyl overhead door. It was one of two sitting side by side, creating between them a giant four-car garage. Something like that would provide a nice, echoey hollow noise if I banged on it hard enough. I desperately wanted to kick at it to attract attention.

It was too dim to make out more than a tiny fraction of the door's embossed rectangles. Why was it so dark here? As I allowed my gaze to wander up and around the structure, I noticed floodlights. They'd either never been turned on or someone had taken the time to disable them.

Scraping noises, coupled with the sound of human exertion, came from beyond the top of my head. My brain sent signals to turn and stretch to see what was happening, but they went unheeded as my body remained paralyzed.

Moments later, the priest and the other guy dragged the funeral director's limp body into view. They dropped him onto his back in a position that didn't allow for eye contact between us, but I could tell that his eyes were open. I hoped that meant he was still alive.

Through it all, the two Armustanians argued. Or, more accurately, the priest barked hushed orders and the other guy answered and complied. Though I couldn't understand any words beyond *Kern*, the two gesticulated with such fervor that the essence of their conversation wasn't difficult to deduce.

Clearly, the funeral home director's unexpected involvement had thrown off their plan. What subsequently became apparent was that they'd intended to drive away with me as soon as I was immobile, but Gray Pea Coat had lost the keys in the grass while dragging the funeral director across the home's front lawn.

The fake priest grabbed the other guy by the collar of his pea coat, baring his teeth and whisper-shouting into his face.

Slowly I began to notice that only one of the two men used the word *Kern*, and every time he uttered it, he did so in obedient response to the fake priest's commands.

Could this man with the white hair and clean-shaven face *be* Kern? Why wasn't he in custody? Had he managed to escape? Unlikely. If he had, Gav and Yablonski would have been instantly at my side.

I studied him as the other guy dug through his pockets for the third time in thirty seconds. The only photo I'd seen of the Armustanian leader had been out of focus and not face-on. Gav had said they thought he was thirty-two. Yes, that was about right.

He used the word *Slager* repeatedly as he chastised his accomplice. I gathered that was Gray Pea Coat's name.

The futility of their predicament gave me hope until Kern came up with the idea of digging through Altergott's pockets. The two of them rocked the large man's body as they pulled open his suit coat, searching it thoroughly, then started in on the pants.

With a quiet exclamation of triumph, Slager hoisted a set of keys into the night air. Sorting through them, he raced around the building and out of sight. I heard the muffled sounds of metal against metal and then a soft slam. A moment later, the large overhead door behind me whirred open, revealing two vehicles, both shiny black hearses.

Kern scooped his arms under the funeral director and dragged the dead weight backward into the cavernous garage. When they passed me, I detected awareness in Altergott's eyes. He stared as though pleading for help, asking me what was going on. I hoped my silent commiseration helped him, but I doubted anything would.

With effort, Kern dragged the man between the two sleek vehicles and out of sight.

From my vantage point on the ground, I watched Slager make a quick circuit of the garage. I assumed he was searching for car keys. Every second the two Armustanians delayed was another moment in my favor, offering the slim chance that we'd be noticed. But before I could count to twenty, I heard his muffled shout and the subsequent jingling of keys. He hurried toward the nearest hearse.

Don't start. Don't start.

Slager turned the key. The engine purred to life.

From the ground, I watched the car's tires roll forward until the vehicle was roughly parallel with my position. Leaving it to idle, Slager jumped out of the car and hurried around to open the back hatch.

Kern stepped over my bent form. I wanted to kick and trip him; I wanted to scream and alert the quiet neighborhood to the terror that was happening in the shadows of this funeral home. But I could do nothing as Kern took my arms and Slager came around to grab my feet. I remained limp and lifeless as they lifted me like a human hammock and shuffled around the car.

With my head hanging forward this time, I had a partial view of Slager as he walked backward. I couldn't see the funeral director, but I could hear his labored breathing as the two Armustanians transported me to the rear of the hearse. With a grunt of effort, they tossed my broken body into the long, lonely compartment of death.

I landed mostly on my left side with my arm pinned beneath me. My body lay on an angle with my face low and my backside high. I imagined my fat purse was wedged underneath my hip. Half my face smashed into one of the metal rollers built into the floor I assumed was to facilitate the transport of heavy caskets. I couldn't see out the windows, but if this hearse was like most I'd encountered in my life, it had been fitted with curtains, meaning no one could see in, either.

My right arm had landed atop my hip and my hand bounced as Slager peeled out of the funeral home parking lot and away. I had no idea what position my legs were in. I couldn't feel them, couldn't see them.

The drug they'd administered hadn't killed me. Not yet, at least. They were keeping me alive. I wondered why.

The two men talked quietly in their native language, and I got the impression that now that they'd gotten what they wanted—me—they were more relaxed. That scared me most of all. While they'd been scrambling at the funeral home because of the unexpected complication of Altergott's presence, there had been hope. With every lighthearted lilt in their cheerful banter, my outlook dimmed.

Gav was out of town with Yablonski, and no one would miss me until tomorrow morning. Bucky and Sargeant knew that I'd planned to attend Margaret's wake. But they wouldn't have any reason to confirm my arrival. Why would they?

I had to face it: I was on my own.

I took in as much of my dark surroundings as I could. How strange, I thought, that my last car ride alive be in the same type of vehicle as my final ride deceased. For the first time ever, I had no doubt: I would not get out of this one alive. There were no means to save myself and I could see no one riding to my rescue.

I missed Gav. Knowing I would never see him again cut my heart to shreds and made my eyes hot. Sorrow overwhelmed me, making it hard to breathe.

We drove for what felt like a long time. More than an hour. Maybe two. Although I tried, I couldn't keep track. My brain still felt foggier than usual. I hated that.

After a while, we hit an extended bumpy patch, letting me know we'd turned off the paved road. We traveled some distance with quick turns and bends so sharp that my right arm got knocked off its perch. It landed with a *thud* in front of me, twisted so that the palm faced up.

I could hear one of the men turn around. Probably Kern. "What are you doing back there?" he asked me in English. That odd Italian/South African inflection he'd adopted as the fake priest had been replaced by a clear Armustanian accent.

If I could have answered, he would have probably shot me right then and there.

Instead I lay staring at my lame, contorted hand, plotting what I would do if I regained control of my limbs.

"How long will the drug keep her immobilized?" Kern's question, directed to Slager, also came in English, which surprised me.

Slager began to answer in Armustanian, but Kern was swift to stop him.

"No. In English. Until we are out of the country, we must minimize suspicion. She is the only one who can hear us now." Kern chuckled. "And it doesn't matter what we say in front of her."

"I do not know how long the drug will work." Slager's accent was much thicker than Kern's. "She did not receive the full portion because of the fat man."

"Long enough to get to the car?"

"I am confident, yes."

"That's all we need."

Another fifteen minutes or so passed before Kern asked, "How soon before we're there?"

"Ten minutes, perhaps less than that."

Whatever they had planned for me would happen in ten minutes. I had ten minutes to save my own life. I wished I knew how.

CHAPTER 28

TEN MINUTES LATER, SLAGER THREW THE HEARSE into Park and shut off the engine. I assumed it was Kern who clapped his hands together because he followed it up with, "Finally, a plan that has gone correctly. It has always been up to us, Slager, to get things right."

"You were wise to follow your instincts," Slager said as he opened the car door.

"Ah, my good friend. You are too modest."

"You have the flashlights?" Slager asked.

I heard Kern shuffle things around as though he was digging through his bag. "Right here."

When they opened their doors, the interior lit up and I blinked in the unexpected brightness. The two men stepped out of the car. I could hear them converse as they walked away, but I couldn't make out what they were saying.

Sweet, fresh, chilly air rolled in over me, and I breathed as deeply as I could to clear the stench of the car from my lungs. I not only retained my vision and hearing, I'd also never lost my sense of smell. Whether it was fear or the exertion of moving me and the heavy-set funeral director, the two men reeked of hot sweat and old clothes.

Drawing another deep breath, I recognized that my left arm—the one pinned beneath me—had fallen asleep. Faint tingles teased down my forearm to my chilled fingertips.

I'd been lying atop my arm for a considerable length of time. The fact that my appendage had fallen asleep didn't surprise me. What made me suck in a breath of astonishment was the fact that I was aware of it. That I could feel something. Could I be regaining control?

Outside I could hear leaves rustling in the wind. Frogs in the distance croaked love songs to one another—a melancholy sound I'd always particularly enjoyed.

Maybe Kern's plan was to leave me in the wilderness and hope I'd die of exposure. But that didn't make sense. Though chilly, the temperature was mild, and it sounded as though they expected the paralyzing drug to wear off at some point.

No, I thought, and instinctively tried to shake my head. Wait, was that movement? A little? I tried moving my jaw. No luck.

My upturned right hand lay like a mannequin's appendage against the shiny burled wood surface that comprised the hearse's floor. I stared at it, willing my fingers to clench. Concentrating, I gave it every bit of energy I possessed. Nothing. My hand remained as fixed and useless as a doll's.

Maybe, I thought, the faster I metabolized the drug, the quicker it would wear off. I had no idea if that theory was medically sound or simply wishful thinking, but I began pushing the tiny control I did have to its maximum. I blinked and blinked and blinked again, all the while breathing as deeply and as rapidly as I could.

When pinpricks of light clouded my vision, I slowed the breathing so I wouldn't pass out. I rolled my eyes up and down and side to side, still blinking all the while. If anyone would have peered in at me at the moment, I'm sure I looked as though I was having a seizure, but it was the only course of action available, and—even given the monumental odds against me—I refused to go down without a fight.

The men's voices grew louder as I continued my fruitless undertaking. I noted that beyond their conversation, the world was quiet. Such stillness, coupled with the rustling leaves and croaking frogs, meant that we were probably far from any other human beings.

I strove to make out what was being discussed and hoped that straining to listen involved another set of muscles I still had access to. Wherever we were, and whatever they had planned, they were clearly in no big rush.

I'd clung to a single hope: that Altergott, the funeral director, had been found and able to alert someone about my abduction. Searchers might be able to use my phone to determine my location. It was still on, thank goodness. Maybe the hearse had GPS installed and that would lead the authorities to my location? Of course, that depended on two things: the GPS being activated, and a strong enough signal to transmit. And all these things could come to pass only if the funeral director had been able to communicate. That was a lot of ifs.

My heart squeezed with almost unbearable pain. Was this a side effect of the drug? Or the realization that I really had no hope at all?

Blinking and breathing hard, I again willed my fingers to clench.

Come on, hand. I'm in control here, don't you remember? Move.

The two men's voices grew loud enough for me to make out what they were saying.

Kern's voice: "You did well."

Don't you understand? Move now or you may never get another chance.

"It is my honor to serve," Slager answered. "I am fortunate you chose to adopt the strategy I suggested in the event the abduction failed."

Laser-focused on my right hand's pinkie, I almost missed my thumb's tiny twitch.

Breathing faster again, this time with excitement, I willed my thumb to repeat the movement. But my concentration faltered when Kern spoke again.

"No need for false modesty, my friend. You saw what others did not—that we needed a backup plan in case our brethren were not successful." It sounded as though he clapped Slager on the back. "We have our proof tonight that they did not succeed. If the Americans hadn't been fooled—if they didn't believe they had captured me, they would never have allowed this troublesome woman to travel unescorted."

So this *was* Kern. They'd fooled us all.

He kept talking. "They would never have dropped the threat level on the president and his family. You have outsmarted the Americans in a way we have never been able to achieve before. When we return to our country, I will name you my first general."

My heart dropped with the realization that we'd been so thoroughly outsmarted. But at the very same moment: a twitch. Another one. Tiny, but real. I'd done it.

With a metallic *clunk*, the back door of the hearse flew open, shooting a gust of snappy air into the death compartment.

"It is time," Kern said. I didn't know whether he was addressing me or Slager.

One of them grabbed my feet and dragged me out, taking no care whatsoever to prevent my nose and cheekbones from banging against the transport slab's remaining metal rollers. Rather than be angry, I was thrilled. I felt every bounce.

The skin on one side of my face burned as it slid along the smooth burled wood surface. Although my triumph was tiny—a half-centimeter thumb movement wouldn't do much good against two muscular terrorists—it gave me what I needed most. Hope.

I vowed not to let them take that from me again.

Once my body was halfway out of the hearse, Slager—with a grunt of effort—grabbed me by the waist and hoisted me over his shoulder. As he swung me into place, I noticed that we were surrounded by tall trees—hundreds of them. Kern's flashlight produced a searingly high-wattage beam as he lit the path Slager followed.

Slager stepped with care, but I got the sense that it was the uneven terrain rather than the added weight that slowed him down. My arms hung like limp things below my head as he made his way down a small embankment.

All the while, Kern kept talking about how pleased he was to have Slager in his camp, and how rich his reward would be once my death was accomplished and the president's fate was sealed.

The president's fate. What could that be? I wanted to know what Kern was talking about. I wanted details, times, dates, whatever. Not that I could do anything even if he'd spelled out all the nitty-gritties. In my present condition, all I could do was stare at the dark grass below me and trust that my pendulous hands were gradually coming back to life.

"Why not leave her in the vehicle?" Slager asked. "Why must I carry her so far into the forest?"

Kern chuckled. "You are a smart man. Can you not figure it out?"

We traveled another ten seconds or so.

"You do not wish the burial vehicle to be destroyed in the blast?" Slager asked.

Blast? Oh dear God.

"Exactly right, my friend. In a very short time, they will begin looking for this hearse. I want them to find it. I want there to be no doubt when they examine the debris. I want the smug Americans to understand that when we identify a target for elimination, we do not give up until we succeed."

My left arm continued to tingle, but I longed for real pain to kick in.

Please, please, please.

Slager dropped me like a construction worker might dump a bag of cement. I landed faceup, happy to have felt the impact's sting. Kern handed a second flashlight to Slager, then crouched next to me. He grabbed my chin with one hand and tilted my head until I made eye contact. He held the torch beneath his chin. The upward-facing beam threw half his face into shadow, blackening the hollows of his eyes.

Cruel highlights accentuated his downturned mouth. I felt the same terror I had as a child when Snow White's evil stepmother consulted her magic mirror.

"I know it galls you to know that we have won," he said with a glint in his eye that sparkled from the darkness. "You are seething, are you not? Feeling helpless. Like my brother did. Will it help you to know that we anticipate that your beloved husband will now attempt to infiltrate our organization? He will fail."

I didn't say anything. I couldn't.

"And when he learns of your death, he will ask himself how he could have been so mistaken, so easily duped. He

will then grieve, as I did for my brother." Wagging a finger
side to side, he said, "But don't worry. He won't grieve long.
He won't see the end coming. Not like you."

Pressing his hands against his knees, Kern boosted himself to stand and started away. Slager shuffled off, too, or so
I deduced from the sound of leafy footsteps and the decreas-
ing level of light.

I stared at Kern's pant legs until they were swallowed by
the dark. I strained every muscle, hoping to expel the drug
from my body by sheer force of will.

"Slager?" Kern called. "Do you need assistance?"

The other man answered from enough of a distance that
I couldn't make out his reply. A hundred feet away, at least.

I heard a trunk slam. The hearse didn't have a trunk, and
its back door made an entirely different sound. Slager must
have accessed that other car they'd discussed earlier.

Kern returned to my side. "You are one of the lucky ones,"
he said very quietly. "Few humans are fortunate enough to
know the precise moment of their death. You have a rare
opportunity to find peace, and to offer your soul to whatever
god you believe in." He leaned down and chuckled. "Or spend
your last few minutes cursing me. Your choice."

Slager's flashlight cut wide swaths of light back and forth
as he trudged down the embankment again. As he came into
view, I could see that he carried the torch in his right hand
and held a backpack close to his chest with his left.

Using gingerly movements, he lowered the backpack to
the ground next to me. "It is highly unlikely that she will
regain the use of her limbs soon," he said. "How far do we
need to be before the bomb detonates?"

"I want to set the timer so that we are back in the city
before it goes off."

"It would be foolhardy to leave her here for that long,

Kern. As unlikely as it is that she will be found, we cannot risk it."

"We are far from the city, yes, but not so far that an explosion of this magnitude will go unnoticed." Kern's voice was strained. "We must not be anywhere nearby. If roads are closed, or blockades are established, we will be stopped. We must not be stopped."

Slager began to pace. "It would be madness to set it for longer than an hour."

Kern crouched next to me again. He lifted my right arm and let go, letting it drop, lifeless, to the ground next to me. He did the same with my leg. "I don't believe she will recover sufficiently in an hour's time."

Slager didn't answer. He took off back up the embankment and returned a moment later. "We can use these," he said.

I couldn't see what he was holding. A moment later, however, it became clear when he wrapped a white nylon tie-wrap around my left wrist and a second one around my right. The two men crouch-shuffled back and forth, rolling me to my side, my bulky purse wedged beneath my right hip.

They ran a third tie-wrap through the backpack's woven carry handle and then through both loops, encircling my wrists. At first I thought they'd left a large amount of slack by mistake, but once they'd made the final connections and locked the third cable, Slager cinched the plastic around my wrists. Not tight enough to cut off circulation, but there would be no wiggling free of these restraints.

"An hour before she might have movement again?" Kern asked as they stood again, and slapped dirt off their hands. "Is that what you believe?"

"Yes, but I would set the timer for thirty minutes."

No, please. I need more time. Please. An hour. At least.
I was on my right side, working hard to keep my extra-deep

breathing as quiet as possible. I couldn't try to stretch, couldn't attempt to move, lest I spasm slightly and they notice.

"We are too far from our safe house. As I said, an explosion will be detected and add to our risk of being stopped," Kern said.

Slager gave an exasperated grunt. "You have depended on me to bring us this far. Trust me. You have seen how these Americans react and how careful they attempt to be. It slows them down." He paced. "They are incapable of assembling forces within thirty minutes. We will not be stopped."

Kern seemed to consider this. "Even if she regains control, she cannot escape her bonds," he said, sliding an index finger along the nylon cables cuffing me. "She will die here." Quietly, almost reverently, he added, "Tonight, I will finally have my revenge."

"Then the timer's detonation must be your decision."

Kern placed his flashlight on the ground next to him. He crouched next to me. "Shine your light here," he said.

Slager complied.

Kern held a digital timer in both hands. About the size of a deck of cards, it was an ordinary device—the kind that kitchen stores sold by the thousands every year. Two kinked wires sprang from the back of the timer's case like skinny blue arms.

Kern shifted his weight to one knee as he thumbed a control level on the right to "set" and then tapped small gray boxes below until the display read 0:30:00. "You see?" he said, holding the timer up for Slager's benefit. "I prove my faith in you. Thirty minutes."

When Slager grunted acknowledgment, Kern reached into the backpack and pulled out a fat PVC cylinder. The shiny white plastic was about six inches in diameter and about twelve inches long. There was a nine-volt battery duct-taped to the side and wires ran from the battery to a long, slim piece of metal. It looked like an expensive pen, but I recognized it as the detonator.

I'd seen similar components, first several years ago when Gav had come to the White House to teach us about bombs, and then again Thursday night during my impromptu class on IEDs.

The thought of Gav made my heart swell with sadness and fire race to my eyes, but I forced myself to concentrate on Kern's movements. He attached the timer's blue wires to the detonator and gently placed the PVC cylinder atop the backpack.

"No need to hide it at this point, is there?" he asked.

I swallowed, fighting to ignore the terror building in my chest. My heart slammed so hard that I was surprised its reverberations didn't catch their attention.

Kern continued working, propping the timer against the white PVC and arranging it so that I could read the display.

Kern looked up at Slager. "You are ready?" he asked.

Slager nodded.

"Give me your flashlight," Kern said.

Slager slapped the heavy-duty instrument into his leader's upturned hand. Kern positioned it on the cold ground next to my head, its beam pointing to the timer, and beyond it, the homemade bomb. "You see? I am a man of my word. You will be given the gift that so few enjoy. You will know the moment of your death."

I stared at the digital readout, still set at 0:30:00.

"I am certain you would wish to thank me," he said with a cruel laugh, "but I cannot wait." He boosted himself to his feet and turned to Slager. "Let's go."

The other man executed a brisk pivot and headed back up the embankment.

Kern leaned down. "Our family will finally know peace tonight."

He pressed one of the small gray buttons on the timer, and with a tinny beep, sent the display into motion. He took off running up the embankment. Moments later the car's doors slammed. Its engine revved. Before half a minute had elapsed, they were gone.

CHAPTER 29

THIRTY MINUTES TO LIVE. NO, LESS THAN THAT.

Though I desperately wished they would have given me that hour, I couldn't waste time lamenting my fate. This situation was the gravest I'd ever encountered, but I fought to keep my bubbling emotions in check. Spending the next twenty-nine minutes crying served no one, least of all me.

I might die trying, but I couldn't *not* try.

I'd never given up before, had I? No. This would be a bad time to start a new habit.

The moment Kern took off, I'd resumed stretching, trying, fighting for control of my body. Although the two men had argued about the timer's duration for only a few minutes, those were a few more minutes in my favor.

My thumb twitched with more consistency. Both hands began responding, the left a little slower than the right. Tingles ran brilliantly up and down my entire left side and though I knew that was the result of lying atop my arm for so long, I willed myself to believe that feeling was truly seeping back into my body. I hadn't the strength or power to clench either hand completely but I could make my fingers move a little bit. They were abbreviated, jerky responses, but they gave me a heart full of hope.

I'd given up on the breathing exercises because my breaths were coming faster on their own as adrenaline flooded my system.

The two men left me lying on my right side with my hands in front of me, attached to the backpack, which lay stretched out just beyond my reach. The timer, resting comfortably atop the backpack, blinked its deadly alert.

Slowly—only because I couldn't move at any other speed—I worked the index and middle fingers of my right hand under the woven backpack handle. Once I'd gotten them far enough in so that the handle rested in the crooks of my fingers, I pulled.

The backpack's weight resisted my paltry efforts. It didn't move.

A sharp breeze swirled over my recumbent form, chilling the perspiration that had broken out at my hairline and down my neck. I'd dressed for the weather, but temperatures had dropped at least twenty degrees. I shivered, but took that as a good sign.

As cold as I was, however, sweat poured off me, pooling around the right side of my waist and leaking down my back.

I pulled at the strap again, maintaining my focus on the backpack, knowing my only hope lay in disabling the bomb. Gav, John, and Jane had done their best to instruct me on the workings of IEDs like this one, but their strongest admonition had involved running away and calling the bomb squad. No chance of that tonight.

Still no movement. If I could only exert enough pressure

with my thumb to get a grip on the woven handle, I'd have better leverage. Alas, my thumb still lacked the necessary strength.

John and Jane had taken care to impress upon me that some bombs are set to fail "open" and some set to fail "closed." That's the main reason why movies relied on "cut or no-cut" scenarios to build suspense. A cut wire could trigger—or cancel—a bomb's detonation. It was all in the design. Only the bomb-maker knew for sure which move was the right choice.

The timer kept up its steady pace. Twenty-three minutes and change.

I remembered them telling me that most bombs are set to go off without interference. That is, they're designed to explode before anyone becomes aware of their existence. And, in the case of remote detonation, if the bomb-maker is able to maintain a line of sight at a safe distance, he can send the signal to explode if anyone so much as gives his creation a second look.

As sweat drenched my right side, I hoped that was an indication that my metabolism had kicked into high gear. I still had no idea if that would help me, but I had no reason to believe otherwise.

I attempted to curl my fingers more snugly into the handle. Closing my eyes, I visualized sitting up, nabbing the backpack, and expediently disarming the bomb. When I opened my eyes, I was still lying helplessly on the ground, but I swore my hand felt stronger.

The frogs in the distance croaked their melody, and I told myself they were singing to me, urging me to persevere.

This time when I tugged, the timer wobbled for a long two seconds before righting itself again.

I'd moved the backpack.

Or maybe I'd only jarred it some.

No, I'd moved it. I had. I couldn't allow myself to believe otherwise.

Belatedly, I realized my jaw was clenched. No idea when that had happened, but as I loosened the tension I attempted a shout. I doubted there were any other humans nearby but I had to try.

The incoherent croak that burbled from my throat rivaled that of the frogs.

Frustration twisted inside me as I tugged again with no result.

The definition of a fool, I reminded myself, was one who attempted the same thing over and over and expected a different result.

I pulled in a deep breath and held tight, using every shred of strength to maneuver myself farther along the ground. My arm inched against the uneven terrain in increments so small my teeth hurt, but the scraping sound of my sleeve—sliding one notch, then another—boosted my optimism and brought my fingers ever closer to the backpack's padded shoulder straps.

I blew out my breath and tried again.

Salty, cold perspiration fogged my vision. I blinked repeatedly, trying to bring the clock into focus. Eighteen minutes? No. Sixteen, and thirty-two seconds.

Please, body. Move. We're in this together.

I slid my two fingers into the small spread between the right shoulder strap and the body of the backpack.

My lips moved now—barely—attempting to bolster myself with unspoken affirmations.

The fabric of the shoulder strap was smooth, but I believed its thickness would work to my advantage. The width of the strap meant that I couldn't get my fingers all the way around it, but I kept at it, working them deeper, inching myself closer.

I mouthed what should have been "All together now," but probably would have looked more like a silent prayer if anyone had seen me.

Of course, if anyone had seen me, I would like to believe they'd cut me loose and we'd both run far, far away.

The timer had counted down another two minutes. I had less than fifteen minutes to go.

When I got my fingers jammed beneath the strap up to the second knuckle, I blew out another breath.

I tugged.

The backpack lurched toward me with sudden and unexpected speed. This time when the timer wobbled, it lost its footing and toppled facefirst onto the ground, angled upward against the tension of its wires.

I gasped, then exhaled in relief when I wasn't blown to bits.

The backpack had moved less than an inch, but the surprise had energized me. I curled my fingers closer, trying to reach the edge of the timer. It had fallen close to my face, nowhere near my hand.

There wasn't enough power in me to lift my head off the ground, but I scooched my face closer to the timer with the intention of pushing it to within reach of my fingers. My angle was off, way off.

I managed to ease my head back again, bringing my nose closer to the timer's edge. I thrust forward in tiny bursts, pushing the timer with the tip of my nose. Little pebbles in the grass scraped at the side of my face but I didn't stop, not even when my grunts of exertion morphed into exclamations of pain. The timer moved about every third try, and then only the barest fraction.

I didn't want to think about how much time was counting down. All I concentrated on was getting my fingers close enough to grab it.

When my fingers finally grazed the plastic, I moaned with relief. I was finally able to lift my hand slightly. My right thumb had gained a little more power in the minutes I'd been struggling and I used it, along with my index finger as a pincer, trying to lift the timer back up.

The plastic casing was too smooth. I got no traction at all.

Summoning all my willpower, I jerked my left hand closer to my right, keeping at it until one hand was atop the other. Using both sets of fingers, I clawed at two sides of the timer at once, dragging it unevenly back to where I might have a chance to lift it up.

I'd planned to turn the device over quickly yet gingerly, but the casing slipped from my nervous fingers, straining against the blue wires once again. It landed faceup, and again, I couldn't see the time at all.

When I finally got it pointed toward me, the display was out of the light. I conked my forehead against the flashlight's handle, like playing kick the can—a solid, heavy can—with my skull. I knew I'd have bruises for weeks.

I *hoped* I'd have bruises for weeks.

I nudged it into place. Fear threatened to take over as I fumbled with my tethered, uncooperative hands until I was finally able to angle the timer into the light.

My heart dropped and my stomach clenched.

Fourteen seconds.

CHAPTER 30

HOLDING THE TIMER IN MY WEAK, TREMBLING hands, I couldn't take time to decide. Without enough strength to yank out one of the wires and without the skills necessary to defuse the bomb any other way, I had to rely on instinct. All I had were my reluctant fingers and a familiarity with kitchen timers.

Moving with inexorable clumsiness, I slid my right thumb up the side of the timer and used every ounce of pressure I could muster to slide the control from "Lock" to "Set."

Eight seconds left.

My breaths coming fast and shallow, my hands moved like they belonged to someone else—someone dosed with sleeping pills wearing giant clown gloves—as my right thumb eased leftward to the first gray button on the right.

Four seconds.

I pressed the button as the display rolled down to three.

Back to four seconds.

As it turned to three again, I pressed the button again.

Four seconds. I pressed again and again and again, as quickly as I could.

Up to eight seconds.

I allowed myself a breath as it dropped to seven, then started back at the little button, hitting it as fast and often as I could until the readout showed that I had fifteen seconds to play with.

With the amount of sweat I was producing, my racing heartbeat, and my panicked breathing, I felt as though I'd run a marathon.

Before the seconds could drop back below twelve, I slid my thumb to the second button from the right and tapped it. A minute added to my total. I breathed a relieved, terrified, half-sob laugh, and went back at it, adding minutes until I'd totaled twenty.

Finally able to relax enough to think, I slid my thumb sideways farther and hit the hour button. One, two, three. All the way up to twelve, the maximum it would allow.

I hadn't realized I'd been able to pull my head up a little. It hadn't been much, but now I allowed it to drop back against the ground. Above me, tree branches obscured some of the night sky, but I was able to find an open patch where the stars shone through. I stared through the leaves at the glittering beauty above and thanked the heavens for seeing me through another close call.

I wasn't free of the bomb yet. I knew I still had a struggle ahead of me. But for now I enjoyed the sound of my breathing. I stared. I smiled. And allowed myself to relax.

When I checked the timer again, we were down to eleven hours and change. I added another hour, hitting the maximum yet again. I didn't want there to be any chance of time running out if I lost consciousness or fell asleep.

Not that there was much chance of that.

I had a little bit more feeling in my legs, and when I tried shifting position, my left leg twitched. My right side was suffering the same fate that my left had on the ride here. Too long in one position. Pain shot up along my thigh, and I tried rocking myself from side to side to get the purse out from underneath.

I was a long way from being able to reach it, but my phone was in there. If I could get even minimal signal, I could call or text for help.

Whether it was because of my small stature or petite build, or if it was because Slager miscalculated the dose, the effects of the drug he'd administered held me tight for another three hours. I shivered in the cold, feeling my already lifeless body growing numb by the minute in a completely different way.

When I moved, it was with such excruciating clumsiness that I growled my frustration. Is this how babies feel when they're first learning to roll over? No wonder they constantly cry. I lay there for hours. The cold and damp seeped through my pant legs, chilling me through every point of contact.

Though it took enormous effort, I eventually managed to raise the upper part of my body, propping myself up with my right elbow. With some effort, I was able to check my watch. Two in the morning. I hesitated to move too quickly—not that I could—because I didn't know how touchy the detonator might be. I knew it needed an electrical charge to blow, and I knew I'd effectively taken the timer's role off the table, but I wasn't about to declare victory yet.

I remained tethered to the backpack, and unless I chewed through its woven handle, or gnawed the tie-wraps off my wrists, I wouldn't be safe. Not until the bomb itself was disarmed.

I tried to speak; nothing came out. My throat remained paralyzed, as did my legs. They were the last, it seemed, to begin this painful, cold reanimation process.

Another several hours passed before I had enough strength and control to completely raise my torso. I navigated up, moving my hands as little as possible and realizing I needed to use the washroom. There clearly wasn't one nearby and likely wouldn't be for some time.

I blew out a breath and told myself to block the discomfort from my mind.

Yeah, like that old quip: "Don't think about a pink hippopotamus."

Sitting up now, I made sure I had the maximum number of hours on my timer, then did my best to scooch my cross-body purse to my lap. My movements were still slow and heavy, so that process took another ten minutes. I fumbled around inside and finally located my cell phone and switched on the sound. I felt as though I suddenly had all the time in the world.

Light began to dawn behind me and I turned myself—to the extent I could—to face it. My legs still didn't want to cooperate, but they had begun to show signs of life. I faced the sun, watching as it slowly rose in the eastern sky. Though the view was mostly blocked by trees, I'd never seen anything so beautiful.

I tapped the phone to bring up the touchpad dialer. Rather than try to provide my location—which I didn't know—to a 911 dispatcher, I dialed the White House.

No signal.

And then I remembered I still couldn't speak.

Texting took less bandwidth, or so I'd been told. I didn't know whether it was true or not, but I decided to try. With Gav out of town, I composed a text to Sargeant. Please help. Kidnapped.

While the phone searched for a signal, I hit Send, and waited for the confirming *whoosh*.

It didn't come.

Two minutes ticked down on the timer while ticking up on my phone before the "No Service" message appeared.

Hardly surprising. I couldn't be annoyed by the inconvenience; the fact that there was no signal out here might have driven the decision to use a timer rather than a remote detonation device. What was a minor nuisance in the moment had undoubtedly saved my life.

As the sun climbed higher in the sky, I carefully tucked the PVC cylinder into the backpack, and ensured the timer was set for the longest interval possible. I stretched my limbs, lifted the backpack to my chest, and prepared to stand. With my throat parched and my bladder swollen, I had to get moving.

The first thing I did was make my way up the embankment to look around. The hearse was exactly where they'd left it, about a hundred yards off. My heart raced as I stumbled my way toward it, hoping they'd left the keys in the ignition, or had carelessly dropped them on the seat. Though it would be difficult to drive with my hands attached to the backpack, I knew I'd figure out a way to manage.

Wedging the fingers of my right hand underneath, I lifted the metal door handle and guided the heavy door until it was fully open. There was plenty of light, both from the sun and from the vehicle's interior but there were no keys. I eased myself into the driver's seat and did my best to examine the space, spending extra time scanning the top of the dash and around the passenger side until I gave up and scooted out again. My last hope was that he'd dropped the keys on the floor. I got to my knees—carefully—and did my best to search under the seat. Nothing.

I did a slow circuit around the vehicle, hoping the sunlight might glint off discarded metal. Still no luck.

With no choice but to walk to safety, I headed east for no better reason than because it felt like the right decision. More than once I wished I could sling the backpack over one shoulder the way it was designed to be carried. Hauling it around with it plastered to my chest made navigating the uneven ground difficult. But with my hands shackled to the bag's top, I had no choice.

My elbows clamped against the bag's soft sides, I hooked both thumbs under the woven handle for leverage, glad now that I hadn't tried to chew it away.

Although I'd regained the control of my limbs, I remained weak. Every step required effort, and not knowing my location or where I'd find the closest civilization could have dampened my spirits. But I was alive when I shouldn't have been and because of that I found the strength to fight my weariness and despair—even when I finally conquered a small rise and still saw nothing but trees in my path. *Every* time I conquered a small rise and saw nothing but trees in my path.

"It's okay," I assured myself aloud, now that I could speak again. "I'm going home."

Every fifteen minutes or so—which I knew because the timer kept me apprised—I stopped. Placing the backpack on the ground, I sat next to it, and went through all the awkward gyrations necessary to pull out my phone and check for signal.

At the fifth such pause in my journey, I spied what looked like an outhouse a hundred feet away.

The sight of the dingy wooden structure with the slanted roof warmed my heart and as I picked up my burden and made my way over, I tried to remember which campgrounds were nearest D.C. Not that it mattered. Unless I encountered a sign, I wouldn't have any idea which forest I was in.

An outhouse like this one, however, made me believe I'd happen across hikers or campers soon. Though I knew it was likely that most adventurers had headed home Sunday night, I didn't allow it to discourage me.

The rocky terrain surrounding the outhouse meant that I half-hobbled the final fifteen steps, but I made it. Inside the stench was overwhelming. The processes required to complete my necessary bodily function were some I hoped never to encounter again.

Though it seemed to take forever, I emerged about twenty minutes later, relieved in more ways than one.

I took the opportunity to check for signal once again. Still nothing.

Hungry, thirsty, and bone-tired, I felt reenergized and determined to succeed. I set off for home.

AT TEN-TWELVE A.M., IT FINALLY HAPPENED. IN the middle of a golden meadow, a single bar of signal replaced the "No Service" alert. Before the overhead satellites had a chance to change their minds, I re-sent the text to Sargeant, adding: Got away. In a national forest, I think. Tell Gav. I then texted a similar message to Bucky and sent a separate one to the White House emergency number, hoping at least one of the missives would hit its target.

Although chances were high that Gav remained out of the country and therefore out of touch, there was also the possibility—however slim—that once the White House became aware of my absence, they may have recalled my husband home. I hoped so.

There was far more I wanted to say to him than I could

properly manage in a text. My emotions shimmered too close to the surface to try. Biting my lip and swallowing hard, I settled for the barest minimum: I'm okay.

I sat in the grass staring at the tiny phone, listening for each *whoosh*, and hoping not to receive a belated "Not delivered" alert in return.

Less than a minute passed before Sargeant's reply dinged in. On our way.

With a whoop of triumph, I crowed my happiness to the skies. A moment later, I texted him again. Send bomb squad.

CHAPTER 31

A MOMENT LATER, I SENT SARGEANT A FOLLOW-UP: Kern in U.S. Plot against president. Gav not safe.

Details? he replied

I shook my head. None.

I had plenty of battery power left in my phone, thank goodness. Rather than keep moving and risk hitting a dead zone, I sat and waited for help to arrive. In the interim, I had two important jobs: ensure I maintained signal and keep the timer well above the danger point.

Sitting in the middle of a wide-open patch didn't bother me. The heavy forest lay behind and another tree line began about half a mile east of my position. The sun warmed my cold, perspiring body, and I breathed in my own acrid scent with gusto.

My phone dinged again. Bucky this time, expressing worry, relief, and anger. I told him Sargeant was sending help and he told me he already knew. Sit tight.

Neville Walker responded to the text I'd sent to the

emergency line with questions asking about my physical and mental state. He assured me that help was on its way and that they were using my phone's GPS to track me down.

Though stretched to the breaking point and thirstier than I could ever remember being in my life, I knew there was nothing Neville could do, so I assured him I was fine. He, too, encouraged me to hang in there. I texted him back asking if he had any word from Gav.

Message sent through channels. Will keep you apprised.

POTUS and family? I asked.

Under control.

Not being able to connect with Gav kept me from relaxing. What did Kern mean when he'd said they anticipated Gav's next move? I pulled my knees up and set the backpack in the space between them and my chest, and studied the plastic tie-wraps, wondering if there was some trick to releasing them.

In the daylight, now that I could see, and now that I had full control of my fingers, I did my best to finagle the end backward through the plastic locking mechanism.

So engrossed in my project, I didn't notice I wasn't alone until I heard someone shout, "Hey there, you okay?"

I glanced up to see two young people. Both wore light jackets, canvas hats, and carried backpacks. From this distance, I couldn't tell if they were male or female. I waved— to the extent that I could—and raised my voice. "Stay back."

They started toward me. "Do you need help?"

Shouting, I held up both hands. "Don't come any closer." Although I believed the bomb wouldn't explode unless the timer went off, the last thing I needed was to risk these people's lives.

They stopped and looked at each other. One asked, "Why not?"

"Long story," I said. "Please give the authorities my position. Where are we, by the way?" If I could text my location to Neville, it would help speed up the process.

The two continued to trudge forward despite my pleas.

"I'm fine, really. Help is coming," I shouted, but before I knew it they were less than twenty yards away. "Please go back. Just go tell someone where I am."

Both young men were in their late twenties. Slim, yet muscular, one was pale and freckled. The other was dark-skinned. He said, "Don't be afraid. My name's Jerold," as he moved closer. "Your lips are chapped."

"Where am I?" I asked again.

"Don't you know?"

Exasperation got the better of me. "I wouldn't be asking if I did."

"We're in Gold Cliff State Forest," he said.

"Thank you." I began tapping into my phone, but begged them both again, "Please, for your own safety, get away from me."

"You're bleeding." Jerold pointed to his cheek.

"Not anymore, it's dry. Just a scrape," I said. "I'm fine, really. Please just go alert the authorities and tell them this location. People are coming for me."

Jerold reached around to the side of the sack he carried. "You need water."

"Water?" I sat up straighter.

He pulled an aluminum bottle out and offered it to me. Both men's eyes widened when they caught sight of my hands bound to the top of the backpack.

"Who did this to you?" the paler man asked. "Don't be afraid. We can help. My name is Kenneth. Did someone hurt you?"

"Yes, but not in the way you think. Please," I said striving to appear rational. "I know this looks strange . . ."

Jerold unscrewed the bottle and handed it to me. He nodded at the backpack. "What's in there?"

My hands trembled with anticipation, and it took several fumbling seconds before I was able to successfully tilt the bottle to my lips. I drank the cool, delicious liquid with greedy joy.

"Slow down," Jerold said. "If you're dehydrated it's going to come right back up."

As though my stomach had heard the warning, it seized and convulsed, threatening to send its fresh contents on a return trip.

I lowered the bottle and took a deep breath, waiting for the spasms to quiet. As they did, I implored the two young men again. "Leave me your names and contact information. I'll see that this bottle is returned to you or replaced. But you must get away from me. As far and as fast as possible. Please."

Jerold regarded me carefully. "Who are you?"

"That's not important," I said. "Please leave. I'm not joking. It's—"

Comprehension dawned on his face. "It's a bomb, isn't it?" He took a step backward. "That's what you're not telling us."

I bit my lower lip, but kept a tight grip on the water bottle. "I'm keeping this. Get out of here now. Run, okay?"

Finally believing me, the two young men took off. I shouted after them. "Don't forget to tell the rangers where I am."

Hard as it was to refrain from chugging the remaining water, I allowed myself a sip every few minutes. I didn't know how long it would take for Neville's team to pinpoint my position or for Jerold and Kenneth to report my location.

Last night, I'd estimated I'd traveled two hours in the back of that hearse, but I could be way off. I had no idea how far out of D.C. the Gold Cliff State Forest was located.

Still wearing the jacket I'd donned for the wake last night and sitting under the clear sky, I grew warm. My face, having suffered miserably against the cold ground overnight, appreciated the sunshine, but the rest of me began to sweat. I shook the bottle to judge the water level. Now that I'd curbed the temptation to guzzle, at the rate I was sipping, I probably had about four hours' worth of refreshment left.

A check of the timer revealed that it had dropped to ten hours and thirty-two minutes. I upped the digital display to its maximum one more time and stared at my phone.

I heard the *whup-whup-whup* of the approaching helicopter before I saw it. Correction. Two helicopters.

I held the backpack aloft to block the whipped-up dust from stinging my eyes. Struggling to my feet, I backed away, moving closer to the tree line behind me in order to give both choppers plenty of room.

The moment they touched down, a dozen people poured out. They all wore green padded body armor and oversize helmets with clear face shields. Six carried high-powered rifles and fanned out to form a rough perimeter around the meadow. Four settled heavy equipment onto the ground while the final two individuals made their way toward me.

As soon as the four with the equipment began unpacking their loads, the helicopters lifted off again. I turned my face away as the choppers returned to the skies. I guessed the government wanted them out of harm's way just in case. Couldn't blame them.

The two bomb experts approached slowly, asking questions in quiet, calm voices, as they surveyed the scene. I was so excited to see them that I began babbling about the bomb in the backpack and how it wouldn't go off unless the timer counted all the way down and how I'd managed to thwart that particular outcome.

They managed to decipher my exuberant ravings and assess the situation. They called to the equipment team for wire cutters and within seconds had freed me from the backpack.

I didn't even have time to rub my wrists or shake my arms out before one of the two threw an arm around my shoulders and hustled me away. They must have radioed ahead because by the time we reached the equipment loading area, one of the helicopters was on its way back.

The bomb expert who had run with me yelled over the chopper's loud approach. "You did well. Now go."

Another armor-clad soldier jumped out and helped me into the helicopter's passenger compartment. The moment my rear end touched the seat, we lifted off again.

From the time they'd first arrived to this moment with me being spirited away, no more than five minutes had elapsed. If that.

The soldier next to me leaned forward to fit ear protection over my head. As we curved into the sky, she removed her helmet and gave me a wide smile.

"Jane," I said, even though she probably couldn't hear.

She leaned over and patted my knee.

CHAPTER 32

THE PILOT LANDED ON THE HELIPORT OF A D.C. hospital. I protested that I didn't need anything beyond my husband and a shower, but as I'd learned too often in the past, there was no arguing with a soldier following orders.

I put my foot down, however, when two hospital staffers tried to get me to lie on the gurney they'd rolled in for my transport. "Not a chance," I said, pointing to my cheek. "A little disinfectant and a bandage and I'm good to go."

Jane had taken off again with the helicopter while I agreed to be checked for injury by an army doctor who'd been called in just for me. Still holding tight to the aluminum water bottle, I was whisked into a windowless room—the better to keep the media at bay, no doubt—where I was poked, prodded, and pierced with brisk efficiency.

I wanted to eat, but they told me I had to wait until they were certain I wouldn't need any more blood drawn.

They offered me a change of clothes, which I accepted

with grateful alacrity. This was the second time in a year that I'd been provided colorful hospital scrubs after an altercation. I hoped this wasn't getting to be a habit, but I was so thrilled to be able to strip off the crusty sweat-soaked outfit I'd been wearing that I didn't care that I now sported a cotton V-neck teddy bear shirt and coordinating purple pants. They were crisp, clean, and felt like heaven.

After I'd shared details of my experience with the doctor, I asked her, "What did they drug me with?"

She sat on a rolling chair as she tapped information into a laptop computer. "We're running tests now. I don't know when I'll have an answer for you."

"Or *if* you'll ever have an answer for me, right?"

She smiled. "It may no longer be in your system, or it may be classified information."

"What if you find out there are lasting side effects?"

"We'll do our best to provide the information you need."

Not the most comforting reassurance on the planet, but I was happy to discover that the abrasion on my face was so mild it needed nothing more than topical treatment.

Before the doctor finished her examination, Yablonski thundered in. "What in the world did you get yourself into this time?" he asked.

I sat straighter on the examining table. "Don't you knock?"

"Sorry." He gave a quick look around as though realizing that he could have accidentally walked in during an awkward moment. "Sorry," he said again.

"Where's Gav? Did you get the message about Kern's plan against the president?"

"We did, and every precaution has been taken to keep President Hyden and his family safe. Thank you for that. How did it happen and how did you know it was Kern?"

"You didn't answer my question. Where's Gav?"

"On his way."

"Does he know I'm all right?"

Yablonski nodded. "He was out of his mind when you went missing. We got a message to him the moment we heard from you."

I stared at the ceiling, feeling relief rise up through my body from the bottom of my feet to the top of my head. "Thank you."

"He should be back in D.C. by the end of the day."

I closed my eyes.

The doctor stood to excuse herself. She reminded me to keep hydrated, get rest, and suggested I take over-the-counter pain medication if I suffered any aches and pains.

I opened my eyes and stared at the speckled ceiling tiles. "I don't know if I can take any more of this."

Yablonski lowered himself onto the low rolling seat and waited for me to make eye contact.

"That's exactly what I wanted to discuss with you," he said. "Now that we know Kern is still at large . . ."

I dropped my head into my hands. *Here it comes*, I thought. *The push for us to disappear.* To abandon the lives we created, to give up everything we'd worked for and adopt new identities, move to a new city, start over. There was no pretending I didn't hear or understand him. Not anymore.

"Ollie." Yablonski's tone was gentle. "Do you know what I'm talking about?"

Without looking up, I nodded and rubbed my eyes. "We can't begin to discuss any of this until Gav gets here."

"I know, but I suspect you're the harder sell on this topic."

I still didn't look up. "You suspect right."

He slapped his hands against his knees and got to his feet. "If you're up for it, there's a roomful of military strategists at the White House waiting to debrief you."

"Of course," I said, finally raising my face. "But could I please get something to eat first?"

CONDUCTED IN THE ROOSEVELT ROOM IN THE West Wing, my debriefing consisted of me recounting in detail every moment of my abduction up to my helicopter rescue. Yablonski hadn't been kidding—the room was packed with big shots plus a handful of assistants sitting in folding chairs along the wall.

Yablonski led me to the only open seat at the table. Dead center, north side. Although no one took the time to introduce all the individuals seated around the massive table, I recognized a number of faces from Yablonski's meeting in the Family Dining Room before the winery adventure.

Yablonski had arranged to have food sent up. As I took my seat a butler provided a cloth napkin, then laid out silverware on the table. He placed in front of me a steaming plate of meat loaf, mashed potatoes, and broccoli. "Comfort food," he whispered. "If you think this is too heavy, I can order in lighter fare."

"This will be wonderful," I said. "I'll eat slowly."

Though ravenous, I waited for everyone else's food to arrive, realizing a half-second later that I was the only person at the table being served.

Awkward.

I took a longing look at the plate before me, then dug in.

Louis Del Priore, who had served as Bill's stand-in at the winery, was the lead interrogator. Between mouthfuls, I answered their questions, describing Kern and Slager, and repeating—to the best I could recall—the conversations they'd shared around me.

I was halfway through the most delicious meal I'd ever consumed—patiently listening to the banter around the table during a questioning lull—when I noticed a folded white paper peeking out from beneath my plate. While the think tank discussed Kern's likely next move, I slid the paper out and opened it.

From Bucky: Good to have you back, Ace. Enjoy.

My heart swelled as I smiled down at my assistant's words. What I wouldn't give to be back in the kitchen right now.

"Ms. Paras?"

I jerked to attention, realizing I'd missed what Louis had asked. "I'm sorry, could you repeat that?"

"Tell us again—the exact words Kern used—when he talked about the president."

I slid Bucky's note into the pocket of the purple scrubs and leaned forward to answer.

An hour or so later, the team either realized I was too physically and mentally exhausted to continue or they'd run out of questions to ask.

"Thank you, Ms. Paras," Louis said with a nod around the table. "I believe we're done here."

The last thing I wanted was to remain in this room a moment longer than necessary, but I had questions of my own.

"What happened to the bomb?" I asked. "Was the team able to defuse it?"

"It is no longer a threat."

"And the two guys who helped me? Who gave me water?"

Louis made eye contact with a person on my side of the table, to my far left. "They have been provided an explanation that doesn't jeopardize national security."

"So you have their names?"

Alarm lit Louis's face. "You don't intend to contact them, do you?"

"I still have Jerold's water bottle. I promised I'd return it. Or at least replace it."

That garnered a ripple of chuckles. Louis glanced over at one of the assistants behind him. She nodded. "I'll take care of it."

"What about the funeral director?" I asked. "Mr. Altergott. Is he all right?"

"He's fine. Fully recovered."

"I owe that man my life," I said. "If he hadn't stepped out the front door just then, I would've gotten a full dose and I doubt I'd be here right now."

Louis scratched his eyebrow as he listened. "Anything else?"

Yablonski had remained standing behind me throughout the meeting. Now he tapped me on the shoulder. "Time to go."

He pulled my chair out and I got to my feet, slowly. Louis thanked me for my cooperation and his kind words were repeated around the table along with occasional kudos for a job well done.

My body ached from every minute of its thirty-six hours without sleep. I made it almost to the door when I turned. "Wait," I said remembering to ask the most important question of all. "What happens now?"

Dead silence.

"What I mean is—will you need my help with anything else?"

Louis flexed his jaw. Still, no one spoke.

Yablonski tugged my arm. I ignored him. "To apprehend Kern, I mean."

Louis cleared his throat. "We will let you know. Thank you again, Ms. Paras."

Outside the door, I looked up at Yablonski. The older man's eyes held pity and concern. "Can I go home now?"

"No, I'm sorry." He shook his head. "You can't."

CHAPTER 33

"WHERE ARE WE GOING, THEN?" I ASKED.

"Sleep first, talk later," Yablonski said as he led me around the Cabinet Room and out the door to the West Colonnade. Outside it was gray with heavy cloud cover and a sharp wind. He put an arm around my shoulders. "You have to be freezing in that light clothing."

I allowed myself to lean a little against his hefty build. "It's not so bad." Thunder rumbled and lightning crackled far to the south, past the Washington Monument. Glancing over the Rose Garden as it began to rain, I suppressed a shiver. "Would have been a lot worse for me if we'd had this weather overnight. I guess I got lucky, didn't I?"

Yablonski tugged tighter. "You really are something," he said.

We walked a little farther. "Let me ask you again: Where are we going?"

"The First Family is back at Camp David," he whispered. "But that information's classified, so don't tell anyone."

A marine sentry stationed in front of the door stepped forward and opened it for us. I thanked him, then whispered back to Yablonski once we were inside, "I thought the sentries were only on duty when the president was in the West Wing."

"Yes, well . . ." Yablonski led me through the Center Hall and to the Family Elevator. "There is something to be said for keeping up appearances. And calculated misdirection."

"You want Kern and his people to believe that President Hyden hasn't been warned."

He pressed the elevator's Up button and nodded. He still hadn't answered my question about where we were going, but I assumed I'd find out soon enough.

I continued to speak softly even though there was no one else around. "But once Kern and Slager discover that the bomb didn't go off, they're sure to know—" The look on Yablonski's face stopped me mid-thought.

The elevator dinged its arrival. I waited until we got inside and the doors closed. "I'm being hidden, aren't I? You're feeding the media, or at least dropping hints, suggesting a bomb did go off, aren't you? Or maybe the bomb squad detonated it themselves. You're making Kern believe that he was successful, so as to draw him out."

"You missed your calling as a strategist," he said, deadpan.

"That's what Gav says."

"Yeah, I can see why he keeps you around."

A laugh burbled out of me, even though I wouldn't have believed I had the energy for it. "Gee, thanks," I said.

The elevator doors opened at the second floor. "Home away from home," he said as we stepped out and into that floor's central hallway.

"Uh, what?" I twisted my head back and forth between the West Sitting Hall and its counterpart across the building. "This is the residence. I don't belong here."

"This is temporary. As I told you, the president and his family are safely away. You won't be bothered."

"*I* won't be bothered?" It took effort to keep up with the conversation but incredulity, I was beginning to discover, is quite energizing. "This is their home. I'm an intruder."

"You're a welcome guest, and until you and I—and Gav— are able to come to an agreement about the future, this is the best we could do for secure temporary quarters." He led me past the Yellow Oval Room and the Treaty Room into the narrow corridor that opened up to the East Sitting Hall. I'd been up here only a couple of times before but never in such a bedraggled state.

Two maids waited for us. "Hey, Ollie," they said. "Glad you're okay."

"Thanks," I said, still not understanding.

Yablonski turned his back to them and faced me. "The Queen's Bedroom," he said, pointing north, "or the Lincoln Bedroom?" He pointed south.

"You're kidding me."

"You're exhausted, you're mentally drained, you saved yourself from being blown to bits, and, quite possibly, performed a similar service for the president of the United States. I wouldn't kid you right now."

I rubbed my temples. Wow, I really wished Gav were here.

"The Lincoln Bedroom is the one with the ghost, right?" I asked.

"So they say."

"Then that's my choice. I could use a spirit watching over me tonight, I guess."

Yablonski got that sad look in his eyes again. "Get some sleep."

I WOKE UP FACING THE WINDOWS, HANDS beneath my cheek. It took a few blinks and memory searches before I remembered where I was. Sunlight streamed in through the sheer window coverings, warming my soul and making me wonder about the time.

When I'd first arrived, I hadn't been alert enough to appreciate my palatial digs, but now I drew in a breath of total relaxation. The clean scent of fresh sheets surrounded me and brightness made this gorgeous room glisten as I studied the elaborate cornice boards above the two windows and smiled at the golden cords and tassels draped below.

Wait. Shouldn't Gav have gotten back by now? Why wasn't he here? No doubt he would be called into meetings, but shouldn't I have been able to see him before he got dragged away again? Had Yablonski lied to me about Gav being on his way? I wouldn't put it past the man.

Wide awake now and decidedly angry, I sat up fast.

"What? Ollie? You okay?"

The moment I turned, all my anger melted away.

Gav reached over, sitting up to grab my arm. His hair was flattened on one side, and it looked as though he hadn't shaved since I'd last seen him. "Are you okay? Did you have a nightmare?"

He was the most beautiful sight I'd ever seen.

"You're here?" I threw my arms around him, knocking him onto his back. I kissed him full on the lips, then pulled my head back. "When did you get in?"

"Pretty late. You were sleeping so soundly I didn't want

to wake you so I crawled in quietly." He stared up at me, pushing my dark hair back behind my ears. "What happened out there?"

I rolled back onto my side of the bed, feeling such uncomplicated bliss that I hesitated to relive the horrors of . . . wait . . . was that last night? Two nights ago? I raised a hand to my forehead. "What day is it? Do you know?"

He sat up. "Tuesday, if I'm not mistaken. Flying back and forth so much, I lost track a little myself." Reaching over to the side table he lifted up his watch. "Eight o'clock."

"That's eight A.M., I presume," I said, flinging a hand toward the windows. "Given the sunlight."

"Tell me everything," he said.

His eyes held fear, love, and worry in their gray depths. I reached up to stroke his stubbled cheek. "You already know it all, I'm sure," I said. "I'd rather hear how things went for you. I mean, once Kern knew that you and I hadn't been captured, he assumed you were flying out to try to infiltrate his faction. You had to be in danger."

"I'm here." He gripped my hand. "And my team is safe. That's all that matters. And yes, while en route I read every report I could get my hands on and talked to everyone with information, but I want to hear what really happened. I need to hear it from you."

I sat up, arranging a pillow behind my back for support. Gav rose, intending to settle in next to me when we were both startled by a knock at the door.

I gave him a puzzled look then called, "Come in?"

One of the maids peered around the door. "I heard voices so I knew you were awake."

A staffer, listening outside my room? I wondered how the First Family dealt with that level of attention every single day. I knew I'd go nuts.

"Is there anything you need before breakfast?" the maid asked. "Anything you care to request from the chef?"

"*I'm* the chef," I said before I could stop the words from tumbling out.

The maid, a middle-aged woman who'd been around for years, smiled. "Today you're the guest. Bucky told me to tell you he'll whip up anything you request."

My stomach growled as I turned to Gav.

He shrugged. "Whatever you want."

"Tell Bucky we're starving," I said to the maid. "I'll take whatever he's got. I guarantee nothing will go to waste."

And while we waited, I told Gav everything.

AFTER BREAKFAST, GAV AND I GOT DRESSED. HE had a change of clothes in his duffel bag. I'd slept in the scrubs from the hospital.

To my surprise, several wardrobe choices awaited me on a nearby Queen Anne–style chair. There were blue jeans, dark cotton pants, a handful of V-neck sweaters, T-shirts, all the necessary underthings, and even footwear choices. The items had appeared, as if by magic, overnight. Clearly, someone had been dispatched to find me suitable clothing.

Gav explained that the U.S. government hoped that Kern believed I'd succumbed to his evil plan. To maintain the charade, the Secret Service couldn't be seen visiting my apartment and leaving with armloads of my clothes. Though Gav wasn't forbidden from entering our home, it was decided a better strategy to make it seem as though he remained out of town.

Whoever had picked out my new attire—and I assumed the task had fallen to a female agent—had done an amazing job. Sizes and fit were spot-on and the combinations were comfortable and just my style.

Gav and I were encouraged to make ourselves at home in the residence until further notice. "Can you imagine living like this?" I asked as we made our way to the Yellow Oval Room.

"No."

"That was a pretty quick answer," I said.

I crossed the room to stare out the windows. Positioned directly above the similarly shaped Blue Room on the first floor, the Yellow Oval Room opened to the Truman Balcony and overlooked the south grounds. Gorgeous day out there today.

He came to stand next to me. "I see how hard it is for the families who move in. They can't let their guard down. Not for a moment. Every decision they make—whether manifested in a word, facial expression, beverage, or book choice—faces relentless judgment."

"I know that. I see it, too. I'm only trying to express how overwhelmed I am by the beauty and all the history surrounding us. And what it must be like to have this be part of your everyday life."

He wrapped an arm around my waist, snugging me close. "I need to feel you near me," he said into my hair. "When I think of how close you came—"

"Don't think about it. I'm here. You're here. That's all that's important now."

"I can't *not* think about it."

We stood together staring out the center window. A giant cloud passed overhead, rolling its shadow over the green grass below.

Gav cleared his throat. "But speaking of living in a fishbowl, do you remember how vulnerable we felt when we knew the Armustanians were listening in on our conversations?"

"How could I forget?" With a sense of what was coming, I blew out a breath and stepped away from the window. "Right now, though, we're in the White House; we're safe. For one day—just one day—I want to forget the outside world exists. I want to forget that there are terrorists and assassins out there with our names on their to-do lists."

Offering a tentative smile, I lowered myself onto one of the twin yellow sofas and patted the cushion next to me.

Gav faced me. I couldn't miss the profound sadness in his eyes.

"Ollie." His voice held a timbre of warning.

"We aren't going to get that one whole day, are we?"

He pulled in a breath.

I had my answer.

"Okay, then," I said with as much energy as I could muster. "What happens next?"

From behind me: "I'm glad you asked."

Yablonski stood in the doorway. He held a leather portfolio and wore the look of a man who'd been up all night. "How bad was it?" he asked Gav.

Gav crossed the room to shake his mentor's hand. "They knew we were coming," he said. "I assume you've already read the reports. We got out with a few scrapes, no serious casualties. That's the best we could have hoped for under the circumstances."

I bolted to my feet. "What happened?"

Yablonski waved me back to my seat. "Your boy here walked into an ambush." He made his way over and settled into the matching sofa across from us as Gav sat down next to me. I felt a peculiar sense of déjà vu. It hadn't been all that long ago that we'd sat facing each other exactly like this in a very different oval room.

I warped back to when Yablonski had shared details about my father's service to the country—classified details Gav and I had sworn never to share with anyone else. And we hadn't.

Here we were again. Though not in the Oval Office this time, everything else was the same: a low table between us and Yablonski looking haggard.

He placed his leather portfolio on the marble tabletop. "You know why I'm here."

Though not a question, it demanded an answer. Gav knew this was directed to me so he waited.

"Kern is still at large, isn't he?" I asked.

Yablonski nodded. "The information you provided—your description of both men and insight into how they work—has been an enormous help. Based on what we know now, we're convinced we will eventually track him down."

"As long as I stay hidden, you mean. As long as he believes I'm dead."

Again, the big man nodded. "We've taken extraordinary steps to perpetuate the charade. We tracked back to the location where they abandoned you and detonated the bomb."

"That seems like an extreme measure. You really think they might have come back to double-check?"

"However unlikely, there remained a remote possibility."

"What about all the beautiful trees?" I asked. "Were they destroyed?"

"The device was designed to maximize the loss of human life," he said. "The flora and fauna suffered damage, but it was minimal."

"How long do you think we have until Kern realizes I wasn't killed?"

"If all goes as planned, he'll never realize it."

"So that means . . ."—I looked from one man to another—"as long as I maintain a low profile, we're in the clear? We can go back to living our lives?"

Yablonski pulled in his bottom lip and sucked on it.

Gav took my right hand in his. "Ollie." His voice was a whisper.

I started shaking my head. "No, no."

Yablonski wrinkled his nose and looked away.

I had to make him see reason. "You have a plan, clearly. You just said as much. So all we have to do is wait for Kern to be caught, right? That can't take long, can it?"

Yablonski met my eyes. "You will never be safe while Kern is at large. Neither will the president. The difference is that Secret Service can't tuck the leader of the free world into an underground bunker until all threats against him are eliminated."

Gav's hand was warm, but I'd never felt so bereft.

"But they *can* hide you," Yablonski continued. "We don't have the manpower to protect you the way we do the president. Kern has shown how little regard he has for American lives and collateral damage. If he knows you're alive, he'll come after you again—and again—until he succeeds in killing you. And he won't care how many others he takes down with you."

I steeled myself to say the words I dreaded. "You're talking about the Witness Protection Program."

"A similar arrangement, yes."

"You tried to break this to me yesterday at the hospital, didn't you?" I expelled an angry breath. "The government is putting us in there, isn't it?"

Gav squeezed my hand. "They can't do it without our consent."

Did I really have any choice?

I faced the sunlit windows, not looking at either man. This couldn't be happening. There were too many loose ends. How could I simply walk away from my life and pretend it never existed? Besides Bucky and Sargeant and the maids who'd brought us breakfast, who would be sworn to secrecy? My head spun with questions.

"My mom, my nana," I said. "What about them? Does this mean I'll never see them again?"

"As long as Kern believes you're dead, your mom and grandmother will be safe. They'll be flown out here to attend your funeral."

"What? No, that's not right."

"Don't worry, they know the truth," he said. "They know you're alive and they understand what needs to be done in order to keep you safe. They're willing to do this."

"How can you say 'They know'?" I asked. "You used present tense. What aren't you telling me?"

Yablonski tried to smile. "I believe you're acquainted with your mother's gentleman friend, Kap?"

I nodded. I'd met Kap some years ago, shortly after a guest at the White House died at dinner. I'd been suspicious of the handsome, slick man—especially when he began paying attention to my mom—but he'd turned out to be one of the good guys.

"He has been made aware of the situation. He's advising your mother and grandmother even as we speak."

I felt as though all the life drained out of me in one painful *whoosh*. "I'm so sorry," I whispered.

"It isn't your fault," Yablonski said, not realizing I meant the apology to my mom.

A million more thoughts raced through my mind. I plucked at the next one in line. "What about the winery?" I asked. "Bill and Erma have plans to bring Gav into the business. How will this affect them?"

Yablonski and Gav exchanged a look that told me they'd discussed all this before. Probably when they'd first attempted to broach the subject with me and I'd resisted.

The large man sighed. "For now, the winery is out of your future. But in time, once we're convinced that terrorists from Armustan are no longer targeting you, then Gav *may* be able to resume working with Bill and Erma again."

"In time," I repeated. "You make it sound as though it could take years."

"There's no way to predict."

Desperate to grasp at any hope, I asked, "This disappearance of ours could be temporary, right?"

Yablonski hesitated, but said, "It could."

"We could be back here within a week, maybe less . . . couldn't we?"

"It's best not to speculate."

"But it's possible, isn't it?"

Yablonski inhaled deeply, then leaned forward. "I know you're fighting this and believe me, I understand. But I've dealt with a fair share of reluctant witnesses and I've maintained contact with some. Those who fully accept their new identities and try not to look back at what's been lost are the ones who find the most success in their new lives."

This wasn't happening. It couldn't be.

"What you're saying is that we not only have to agree to this, we have to embrace the complete upheaval of our lives. We have to go to a new city with new names, new histories, and forget that this life exists." Thinking of Bucky in my kitchen two floors below, thinking of Sargeant, who I'd miss more than I'd ever allow myself to admit, I let my gaze rove the room.

"Yes."

"And you can't force us. We have to agree."

"That's right. This is a difficult decision, Ollie," Yablonski said. "One not made lightly. Take a look." He pushed the two folders toward us. Gav and I picked them up. When I opened the front cover, my photo stared back at me.

"It's the file we'll keep on you," Yablonski said. "It's the only place in the world where your real name and information is tied to your new identity. The president, the attorney general, and I will be the only ones with access to it. The U.S. Marshals you encounter will not be advised of who you actually are."

I paged through the file, skimming a dossier that provided a name I immediately despised and a background I couldn't recognize. "This is who you expect me to be?"

Yablonski didn't answer.

I nodded toward the closed file on Gav's lap. "Aren't you curious?"

"I don't care if my name changes. I never liked Leonard anyway." He gave a smile, trying to lighten the moment, but my heart hurt. "What matters to me," he said, "is your safety. I'll give anything to protect that."

"But all you've worked for," I said. "Your career." I lifted my hands. "All this."

"Not just me, Ollie. Both of us."

I placed the file on the table and got up to walk to the windows. This could very well be the last time I ever looked out over my beloved Washington D.C.

Bucky would likely be named executive chef. I hoped so, at least. He'd be the one hiring someone to fill Cyan's position. He'd handle the state dinners, official events, the Egg Roll, the family's meals.

I spun. "What will they tell Josh?"

Yablonski ran a hand through his sparse hair. "That's being discussed. I don't have an answer for you yet."

"I think he should be told the truth," I said. "He can be trusted."

"Does that mean you've come to a decision?"

I turned to stare out the window again. "So, what happens if Kern is found in the next few weeks?" I faced Yablonski.

"Do I suddenly show up and terrify everyone who came to my funeral? Or am I supposed to treat this *invitation* to join the Witness Protection Program as my permanent walking papers? Am I being summarily dismissed?"

Yablonski shook his head. "The president agrees with you about being truthful with Josh, but no decision has been made yet. For the record, he wants you back as soon as possible, but more than that, he wants to know you're no longer a target. Until all threats from Armustan are neutralized, we can't take any chances."

Gav came to stand next to me. "I'm sorry," he said quietly.

I pressed against him. He wrapped his powerful arms around me and I waited there, allowing his warmth and strength to envelop me.

"Time is tight," Yablonski said from behind us. "We need a decision."

I looked up at my husband. "Gav?"

He ran a fingertip along my cheek and tried to smile. "You tell me."

My decision today would determine our future: live in constant fear or start over in sheltered secret.

Drawing a deep breath, I leaned closer to Gav, "We can do this, can't we?" I whispered. "We can do anything we set our mind to, right?"

He nodded. "As long as we're together."

Exactly, I thought. *As long as we're together.*

With a tight grip on my husband's arm, I turned to give Yablonski our answer.

RECITES

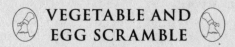

VEGETABLE AND EGG SCRAMBLE

1 tablespoon grapeseed oil
⅛ cup diced onion
⅛ cup diced portabella mushrooms
Kosher salt
Freshly ground black pepper
⅛ cup yellow squash, sliced
⅛ cup zucchini, sliced
3 large eggs

Heat skillet on stove over medium to medium-high heat. When skillet is hot, add in oil and heat until the surface shimmers slightly. Add in onions and mushrooms, hit them with a little kosher salt and freshly ground pepper, and sauté for 3 to 4 minutes. Add in yellow squash and zucchini, season again lightly, and sauté for 1 to 2 minutes. Add in eggs, season lightly with salt and pepper, and scramble in the pan (use a spatula to break the yolks, and then slowly and occasionally stir the eggs, allowing them to scramble). Serve on a plate.

You can also add in some diced meat (usually leftover chicken breast, pork chop, or steak, but almost any lean meat will do here). The key is to use diced, not shredded, meat, and to use leftovers or previously cooked meat so all you need to do is let it reheat. Simply add it in with the onions and mushrooms. One-quarter cup of meat should be sufficient, but like everything else in this recipe, that can be adjusted up or down to your taste.

Yield: one serving

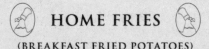

HOME FRIES

(BREAKFAST FRIED POTATOES)

2 medium russet potatoes (fingerlings or Yukon
   Gold work, too)
1 tablespoon grapeseed oil
Kosher salt
Freshly ground black pepper
½ medium white onion, diced

Peel the potatoes and cut them in half lengthwise, then slice each half into smaller half-disks about one-quarter inch thick.

Heat skillet on the stove over medium to medium-high heat; add oil, and heat until the surface starts to shimmer.

Add in potatoes (oil should be hot enough to sizzle when the potatoes drop into it), season with salt and pepper, and toss to coat evenly. At this point, the potatoes should be spread out fairly evenly in as close to a single layer as possible.

Cook, without stirring, for 5 to 8 minutes, or until the potatoes start to get some nice color on the bottom. If the potatoes are browning too quickly, turn the heat down slightly. Toss or flip, making sure to turn all the pieces over so that they're evenly browned.

Add in onion. Cook for another 5 minutes without stirring, then toss (or stir), mixing the onions and potatoes.

Continue to cook until potatoes are done. Total cook time is typically 15 to 20 minutes.

If you don't like the taste or feel of oil, transfer the potatoes to a paper towel–lined platter and allow the potatoes to drain for 1 or 2 minutes, but I usually just serve them right from the pan.

Yield: one serving

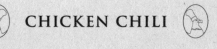

CHICKEN CHILI

¼ cup vegetable oil or extra virgin olive oil
2 pounds boneless, skinless chicken breasts, cut
   into ½-inch cubes

4 medium sweet bell peppers (red, yellow, green,
   or a combination)
2 large onions, chopped
4 cloves garlic, minced
3 tablespoons chili powder
2 teaspoons ground cumin
¼ teaspoon cayenne pepper
1 (28-oz.) can diced tomatoes, undrained
2 (14.5-oz.) cans chicken broth
2 (16-oz.) cans kidney beans or chili beans
   (in mild or medium sauce)
1 (12-oz.) jar medium salsa
1 (10-oz.) package frozen corn
½ teaspoon kosher salt
½ teaspoon pepper

Heat oil in Dutch oven over medium heat. Sauté chicken, peppers, onion, and garlic until chicken is no longer pink and the vegetables are tender, approximately 5 minutes. Add chili powder, cumin, and cayenne; cook, stirring, 1 minute. Add tomatoes and broth; bring to a boil. Reduce heat and simmer, uncovered, for 15 minutes. Stir in remaining ingredients and return to a boil. Reduce heat, cover, and simmer for 10 to 15 minutes or until chicken is tender.

Yield: 6-8 servings

MUSHROOM-TOMATO BISQUE

¼ cup extra virgin olive oil
1 cup onion, diced
1 cup (approximately 2 stalks) celery, chopped
4 cloves garlic, minced
8 ounces baby bella mushrooms, cleaned and
*   sliced*
1 (28-oz.) can diced tomatoes, undrained
4 cups chicken broth
1 cup whipping cream
1 teaspoon dried dill
Kosher salt and freshly ground black pepper,
*   to taste*

Heat a large saucepan over medium-high heat, then add in oil. When the oil starts to shimmer, add in onion, garlic, and celery and cook until tender, approximately 5 minutes. Add mushrooms and cook for another 5 minutes, or until mushrooms are tender. Add in undrained tomatoes, chicken broth, whipping cream, dill, and salt and pepper to taste. Bring to a boil, then reduce heat and simmer for 30 minutes.

Remove from heat. Puree with a handheld immersion blender until nearly smooth (or, alternatively, use a standard blender, pureeing small batches of the soup at a time—be careful not to fill the blender more than half full with any one batch).

Note: Because of the whipping cream, this is a soup that should be enjoyed only occasionally, but the taste is worth the relatively small amount of increased fat and calories.

Yield: 6-8 servings

PORK CHOPS WITH APPLE, WALNUT, AND GORGONZOLA SALSA

¾ teaspoon pumpkin pie spice, divided
1 tablespoon freshly squeezed orange juice
⅓ cup firmly packed brown sugar
½ cup toasted walnuts, coarsely chopped
2 medium red apples, cored and coarsely chopped
1 tablespoon extra virgin olive oil (or grapeseed oil)
4 ½- to 1-inch-thick boneless pork chops
    (approximately 6 ounces each)
Kosher salt
Freshly ground black pepper
¼ cup crumbled Gorgonzola cheese

Combine ¼ teaspoon of the pumpkin pie spice with the orange juice, brown sugar, walnuts, Gorgonzola, and apple. Set aside.

Heat the oil in a 10-inch nonstick skillet over medium-high heat. When the oil is hot, add in the remaining ½ teaspoon of pumpkin pie spice and stir to combine. Season pork lightly on both sides with salt and pepper and add to skillet. Cook until golden brown, about 6 to 8 minutes, then flip and cook until done, another 6 to 8 minutes, depending on the thickness of the chops).

Transfer chops to serving platter. Spoon salsa over them. Allow the chops to rest a couple of minutes before serving.

Yield: four servings

GRILLED SPICY CHICKEN BREASTS

1 clove garlic, smashed (or minced)
1 tablespoon finely chopped fresh cilantro
3 tablespoons freshly squeezed lime juice
2 tablespoons extra virgin olive oil
½ teaspoon chili powder
Kosher salt
Freshly ground black pepper
8 boneless, skinless chicken breast fillets
    (approximately 4 ounces each), trimmed of all fat

In a small bowl, make marinade by mixing together garlic, cilantro, lime juice, oil, chili powder, salt, and pepper. Whisk to combine thoroughly. Set aside.

Wipe down chicken with a damp paper towel and place in a shallow glass dish. Add marinade, turning chicken over several times to coat thoroughly. Cover with plastic wrap and refrigerate for 2 to 3 hours, flipping chicken occasionally to keep well coated.

Twenty minutes before cooking, remove chicken from refrigerator to allow it to come to room temperature. Preheat grill to 350°F and cook chicken 4 to 6 minutes, then flip and cook another 4 to 6 minutes or until thoroughly cooked through.

Serve with long-grain and wild rice and fresh fruit.

Note: This makes excellent leftovers, especially in pita sandwiches. It also works very well as the basis for chicken fajitas.

Yield: four servings

 CHOCOLATE ÉCLAIRS

FILLING:

> 2 cups milk (whole, 2 percent, and 1 percent will
>   all work fine)
> ½ vanilla bean, split lengthwise
> 6 egg yolks

⅔ cup sugar
¼ cup cornstarch
1 tablespoon unsalted butter, chilled

PASTRY:

1 cup water
8 tablespoons (1 stick) unsalted butter
½ teaspoon salt
1 ½ teaspoons sugar
1 cup all-purpose flour
3 eggs, plus 1 extra, if needed

EGG WASH:

1 egg
1 ½ teaspoons water

CHOCOLATE GLAZE:

½ cup heavy cream
4 ounces semisweet chocolate, coarsely chopped

Filling: In a medium saucepan, heat the milk and vanilla bean to a boil over medium heat. Remove from heat and set aside to infuse for 15 minutes. In a medium bowl, whisk the egg yolks and sugar until light and fluffy. Add the cornstarch and whisk vigorously until no lumps remain. Whisk in ¼ cup of the hot milk mixture until incorporated, then whisk in the remaining hot milk mixture, reserving the saucepan. Pour the mixture through a strainer back into the saucepan. Cook over medium-high heat, whisking constantly, until thickened and slowly boiling. Remove from the heat and add in the butter, stirring until well combined. Let cool slightly. Cover with plastic wrap, lightly pressing the plastic against the surface to prevent a skin from forming. Chill at least 2 hours or until ready to serve. The custard can be made up to 24 hours in advance. Refrigerate until 1 hour before using.

Pastry: Preheat the oven to 425°F. Line a sheet pan with parchment paper or a Silpat and set aside.

In a large saucepan, bring the water, butter, salt, and sugar to a rolling boil over medium-high heat. When it boils, remove from heat and add all the flour at once, stirring vigorously with a wooden spoon for 30 to 60 seconds or until all the flour is incorporated. Return to the heat and cook, stirring, for an additional 30 seconds. Scrape the mixture into a mixer fitted with a paddle attachment (or use a hand mixer) and mix at medium speed. With the mixer running, add 3 eggs, one at a time. Stop mixing after each addition to scrape down the sides of the bowl. Mix until the dough is smooth and glossy and the eggs are completely incorporated. The dough should be thick, but should fall slowly and steadily from the beaters when you lift them out of the bowl. If the dough is still clinging to the beaters, add the remaining 1 egg and mix until incorporated.

Using a pastry bag fitted with a large plain tip, pipe fat lengths of dough (about the size and shape of a jumbo hot dog) onto the prepared baking sheet, leaving 2 inches of space between each. You should have 8 to 10 pastries.

Egg Wash: In a bowl, whisk the egg and water together. Brush the surface of each éclair with the egg wash. Use your fingers to smooth out any bumps or points of dough that remain on the surface. Bake 15 minutes, then reduce the heat to 375°F and continue to bake for an additional 25 minutes or until puffed and light golden brown. Don't open the oven door too often during the baking. When done, remove from oven and allow pastries to cool on the baking sheet. Fit a medium-size plain pastry tip over your index finger and use it to make a hole in the end of each éclair (or just use your fingertip). Using a pastry bag fitted with a medium-size plain tip, gently pipe the prepared custard into the éclairs, using just enough to fill the inside (don't overstuff them).

Glaze: In a small saucepan, heat the cream over medium heat just until it boils. Remove from heat. Put the chocolate in a medium bowl, then pour the hot cream over the chocolate and whisk until melted and smooth. Set aside and keep warm. (The glaze can be made up to 2 days in advance. Cover and refrigerate until ready to use, and rewarm in a microwave or over hot water when ready to use.)

Dip the tops of the éclairs in the warm chocolate glaze and set on a sheet pan. Chill, uncovered, at least 1 hour, to set the glaze. Serve chilled.

Yield: 8-10 pastries

CHOCOLATE MOUSSE DESSERT SHOOTER

4 Double Stuf Oreos
1 teaspoon unflavored gelatin
1 tablespoon very cold water
2 tablespoons boiling water
½ cup sugar
¼ cup Hershey's cocoa
1 cup heavy cream, very cold
1 teaspoon vanilla
¼ cup chopped pecans, toasted
1 can Reddi-Whip or 2 cups homemade whipped cream
5 fresh, whole strawberries, sliced in half lengthwise

Place a small mixing bowl into the freezer for a minimum of thirty minutes.

Crush the Oreos. Line the bottoms of 9 small wineglasses or jiggers (2 to 3 ounce glasses work best). Set aside.

Make the mousse: Sprinkle gelatin over cold water in a small bowl; stir and let stand 1 minute to soften. Add boiling water; stir until gelatin is completely dissolved (mixture must be clear). Set aside. Stir together sugar and cocoa in a small chilled mixing bowl; add heavy cream and vanilla. Beat at a medium speed until stiff peaks form; pour in gelatin mixture and beat until well blended.

Pipe the mousse into the glasses. Add a layer of toasted pecan pieces.

When ready to serve, pipe the whipped cream onto the pecan pieces (or, if using Reddi-Whip, just add), garnish with a strawberry half, and serve.

Makes 9 servings

FROM *NEW YORK TIMES* BESTSELLING AUTHOR
JULIE HYZY

ALL THE
PRESIDENT'S MENUS

*It's an old adage that too many cooks spoil the broth. But when a
tour of the White House kitchen by a group of foreign chefs ends
in murder, it's Olivia Paras who finds herself in the soup...*

Due to a government sequester, entertaining at the White
House has been severely curtailed. So executive chef Olivia
Paras is delighted to hear that plans are still on to welcome
a presidential candidate from the country of Saardisca—
the first woman to run for office—and four of that nation's
top chefs.

But while leading the chefs on a kitchen tour, pastry
chef Marcel passes out suddenly—and later claims he was
drugged. When one of the visiting chefs collapses and
dies, it's clear someone has infiltrated the White House
with ill intent. Could it be an anti-Saardiscan zealot? Is
the candidate a target? Are the foreign chefs keeping more
than their recipes a secret? Once again, Olivia must make
sleuthing the special of the day...

juliehyzy.com
penguin.com